Tomcats
Killers of Innocence

Patsy Shook
6/30/2024

IBSN: 979-8-218-37334-4 (paperback)

"Grandma, where are the baby cats?"

"The mama cat must have hidden them so the tomcat can't find them."

"Why doesn't she want the tomcat to find them?"

Grandma was silent for so long that I thought she wasn't going to answer, and then she said in such a low voice that I almost couldn't hear, "Sometimes daddy cats kill the babies."

"Do human daddies kill their babies?"

Grandma pulled a handkerchief from her apron pocket and wiped my wet cheeks. "No, Child, your daddy loves you and would never hurt you. You just get that notion right out of your head. The kittens are just fine—the mama cat has them hidden somewhere safe. Sarah, I don't know what's gotten into you, you've been taking things too seriously for an eight-year-old. You act like you're older than me. What happened to my happy grandchild?"

I couldn't tell Grandma that no one laughs in our house anymore. Daddy doesn't sing anymore. He's been on a long drunk—this time it's lasted longer than usual. Grandma and Grandpa know that daddy drinks too much. They were at our house the day before to check on him because he was drunk and had been in bed for three days. They just didn't know how bad things really were, and Mama said I couldn't tell them. They didn't know we ran out of food and money days before. Mama said, "We'll make do. You can sell some more salve."

A year before I answered an ad in the back of one of the *True Romance* magazines Mama was always reading. The ad said it was easy to sell Cloverine and Rosebud salve so I decided to give it a try. A couple of days later, I received two cardboard containers of each salve with instructions to send the company their share of each sale. I sold several containers of the stuff, but never sent them any money because I needed it to buy food. They kept sending more salve. The day before the tomcat, I walked into town and knocked on doors all day before making a sale. Then I had just enough money to buy two cans of condensed tomato soup, and after watering it down, there was enough for the whole family to have a bowl of watery soup.

Grandma put the wet handkerchief back into her pocket and said, "Here, take this jug of milk and pot of green beans. I cooked them with some good ham—made way too much for me and your grandpa. Now, run along home before the food gets cold, and try to be nice to your daddy and help your mama."

I lifted the lid to have a look. The aroma almost made me faint from hunger, and the milk was still warm—freshly milked. I thanked her for the food and the milk, and headed home.

So that I could get home before the food got cold, I decided to take the short cut home which took me down past the wood shed and a short walk through the woods. As I neared the wood shed, I heard a noise that was a cross between a growl and a scream.

I'd heard that sound once when I was with daddy, and he had said it was a banshee scream. I felt the chills lift the hair on the back of my head. It appeared to be coming from inside the wood shed. Just inside the doorway, a large black tom cat loomed over a litter of kittens. He sank his teeth into a kitten's neck, and then gave a sharp twist which broke the kitten's neck, and silenced its frightened cries. The tomcat dropped the lifeless body to the ground, and then picked up another mewing baby from the pile. I didn't want to watch this horrifying scene, but couldn't tear my eyes away. Finally, after the last of the seven babies had been silenced, the tomcat gave one more banshee cry and slinked away. I managed to force my shaking legs to move away from that carnage, and bent over and vomited so many times that I was only bringing up bile. I ran all the way home. For the sake of my little brother and sister, I pushed the nightmare from my face and managed to carry the pot without any spillage.

When I got home, Mama grabbed the pot. I watched her hands shake as she began spooning it onto four plates. "Mama, why can't we have a garden and a cow like Grandma?"

She said, "That's a lot of work—I don't seem to have that kind of time or energy anymore, but if you'll promise to help me, and if I can get some seed from your grandma, I'll give it some serious thought."

"Mama, you didn't serve Daddy a plate, can I get him to come eat?"

"Here," she said quickly serving another plate, "Take this up to him and keep him upstairs—I'm expecting someone to come by. I don't want her to see your daddy in a drunken state."

"Mama, who's coming over?"

"It's that welfare lady. She says she wants to check up on you kids."

"I don't want to see her. All she ever does is make us walk across the room, and then she says we are either flat footed or pigeon toed. She never does anything about it, like give us shoes or anything else."

"Well, go on upstairs, and take that to your daddy. Keep him up there, and I'll tell her you're asleep and not feeling good."

Daddy wasn't always a drunk. I was three years old before I met him. That's when he came home from the war. People said you couldn't remember things that happened when you're that young, but I remembered that day—at least I thought I did. Maybe I'd just heard Mama and Uncle Ronald talk about it so much that I just thought I could remember.

Uncle Ronald was in the war too, but he came home months before Daddy, and moved back in with Grandma and Grandpa. He helped Mama with things around our house when she couldn't manage, and brought us a gallon of milk from Grandma every day.

I heard them talking that the war was over, but Daddy couldn't come home yet because he had been captured by the Japanese in the Philippines, and he needed extra care in some Army hospital.

When that day came, Uncle Ronald took Mama, Grandpa, Grandma, and me to the train station. He said, "You're going to meet your daddy—he's a real hero. Everyone is so proud of him."

I sat touching Mama on the bench at the train station, and could feel her shaking. I asked if she was sick, she answered, "No, I'm just happy and excited honey. I've been waiting for so long for him to come home."

There was such a big fuss--parades, flashing lights, and people carrying signs that Uncle Ronald told me read, "Welcome home returning hero."

After what seemed hours, a real skinny man stepped off the train. Everything went crazy with excitement. News people shoved little black boxes at him and asked him questions. One news person said, "I've heard you were held prisoner by the Japs, where were you?"

Daddy answered over his shoulder but continued walking toward us, "I've been to hell and back."

He lifted me up to eye level. "Let me see my little princess." He swung me onto his shoulders, ignoring all the calls for a speech, and led Mama to the car. I felt safe and excited to have a dad. I sat as close as I could get, and stared at him for the rest of the day.

Sometime in the night, I awoke suddenly to hear a mournful wailing sound. At first, I thought it was a hurt animal, but sat up in terror when I realized it was Daddy. He was yelling about a place called Bataan, and snakes, and marching with blood spilling out of his boots. "Why do we have to keep marching? Oh God, I held his brains in my hands. John, John, I told you to shut up. I told you the Japs would shoot you."

I cried out to Mama, but she just stuck her head in my door and said, "Hush, go back to sleep. Your Daddy's just having a nightmare." I curled into a trembling ball beneath the covers trying to block out his cries.

I don't remember how long Daddy was home before he started drinking. I just remember one day he sat down and drank a large bottle of something and then fell over on the couch asleep.

Mama said he'd passed out. That night was silent and empty of his screams. I slept through the night, and began looking forward to those nights.

One evening about four or five months later, Daddy was sitting on the front porch, rocking and staring into nothing. I knew he wasn't drunk because we had food, and he'd been going to work every day. That's how it was, weeks with enough, and then days with nothing.

"Come, sit with me," he said, I've company coming—someone who was in the war with me." He motioned me to his lap.

I loved sitting in his lap when he was sober because then he sang to me. It didn't matter that he always sang the same song:

Little girl, little girl, where'd you sleep last night?
Not even your mother knows
I stayed in the pines, in the pines, where the sun never shines
I shivered where the cold winds blow.

Soon a man came up the path holding out his hand to Daddy and smiling.

"Howdy Buster, nice to see you again."

"Good to see you too, Melvin."

When Mama made me go to bed, they were still swapping war stories. The next day, Daddy told Mama that Buster was coming back that evening. Mama started to complain, but Uncle Ronald, who always seemed to be hanging around, said, "Don't stop them Lilly, that's the most I've seen my brother open up since he came back. Let them talk it out. Maybe if he gets it out of his system, he'll stop drinking."

Within a week of Buster's first visit, three more men showed up on our porch. They too, had been in the war. It became a nightly ritual with Daddy and his four visitors. They took turns telling their war stories and I'd listen from the comfort of Daddy's lap until I had to go to bed.

Daddy didn't drink and he went to work every day for the four or five months that the visits lasted. One night, one of the men pulled a bottle from his jacket and passed it around. Then the stories were told through sobs. Mamma pulled me from the porch saying, "That's no place for a kid—stay in the house tonight."

That was the last visit. It seemed like such a long time ago, and Daddy was drunk most of the time after that evening.

Mama poured out his booze when she found it. One Monday night, she found several bottles hidden around the house and poured them out. Tuesday morning, Daddy said, "You've time before school, run down to the store. Get me a bottle of rubbing alcohol—my shoulder's been killing me." I raced to the store and then home again glad to be doing him a favor.

When I came home from school in the afternoon, Mama screamed at me, "How stupid can you be—letting him talk you into buying that rubbing alcohol?"

"Mamma, he needed it for his shoulder."

"He drank it. He drank it. It's not meant to drink—don't you know that? Besides, where did he get the money? He didn't have a dime yesterday."

On Friday, Daddy was still lying around upstairs. Grandpa and Grandpa were worried that maybe Daddy was sick.

They told Mama he should be up and about—that he'd had plenty of time to sleep it off. Mama didn't tell them that Daddy had drunk the rubbing alcohol.

Mama asked them, "If he's not up and about this afternoon, will you help me get him a doctor?"

When Grandma handed me the pot of food, she said, "I'll be down to check on your daddy in a bit. If he doesn't eat or isn't up, then we'll have to have your Uncle Ronald go fetch Doc Barstow."

I balanced the plate against my chest as I pushed open the bedroom door. "Daddy, I brought you something to eat. This'll make you feel better."

He sat up in bed and held his head in his hands. "Oh, my head hurts so bad, I can hardly sit up."

I picked up the fork and fed him a bite. He chewed slowly and swallowed with effort. I tried to give him another bite, but he pushed my hand away.

"What a rotten life you've had—taking care of your little brother and sister like you're the mama and daddy. You're a good kid and deserve better. I'm going to straighten up and start taking proper care of you."

His words were slurred and he was crying, holding his head and swaying back and forth. "Get your Mama. I can't see, my head is killing me."

I rushed down stairs. "Mama, Mama, something's wrong with Daddy. His head hurts real bad and he can't see."

"Oh, I'm real glad he's awake, but for God's sake, he's just got a hangover—let me go see. Stay here with Barbara and Eddie."

I hadn't finished eating when I took Daddy's plate up to him so I sat down with my little brother and sister and tried to eat.

Then Mama's screams filled the house. I ran as fast as I could, and met her at the top of the stairs. "Run next door and get Mrs. Johnson to call a doctor—quick!"

"Grandma said if Daddy needed it, she'd have Uncle Ronald go fetch a doctor."

"We can't wait, the Johnson's have a telephone, run as fast as you can."

Mr. Johnson answered the door, and responding to my breathless message, yelled, "Quick Betty, call for a doctor, I'll go see if I can help. He headed for our house with me on his heels. "You keep your brother and sister down here—I'll go see if there's something I can do to help."

I heard him trying to calm Mama and then the bedroom door closed. It seemed no time at all before the doctor came. He had another man with him, and they too went upstairs and closed the door.

Barbara and Eddie were whimpering and huddling close to me. "The doctor's here now, he'll make Daddy all better." I put an arm around both of them and we watched the kitchen door.

Mama's screams filled the house again, and I ran toward the stairs, but Mr. Johnson blocked my way. He put an arm around me and said, "Get your little sister and brother, you're going to stay over at my house tonight."

He left us on the sofa and took Mrs. Johnson into the kitchen, but I could still hear him say, "Vera, he's dead. They're getting ready to take him out of the house, and I don't think the kids should see it."

Barbara and Eddie didn't understand what was happening. I figured they were too young, and excited over the cake and milk that Mrs. Johnson put in front of them. They were busy shoveling it in, but I pushed mine aside. I felt numb and not sure what was happening.

We spent the next two days with Mrs. Johnson. She tried her best to interest us in games and reading, but all I could think about was home. "I want to go home—Mama needs us at home, I want to see my daddy," I pleaded.

"Your mama needs to rest now, Honey. You can go home with her tomorrow after the wake."

I overheard Mr. Johnson say, "They're doing an autopsy—says it's because he was so young."

"Oh, for heaven's sake," Mrs. Johnson said, "It's all the drinking. He cooked his liver with all the drinking."

"No, the doctor said it was something else. Said he didn't know what, but it wasn't the liver."

I had never seen a dead person or been to a wake. When we entered the funeral home, it seemed more like a party with so many people laughing and talking. I noticed Mama in a big chair near what Mrs. Johnson said was Daddy's casket. I rushed up to Mama hugging her, but she didn't hug me back. Her eyes were dull and puffy. I didn't think she really saw me because she pushed me away.

Grandpa quickly moved over to guide us to chairs on the other side of the room. "You kids sit over here, and I'll get you something to drink."

I watched him walk away and heard someone behind me say, "They did an autopsy, you know. Found that he drank isopropyl alcohol—that's what killed him. Cooked his brain, poor bastard."

Grandpa handed me something in a paper cup. Although I thought I already knew the answer, I asked him, "What is isopropyl alcohol?"

In the days following daddy's funeral, mama paid no attention to us or much of anything. All she wanted to do was sleep. As the weeks went by, things didn't get any better.

Sometimes, I'd go looking for her and find her in the back yard swaying back and forth praying, "Dear God, what am I going to do?"

Uncle Ronald had been coming around lots, and sometimes, I'd see him and Mama talking real low outside on the porch. A couple of times, I overheard Mama raising her voice, she sounded really mad, then he didn't come around, and Mama said she wanted me to go fetch the milk every day.

Miss Diane Greer from Social Services came by every week to check on us. She always brought bags of groceries, but everything that needed cooking spoiled on the kitchen counter. I tried to cook what she brought, but Mama chased me from the kitchen. She said she didn't want to clean up my messes. No matter how much I promised to clean up after myself, Mama wouldn't relent so I took Barbara and Eddie over to Grandma's to eat.

Miss Greer visited Mama several times, and she also went over to talk to Grandma and Grandpa, and Uncle Ronald. I heard Uncle Ronald tell her that Mama was not able to take care of us. Later, Miss Greer told me to pack my things, that she was taking me and Barbara to an orphanage. Mama just sat in her chair wringing her hands, and saying over and over, "Lord, have mercy."

I ran through the house searching for something that I could take with me that would tie me to the house and my family. All I could find was Mama's scissors. I asked her if I could take them, and she nodded. When Barbara and I were in the back seat, I asked Miss Greer, "Aren't you going to get Eddie?"

Miss Greer said, "Eddie is too young to go to the place you are going, he has to go to another home."

"Why can't we stay with Grandma and Grandpa?"

"Honey, the welfare has some silly rules we have to follow."

"Where's Mama going?"

"Your mama is going to Florida to visit your uncle Don. He's going to help her get back on her feet, and then she'll bring you kids home."

I watched the scenery pass and wondered, what does get back on your feet mean?

Miss Ann was head of the orphanage. She had white hair, a kind face, and her voice sounded like music. She talked to Miss Greer for awhile, then she told me I would be in the building where the middle-sized girls lived, and Barbara would live in another building with the little girls. I sat on the bed assigned to me and feelings of hopelessness and longing came over me. I had never been homesick before. It was a terrible sickness. All the faces around me were those of strangers. I didn't even see Barbara. She was taken to a different part of the orphanage where I wasn't allowed to go.

I balled up the sick and sad feelings and stuffed them deep inside just as I had done when daddy died.

"I will not cry," I told myself, "Do not cry or you will drown, and not be able to think straight." I started thinking how I could sneak Barbara out of her building and we could run away. I would find the way back to our house. I didn't care what those old welfare people said, Grandma and Grandpa would take care of us.

I lay down on the bed with the scissors under me, and let my loss cover me. The house mother called me for dinner, but I didn't care if I ever ate again, so I ignored her summons. She sat down on the bed and stroked my hair then asked, "What are you holding so close?" I showed her my scissors—my only connection to home and family. She gently took them from me and said she was afraid I might accidently hurt myself. She said she would keep them safe in her office until I needed them. I objected at first saying, "Mama gave them to me, I need to keep them safe." I overhead her asking someone in the office, "What was her mother thinking giving a young kid a pair of scissors to carry around?"

For the next two years, I only saw glimpses of Barbara. I tried to see her. I went over to her building, and her house mother chased me out telling me not to come back, but most of the other grownups were kind, and we were fed three good meals a day. We went to church every Sunday, and we saw a doctor if we were sick, but most of the time I was very lonely.

Grandma and Grandpa came to visit as often as they could, but it was hard for them to get a ride. Mama came to visit once, but the visit just made me lonelier. Someone sent word that my mama was there to see me—they said she was waiting outside the administration building. My heart leaped with gladness. I ran as fast as I could to fling myself into her arms, but she just stood there arms limp by her side with a blank stare. Without any joy in her voice, she said, "I came to tell you that I've moved to Burnsville. It's near Marion where my sister Mary lives—you remember your Aunt Mary?"

I was so startled, "Away from Grandma? Away from our very own house? Miss Greer said that when you got yourself straightened out, that we could go back home and be a family again."

"I don't live there anymore. Your uncle Ronald and his new wife, Ruby, moved into our house. It's their house now. Your grandma is real upset with him, and she doesn't much like Ruby, but that's not why I came. We're going to be a family again. I got married. His name's Al Cantlin--he wants to make a home for us all—we've already gotten Eddie. I'll come back soon to get you and Barbara." She gave me a piece of teaberry chewing gum, and then she was gone again—hardly a visit, but I hung on to that promise.

"I'm going to have a home, a real home with a mama and daddy, and my brother and sister," I kept repeating to myself. Every night I prayed that it was true.

Soon afterwards, Uncle Ronald brought Grandma and Grandpa to visit. I asked Uncle Ronald, "Mama said you got married, where is she?"

The three of them exchanged looks that seemed like they were hiding something they didn't want to tell me. Then Uncle Ronald said, "She wasn't feeling like going anywhere."

They took turns hugging me and telling me how much they missed me. Grandma said, "I haven't seen your mama since she sold the house to your uncle Ronald, and moved down somewhere near Marion close to your Aunt Mary. Your Aunt Mary came up the other day to visit your Aunt Ovela, and then she came over to see me. She said your mama met this fella named Al through the Lonely-Hearts Club--she picked him out of a catalogue and started writing to him. He just showed up on her doorstep one day with a ratty old suitcase and moved right in. He told her a bunch of lies saying he was some big war hero and had a metal plate in his head. He said he had lots of money that was tied up somewhere, but he would get it later because he wanted to take good care of all of you. Your Aunt Mary said she didn't believe a word he said. She told us your mama is practically starving because he takes her Social Security money and spends it all on liquor and cigarettes."

"Mary said that when they got married, your mama's Social Security check stopped, but this old feller found out that you kids got a check., and he high tailed it over to get Eddy. I'm pretty sure he just wants to get his hands on those checks. We know folks in Marion that see what's going on, and old man Jestes says he knows for a fact the war story isn't true. I don't know how he knows, but I don't trust this feller. It's not right. Sarah, I don't feel right about this—maybe you should think twice about going home with them. He told her he won't let you kids visit us—says we're a bad influence."

A few days later, Mama, Eddie and my new step daddy came back to fetch me and Barbara. Eddie sat between me and Barbara in the administration office with his eyes downcast. I hugged him and tried to get him to talk to me, but he just muttered and kept his eyes in his lap. Miss Ann, the head of the orphanage, always had a kind look about her, but today she looked worried— maybe even a bit angry at something. She kept glancing at Eddie while Al tried to convince her he would be a good father and should take us home. "I want them to have everything that I didn't have."

Miss Ann asked Al some questions and listened to him talk for a long time—he talked a lot--then she stood up and nodded to me. "Sarah, could I see you in the other room?"

Miss Ann closed the door softly, "Sarah, if you want to stay here, I'll make some phone calls to see what we can do. I don't feel good around him—something's not right, but until I get more information, I have no choice but to let you girls go. If you just say so, I'll make them leave you here until I can find out more about him."

"Oh no, Miss Ann, I wanna go! I want to live with my little brother and sister."

She gave me a quick hug, "If things don't work out, get in touch with Miss Greer from the welfare office. Here, put her phone number where it'll be safe—on second thought, see if you can memorize it."

The back seat of Al's rickety car reeked from cans of oil and greasy car parts stuffed everywhere. I sat with my feet propped up on them with my knees in my chest. Eddie sat in Barbara's lap with his little legs propped against the door. We bobbed and swayed as the car bounced along. I tried to make time pass faster by watching the heat waves rise up from the pavement, and moving my head to catch every breeze through the open windows. I thought about what Grandma had said—that we couldn't visit her, but I decided it couldn't possibly be true.

At the top of every hill, Al turned off the engine to coast down. "We'll save gas—maybe we can get home before running out." He glanced at the darkening sky, "Maybe we'll still get home before the storm hits."

Every afternoon during the summer, there was a thunderstorm--the hotter the day, the more violent the storm. It must have been at least a hundred degrees, and the skies had been roiling since noon. Thunder bolts were hurled to the ground so close I could smell Clorox. Grandma once told me, "That means the lightning is real close." Barbara shifted Eddie's sleeping weight on her lap, reached for my hand, and tried to move a little closer.

After what seemed an eternity, the car left the paved road, crunched down a long rocky driveway, and came to rest in front of a shack that appeared to be an old barn. We could hear the rains roaring and closing in as we rushed into our new home. Mama grabbed buckets and tubs just in time for the rains, but she only had enough for the major leaks.

The house only had two rooms. One was a kitchen and living area and the other was the bedroom. Someone had strung a clothesline across the room and hung an old blanket over it to mimic privacy. Barbara, Eddie, and I were to share the only bed on our side of the blanket. As I dumped my clothes onto the filthy mattress, I thought about my clean--sheeted bed back at the orphanage.

Barbara and Eddie were scuffling with Al whose tickling was making them squeal with laughter. I wanted in on the fun and jumped in the middle of the fray. Al rolled me on the floor tickling me in the ribs. I screeched with laughter, partly from the play, but also from happiness to have a family again and a dad.

Mama stuck her head in the door, "Sarah, come in here, I need you to do something for me." She lowered her voice so Al couldn't hear. "You're almost eleven and much too big to scuffle with him. Don't do it anymore."

I couldn't understand the harm or why she was so agitated. When I returned to the bedroom, Al grabbed my ankle inviting me back into the play, but I stepped back.

"Mama told me not to scuffle with you—she says I'm too old."

Al's face went from smiling to menacing in a flash. He grabbed my braids and yanked so hard that the elastic holding them in place broke leaving the braids uncoiled and my head smarting with pain. "Maybe I don't want to play with you—that's a stupid hairdo anyway."

Barbara tripped and fell against Al. He scooped her up and threw her on the bed with such force that she bounced against the wall hitting her head. "Stay there! I've had it with you kids—that means you trouble maker and the little turd there," he said pointing his finger at me, and motioning at Eddie. I grabbed Eddie's hand and we slinked into our side of the bedroom. I lay between them cuddling their trembling bodies close. Eddie whimpered and started to say something, but I quickly put my hand over his mouth and motioned for him to be quiet. He was still a baby. His little body shook so hard from fright that I could feel the bed shake.

Out in the kitchen, Al grumbled at Mama and then I heard heavy steps and the door slammed.

"He's gone," Barbara said hopefully.

"Mama, I'm hungry," I called out.

She stuck her head in the door and cautioned in a low voice, "Be quiet. He could be back at any time. There's nothing in the house to eat. I'll see about getting something tomorrow."

I don't know how long I lay there staring out the window into the night sky, acutely aware of my grumbling stomach, but one thing I did know, I had never known misery so bad.

No one ever treated us that mean at the orphanage, we had food every day, and there were sheets on the beds--clean sheets. Nobody ever treated us mean before Daddy died. Even when he was drunk, he was kind.

Mama arranged to start getting the Social Security check again for us kids. The check came every month, and every month when it was due, Al watched the mailbox like a hawk. When it came, he took Mama to the store to cash it, letting her buy some groceries before he pocketed the rest. Then he disappeared for a day or two, and then he'd come home in a foul mood smelling of alcohol. The groceries never lasted until the next check came, but it was her only shopping trip.

One day I heard Mama and Al arguing in the living room. I was sitting outside on the stoop minding Barbara and Eddie.

Mama was almost wailing, "What are we going to do? Oh Lord, what can we do? If you didn't do anything wrong, then why would the law be after you?

I couldn't hear all that Al had to say, but I did hear that he wanted them to go somewhere but leave us behind.

Mama started crying again, "No, I'm not going without my kids."

Sometime in the night, Mama shook me awake, "Get up. Get your brother and sister dressed, we're going on a long trip."

I sat in the back seat of Al's rickety old car with my little brother and sister. Mama had wadded up our dirty and raggedy clothes and stuffed them around us. They were the only possessions we had. The only shoes we had were on our feet. I don't know why we still wore them because they had large holes in the soles and we walked on the bare ground.

We rode in that cramped half-sitting position for over two days until we arrived at Al's parent's house in western Massachusetts. We stood behind Al waiting for someone to answer the door. Al's Mother came to the door, and snarled at Al for bringing us. She looked like all the witches I had read about in fairy tales, and her voice was crackly like a witch.

"No, they can't stay here! If you can get rid of them, then you can sleep on the couch."

Al was asking where he could get an apartment real cheap for a short while, "I've gotten myself in a bit of trouble, and just want a place to lie low until it blows over-–then we'll go back south, or on to Vermont to settle close to Francine."

His mother answered, "There's an old abandoned building over on First Street that I know people squat in sometimes. Your dad says some of the apartments are still decent, but they all have rats. He'll take you on over there so you can find something before dark."

Al's dad was just as short tempered as his mama, but he took us to the old building, and showed Al a couple of apartments. They were strewn with trash and broken-down furniture. Al picked the one on the first floor. There were no locks on any of the doors. It looked like someone had stripped them all out. They both went out to prowl the empty building and found two old abandoned beds and an old wood stove. There were two very soiled mattresses that were losing stuffing through large tears. They hooked up the stove in the only room that had an opening for a stove Pipe. Al's dad had found a couple of old scratchy and smelly blankets that he threw on the beds. Lots of times I'd heard Beggars can't be choosers, but I didn't think those beds or blankets were fit even for my granny's pigs. He called over his shoulder as he was leaving, "There's still some coal in the basement where the furnaces are, you could use coal in that stove. We were restless all night from the cold. The stove didn't give off much heat, and none of us had ever experienced such extreme cold. Early in the morning, Al told us to stay where we were because he and Mama were going to the Social Security office to get our checks sent, and then he would send Mama into the Catholic Church to beg for food. "That's the place you'll go to school when your mama registers you."

We stayed beneath the covers shivering until they returned. Al built another fire in the old stove with some more coal he found downstairs, and pulled a coffee pot, coffee, cans of beans and franks from the bag. Mama pulled our bed as close to the stove as she dared, and the three of us kids huddled together sharing body heat. It wasn't quite as cold that night and we had a little food in our bellies. I could hear the rats thumping around all night. I tried to stay awake.

The next day Al told me and Barbara to get ready for school that he was going to register us for the Catholic School in town. We'd never been to a Catholic Church nor had we ever seen a nun. They taught all the classes. I found it strange that there was someone called Mother Superior instead of a principal.

Al had figured out what our address was, and he and mama talked about whether if they used that address the mail man would ever deliver it, so they put down his mama's address at the Social Security office. The first check came in the mail.

After taking mama to cash the check and buy a little food, he took the rest and disappeared for the evening. Mama woke me up sometime late in the night and had me get up to worry with her. She tried to bribe me awake with coffee. "I have coffee on the stove perking. I'll pour you a cup when it's done."

Before I could get my coffee, Al came in. He grabbed the coffee pot and threw the boiling contents in my eyes. Then he stripped my clothes, beat me with the buckle end of his belt and made me sit outside for hours in freezing cold. By the time he brought me inside, I was shivering badly, and my feet and hands were numb. My eyes were burning, and everything was so blurry that I figured they must be bleeding. I was coughing up congestion and feeling real sick. Mama put her hand on my forehead, said I felt hot and should not go to school, but old Al insisted.

At school, I was feeling sicker and sicker, and when I put my head on my desk, Sister Mary Margaret took me to Mother Superior's office. She had a cot in her office and wanted me to lie down. She and the sister pulled my dress over my head to put me beneath the covers. They gasped when they saw the welts and bruises on my body. I confessed that my stepfather had beaten me, and made me stay outside last night. They fussed and fumed saying they were notifying the authorities. Mother Superior said,

"Don't you worry, we'll make sure you never have to be treated like this again."

I was afraid that we would be split up again in different orphanages, and nowhere near Grandma unless I could get home to warn mama.

I saw my chance when both the Mother Superior and Sister Mary Margaret left the room. I stuck my head in Barbara's classroom and motioned for her to come out to speak to me. She didn't ask questions but took my hand, and we ran like the wind home to warn mama. I felt like I would collapse and my throat was so sore I could hardly talk, but I managed to get out the warning. I didn't know old Al would be there, and didn't see him until after my warning. He didn't say a word, but started gathering up our few belongings, mostly ragged clothes and the old salvaged blankets. He hustled us all to the car. We stopped at his mother's house only long enough for him to get the address of his sister Francine in Vermont. We were on the road in no time heading for Vermont way up near the Canadian border. Everything was covered with snow, and I didn't think any of us could survive the cold because none of us owned a coat, or gloves, or a hat.

Francine was not happy to see us. She barely acknowledged Mama, and took Al in the next room to talk. When they came back out, Al told us that we would have to stay in the attic. There was nothing up there but a couple of mattresses on the floor, but it was warmer than the apartment we had left--I guess from the rising heat from the stove under us. Al told us he would stay downstairs with his family, but we were ordered to stay up there until called. He said we could come down to use the bathroom at the foot of the stairs, but go right back into the attic. Around meal time, we could smell something good cooking, and half-starved, we went downstairs. Al shooed us back upstairs saying his family was eating first, and we would be called to eat later. After the enticing odors of the meal Al was eating, there was a different smell like something rotten cooking. It seemed to penetrate even our pores. Al called us down to eat. I could see on the counter a pile of foil wrapped squares that were about two inches long and an inch wide. Francine had unwrapped one of these brown squares and was boiling it in a pot of water. The odor was disgusting even to someone starving. I asked her what it was. She answered that it was bouillon as she served us all a bowl. Even Mama had to stay in the attic with us.

Supposedly, during the day, Al was out trying to find a job.

We had been in the attic for about a week when I dreamed Al took me for a ride—just the two of us. He stopped the car somewhere and tried to take my clothes off and grab my private areas. I fought hard kicking him between the legs until he stopped. When I woke up, I was shaking all over. I lay there in the dark wondering about the dream. Why had I dreamed this? I'd never experienced such things or heard about such things. But the dream seemed so real, almost like a premonition.

Mama and Al were arguing in the corner about something. I could hear some of the words. "Al, why can't you take Eddie with you instead of her—seems that would better serve your purpose."

"I told you why. What do I have to do to get it in your thick head? It needs to be her."

He turned to me, "Get your shoes on. You're going with me over to Burlington. I'm supposed to see a man about a job this afternoon and if I have a kid with me especially one that's as skinny and gawky looking as you, then he's sure to give me the job."

My heart jumped into my throat threatening to cut off my breath. "Mama?"

She wouldn't meet my eyes but said in almost a whisper, "Go, he needs this job—he'll be more apt to get it if they see he has kids to support."

With the dream fresh in my mind, I slid into the car pressing as close as I could to the passenger door and kept my hands tight in my lap. We rode in silence for about half an hour or so until Al pulled into the parking lot of a bar.

"Well, come on get out—this is where I'm meeting him." We joined two men in a booth who seemed surprised to see me.

"This is my stepdaughter, Sarah—isn't she a pretty little thing?"

One of the men—he said his name was Ted—asked what we were drinking. Feeling the emptiness in my stomach, I answered, "Milk."

The three of them laughed and Al mocked me, "Milk? They don't serve milk in here. I'll get you some beer—come on, take a taste."

Reluctantly I took a small sip. It was the most vile tasting thing I'd ever had. I resisted the urge to push it away, knowing it would anger Al.

He handed me some coins, "Here, go put these in the music box—pick out some songs."

I was glad to get away from them, and lingered by the juke box as long as I thought I could. I overheard bits of their conversation. Ted said, "No way, man. That's jail bait." The other man—I never got his name—said, "You're playing with fire, if you get caught, they'll throw your ass in jail."

I knew they were discussing me. I feared the evening would never end, and kept my eyes in my lap with the beer in front of me untouched. "Please, please, God," I prayed silently, "Let us go home."

After what seemed an eternity, Al stood up to leave. "No use wasting good beer," he said as he drank my full glass in one big gulp.

He turned the car out of the parking lot and looked over at me pressed against the passenger door. "Don't sit so far away—scootch over here closer." He unzipped his pants with one hand so that his privates fell out.

My heart raced with terror. "I'm ok here," I managed to say without my voice trembling. I told myself not to look in his direction and stay close to the door—maybe he would continue driving home, but he yanked the steering column to turn off the road. It was a very dark place.

Before it registered what was happening, Al was on top of me lifting my skirt and clawing at my panties. The smell of beer and cigarettes on him made me gag. He slung one leg across mine, and using one arm penned me down. He fumbled at my panties with his free hand.

It felt as if I were floating above what was happening, being instructed by the dream. I managed to free a leg and with all the force I could muster, kicked him where his zipper was open. Yelling and holding himself, he jumped from the car and slid onto the ground. He groaned and rolled around for awhile then he began cursing me. "You little bitch, I ought to kill you for that. I'll get to you yet." He climbed back into the car and started the engine. "If you tell anyone about this, I'll kill you."

The police must have been after Al for something because he piled us into the car and slinked away again under cover of dark. Mama had been sitting on the mattress when he told her to get up and get us all into the car. I saw blood trickle down her legs and land on the floor in a little puddle. She looked up at Al and begged him to send Francine up to see her. I felt my mama's humiliation when Francine tossed her a couple of old towels telling her to clean up her mess, and use the rags to catch the blood. Mama bent to the floor and started wiping, and when she stood up, she looked shriveled like something had let all the air out of her. I grabbed Mama's hand, "Mama, are you sick? What's wrong?"

She barely whispered, "I have my period."

. I wasn't sure what a period was but I knew it must be something shameful by the way Francine had acted.

We rode through the night toward North Carolina, and arrived at Aunt Mary's house almost two days later unannounced. She welcomed us, and hustled to cook us a meal. Aunt Mary had a reputation that she would never let anyone leave her house without a full stomach. She did not have rooms for us or beds, but found a place for each of us to sleep. Al slept in his car, Mama slept on the couch, and Barbara, Eddie and I slept on the floor.

Aunt Mary found every available quilt to pad our bed. Al seemed put out over having to sleep in the car which hastened his search for some place to live. By the end of the day, he had found an old run-down shack not far from Aunt Mary. I knew he didn't have any money for rent so he must have told one of his whoppers.

We had been living there for almost a month before mama got a Social Security check. We had been living on handouts and lies. Al disappeared with most of it and came home drunk. He fretted about paying the rent saying that it was past due and the landlord was pushing him so he had found someone to rent a cot in one corner of the living room. Jessie Blankenship showed up with only a suitcase which she said contained her only possessions. She said she just needed a place to stay for a few weeks until she could get on her feet. I had never heard of Jessie, but Mama and Al seemed to know her. Al said she was paying rent so he borrowed or stole a folding cot from someone. She didn't stay a week. She told Mama and all the neighbors that Al tried to molest her. She told Mama that she didn't have anywhere else to go, so would she just make Al leave her alone. Al raved and stormed around the place insisting he was innocent and that Jessie was lying. Mama cried and wrung her hands saying that she believed Al, and Jessie would have to leave.

I didn't want to see her go. Jessie was the best thing in my life. She pulled a book from her suitcase and said it was her prized possession. She read us a story from it every night and seemed to take pleasure being around us. I told Mama that I believed Jessie, but she just shrugged her shoulders. I had not meant to tell my secret, but I just blurted it out, "Mama, he tried to molest me too."

Mama cried and wrung her hands some more until Al came home. Jessie and I sat on the bed listening to them in the kitchen.

"Sarah says you tried to molest her in Vermont, is that true?"

"Hell, no it's not true. Where's that lying little cunt? He raised his voice to us, "Both of you get in here right now!"

I was shaking all over with terror unable to move forward. Then Jessie took my hand and squeezed it like she was pouring some courage up my arm. Hanging on tight to her hand, I walked into the kitchen keeping my head down, but Jessie stood stiff and defiant.

Al shook his fist at Jessie, "You get your stuff and get out of here." He then pointed at me, "Get a bucket of soapy water and some rags. You're gonna stay up all night scrubbing the walls in this place—every inch of space, and while you're scrubbing, I want you to think about what happens to liars."

From the corner of my eye, I watched Jessie leave--glad my back was toward Al so he couldn't see the tears flowing down my cheeks. I heard the whistle of his belt before the buckle end cracked against my back with such force that it knocked me to the floor. He kept coming after me so that I couldn't get up--slashing the belt against my whole body—even my face and head. I knew he'd drawn blood by the salty taste in my mouth. Mama stood in the doorway wringing her hands, and saying, "Stop. Oh, please stop."

I mentally traced the steps to the knife drawer. The image of twisting the butcher's knife in his ribs kept me lunging forward, ignoring the pain that was starting to spread throughout my body. I heard the whistle of the buckle again as it sliced through air knowing that it would land on my back, and in a split-second decision, I whirled and ran from the house.

I ran as fast as I could for about ten minutes, but realized that I didn't know where I was running. I was glad of darkness so Al couldn't see me if he was out there—I needed to figure out where to go. Grandma, Grandpa, Uncle Ronald, and Miss Greer lived in Banner Elk—much too far to walk. Even the orphanage was in Banner Elk. I had to sit somewhere to catch my breath and figure it out because I was never going back to that house. Then my little brother and sister's face came to mind and with a start, I thought, oh no he'll do to Barbara what he tried to do to me and Jessie. Somehow, I have to find a way to protect them. I started walking in the direction of down town.

There were only a handful of buildings in town so the police building stood out with its dimly lit sign. When I walked in, one of the fattest men that I had ever seen stood up and sucked in his breath noisily when he saw me. He came around the desk and took one of my arms staring at the bloody welts, then he touched my face and I jumped from the pain. He motioned for me to sit while he dialed the telephone on his desk. "Myra, you'd better get over here. There's a little girl here who's been beaten to an inch of her life. I'm sure she could use a woman's help."

I told Myra and Sgt.Tucker about my life, and about the beating. They exchanged angry looks while I talked. Myra stood up and made for the door, "I'm going out there to get those kids and take care of that monster."

"Myra, sit down," Sgt Tucker ordered, "You'll only make matters worse. We have to do everything above board. We need to get testimonies from this Jessie and from Sarah's sister—I know that she's only seven but if we get all three stories to match, then I believe it'd hold up."

"Look at the child! How much more evidence do you want?"

Sgt. Tucker sighed, "Take her over to the medics—have them look her over, and call the welfare department to come get her."

I spoke up, "Please. If you're going to call welfare, I know Diane Greer up in Banner Elk. She helped us once before."

"Alright, I know Miss Greer, Myra—see if she can drive over to get her."

I shrank back, "No, I want to get my little brother and sister first."

"We'll take care of them—I promise. We'll come after you when we need you to talk."

A nurse daubed stuff on me that made my body sting and then she said my head needed stitches. After she'd finished fixing me up, she told me to wait in the hall for Miss Greer.

When Miss Greer arrived, she gasped when she saw me, and taking care not to hurt me, took me into her arms. This kindness pushed me close to tears, but I bit my lip to keep them away. I figured that once a person started crying, they couldn't do anything else.

"It's going to be okay. The police are looking for Jessie and they're going out to talk to Barbara and your Mama. They'll put him in jail—he'll never get out again."

I didn't think the ride to Miss Greer's would ever end. My body got sorer and stiffer with each passing minute. When we got to her house, she fixed me supper while I took a hot bath, then she told me to serve myself as much as I could eat.

I looked at all the food in front of me and shoved my plate away. "I can't eat. My little brother and sister are hungry."

"Honey, going hungry isn't going to help them one bit. You need to keep up your strength so you can go testify to help them."

I considered this logic, and filled my plate to overflowing.

The telephone started ringing even before I got out of bed. Miss Greer didn't seem happy with the people calling her and her face showed worry. I edged closer and tried to eavesdrop, but she lowered her voice so I couldn't hear. After lunch, she didn't even try to keep me from hearing. When she hung up, she said, "Honey, I'm so sorry. Last night a couple of deputies went out to your house to talk to your mama and Barbara. Your mama wouldn't let them talk to Barbara saying that she had nothing to tell them--that you were making things up. She wouldn't even tell them where Jessie was from, or where they might find her. She said she didn't even know a Jessie. This morning, they went back out there to try again and found the house empty. They were all gone. Doesn't your mama have a sister somewhere in Marion that might know where they are?"

I couldn't believe this was happening. Gone? I should have known this would happen. Any time Al sniffed trouble, he slinked away. If only I'd not run off.

"Maybe Aunt Mary knows where they've gone. Al didn't let us go over there except when he sent one of us to borrow coffee or cigarettes--sometimes money. Once I tried to tell Aunt Mary what Al was doing, and asked why she let him borrow when she knew he'd never pay her back. She said she knew that, but didn't want to cause trouble, and it was the only reason Al let her see Mama."

Aunt Mary was rocking in the porch swing when we pulled into her dirt driveway.

"The police have just left," she said, "I figured you'd be here--let's sit here on the porch—it's cooler out here. I'll tell you what I told the police and it's all I know about it. Last night, Al sent your mama over here to borrow gas money—said they were going up north where he's from—somewhere in Massachusetts. They left in the middle of the night. Said she'd write me later."

Aunt Mary suddenly stopped talking and stared at me. "Oh my God, Sarah, what happened to you?"

"Al beat me up."

"Your mama told me last night that you'd run off to the police and told them some big tale—said that's why they had to leave so Al wouldn't be locked up."

I felt the weight of what she said, "Mama never did take up for me."

"Oh, Honey, your mama's afraid of him. She never let on that anything was wrong, but she changed after she married him. I knew he was worthless, but I didn't know he was abusive. I figured he was just real strict. I don't know what happened up north, but when you all came back, she wasn't herself. She's like a walking ghost."

I wanted to tell Aunt Mary that I knew what happened. I wanted to tell her of the awful way Francine had treated mama, but I didn't understand myself, and didn't have the words to tell. I just knew Mama wasn't mama anymore after that morning.

Miss Greer hadn't asked any questions or made any comments. She suddenly stood up and said, "We have to go now Sarah. I want to go by the police station and see what they have to say before we head back home."

Sgt. Tucker was at the station with two policemen who weren't there last night. I was disappointed that Myra wasn't there. Miss Greer asked Sgt. Tucker, "What do you intend to do?"

He shrugged his shoulders, "Nothing I can do. Can't go after a man in another state—can't have him sent back with no more to go on than we have."

"How about Jessie," asked Miss Greer, "Have you been looking for her?"

Sgt. Tucker seemed irritated, "No use. We have bigger fish to fry around here than chasing down lost causes."

I thought Miss Greer would hit him. She moved toward him with her fist raised, and her face was beet red. "Women and children don't count for much do they? You don't give them much thought."

She stormed out the door with me right behind her. We sat in the car for a few minutes in silence until her hands stopped shaking so she could drive.

She had promised to take me to my grandma's and grandpa's, but when we pulled into their driveway, she asked if I would stay in the car while she talked to them. Miss Greer said, "You know, I just live a piece down the road, and if you can get over there sometime, you can use my telephone to call your Aunt Mary, and I'll keep my eyes on what's happening and let you know."

"I thought I the welfare wouldn't let me live with Grandma and Grandpa."

"Those were the rules back then when you were younger. Let's just say I don't know the rules now, and I think you'll be better off with your grandparents."

Grandma looked me over clucking her tongue. "Poor child. Your daddy's rolling over in his grave. If he was here right now, he'd kill that feller. Well Child, you're gonna need some proper clothes. Are those clothes on your back all you have?"

The next day, she made me as presentable as she could. There was nothing she could do for my feet. I wore an old pair of shoes, too big, and missing shoe strings. I had been tying them on my feet. She said we were going shopping at Pearl's Rag Shack to get some proper clothes. Uncle Ronald took us in his old truck. On the way over there, Grandma explained that Pearl's Rag Shack was a second-hand place. If you prowl the big boxes, you can usually find some good stuff, and it's all real cheap."

Within minutes, grandma had fished a couple of dresses from boxes that looked real pretty except one was missing buttons, and one had a rip in one seam. She said, "These will look real purty on you, and I'll have them looking like new."

It took longer to find shoes that would fit and looked like they were for a kid and not for an old woman. The best thing about them was they fit me and had real shoe laces that stayed tied.

I didn't want to burden Miss Greer with big phone bills so I walked over to her house to call Aunt Mary only once a week. I always asked the same question, "Have you heard from Mama?"

Aunt Mary promised to call Miss Greer immediately if she heard anything at all. Weeks went by without a word. Panic turned into despair, and time-dulled despair became acceptance.

Life with Grandma and Grandpa was good but lonely. There was always plenty of food, clean clothes, and clean beds. They worked hard almost every day. Grandpa got up at four in the morning to build a fire in the cook stove and make coffee, and then he would wake up Grandma who got up and started baking biscuits and frying eggs. Every morning I'd pile lots of butter on a biscuit and load it down with homemade blackberry jam. The jam and butter dripped down my arm and smeared my face. Grandma looked on smiling, always urging me to eat more. Sometimes after eating so much, I'd feel like I'd throw up thinking that my brother and sister might be hungry, but as the months went by, guilt became less.

Grandma and Grandpa grew everything we ate. Grandma canned vegetables, made jellies and jams, they tended chickens, gathered eggs and milked the cow. Grandpa split wood for the stoves, and my chore was to keep the wood box full. After awhile, grandma gave me the chore of gathering eggs, and feeding the rabbits. I wondered how grandma could do all these things when she only had one eye and she needed glasses for that eye. Also, one of her hands was deformed. It resembled a fist she couldn't open to hold anything. She said she had fallen into a fire when she was little and lost one eye, and the doctors had folded up her hand and bandaged it shut. It grew balled up like a fist. She could do anything anyone else could--better than most.

Grandpa was really tired at the end of his work day, and it showed on his face, but he was always in a good mood, and always smiling over something. He never seemed to be too tired to tell me a story. He loved dogs and always had three or four hanging around. Strays knew they could get fed at his house, and a bed on the front porch. After a breakfast of biscuits and gravy and a night on the porch, they didn't leave. They followed him everywhere.

It didn't take long for me to feel comfortable with the routine. For the first time in ages, I felt safe and like I was home. I had never told anybody about watching the tomcat killing the kittens. I still saw the kittens in dreams sometimes that were as vivid as if they were real. One day when Grandma and I were weeding the vegetable garden, we took a break and sat under a shade tree handing a mason jar of water back and forth. The dogs suddenly came flying past us barking and chasing one of the barn cats. They disappeared down a bank that was thick with brush. I heard the growling scream from the cat and knew the dogs had caught it. I bent over and threw up water. The memory of the tomcat came flooding back, and I told Grandma what I had witnessed that day long ago. She seemed startled and upset when she said, "Oh dear child, I'm sorry you saw such a thing, but that ain't normal. I've known tomcats to hide the kittens, but never tear them apart like that. There must have been something wrong with that old cat. Put that right out of your head cause that just ain't right."

Maybe she was right—that wasn't normal, but witnessing that scene had left me traumatized, and there was no way I could put it out of my head.

Al and my family returned to Marion. Aunt Mary called Miss Greer and asked her to get word to me that if I'd come to her house, she'd arrange for me to see them when Al wasn't around. "He got some sort of job—don't know how long it'll last, but we can go over to visit during the day."

I was giddy. Miss Greer said she'd take me to visit, and then we'd take Barbara and Mama to the police station. She said that was the first step to put my family back together, and she'd do what she could to help.

Mama met me at the door, not with happiness to see me, but with anger. "How could you do this to me? You caused us so much trouble." She shut the screen door between us.

"Mama, I was trying to help you. I wanted to keep Al from hurting us. I want us to be a family again—without him."

"He's my husband. A woman has to stand by her man." She noticed that I wasn't alone, and nodded a greeting to Aunt Mary and Miss Greer.

Miss Greer asked, "Lilly, can we come in and talk for a minute or two?"

Mama made a motion to shut the door, and Miss Greer stuck her foot in the way. Mama had a terrified expression on her face, and Miss Greer backed out onto the porch and asked Mama if she would sit out there for just a minute. I saw her mouthing to

Aunt Mary that Al was in the house, and Aunt Mary nodded that she understood.

Mama stepped out onto the porch, "We can talk out here." She motioned to a couple of chairs.

"Are the kids here? Could you call them out to visit with Sarah?"

Neither Barbara nor Eddie hugged me back. They sat on the porch steps with eyes downcast while I attempted without success to draw them into conversation. Miss Greer had less success with Mama. She refused to discuss Al, and she was talking really loud when she said, "I'll never testify against him and neither will Barbara."

Miss Greer said, "Lily, you know that I can't let Sarah come home now. I took her to her grandparents--she has to stay with them or go back to the orphanage."

Mama shrugged her shoulders, and I couldn't understand why she kept talking so loudly, "Well, she's brought it on herself. When she ran off, and went to the police, she caused us all kinds of trouble. She's always been trouble—did you know she gave her daddy the alcohol that killed him."

The blood drained from Miss Greer's face, and her gasp sounded almost like a hiss. She took my hand and nodded to Aunt Mary, "Come, we have to go now."

We rode in silence until, without leaving the car, I said my goodbyes to Aunt Mary. She put her hand on my shoulder and said, "You know that Al was skulking in the house listening to every word we said. That's why your mama talked so loud so he could hear that she wasn't saying anything bad about him. You can come to see me as often as you can get a ride from Banner Elk, and you can stay with me. I'll get Barbara and Eddie over here to see you. Your mama too. Sarah, she really does love you. She doesn't mean what she's saying, she's just in a bad situation right now. She's terrified of Al. You know when your daddy died, she had a nervous breakdown. She couldn't take care of you kids."

Miss Greer and I didn't say anything for several miles, until I thought I'd break if I didn't say it out loud. I bit my lip hard and stuffed the tears down deep.

"I killed my daddy."

"Sarah, you didn't do any such thing."

"I bought the alcohol that poisoned him."

Miss Greer put an arm across my shoulders, "It wasn't your fault. You didn't know what it was—besides, he would have gotten it some other way."

"Because I ran away and talked to the police, Old Al will hurt Barbara like he tried to hurt me. Can't you just go back and get her?"

Miss Greer sighed deeply. "Honey, sometimes I don't like my job much-—times like now when my hands are tied to do anything legally."

I thought she had forgotten that I was in the car because she was silent for so long, but then she said, "I'll tell you what I can do. I'm a social worker for Banner Elk and I'm not really authorized to work in Marion, but I have a friend who is a social worker there. I'll get her to unofficially check in on Barbara once or twice a week. I think that would make us both feel a little better about the situation."

I visited Aunt Mary as often as I could get a ride. It was an hour's drive from Banner Elk to Marion, and it wasn't often that I could get anybody to make that drive, and then, it was only if they had other business there. In the beginning, Barbara and Eddie would come over for brief visits but Mama never came. Gradually, the visits dropped off. There was always some excuse.

I'd been living with Grandpa and Grandma for almost two years when I awoke one night to hear them arguing. Grandpa was grumbling about how much noise I made and didn't do enough work around the house, "She's just too much trouble."

"She's just a kid, Jake, a good kid, she's no trouble to me," Grandma said.

"Well, how long do you intend to keep her here?"

"Shame on you Albert, that's your dead son's oldest child--
she'll stay as long as she needs us—she's a good kid."

Before I turned to bury my head under the pillow, I heard
Grandpa say, "As soon as she turns eighteen, she's expected to
go find her own way."

What Grandpa had said kept running around and around in
my head and kept me awake, especially the part about having no
home when I was eighteen. My thoughts lasted well into the night
and I was only able to sleep when I thought I had a plan to get
Grandpa to love me again.

"I'll never make noise, and I'll do Grandpa's chores for
him," I promised the night. I was awakened many nights after that
to their arguing--mostly it was just Grandpa growling about
something that someone had done to him. I didn't remember him
being mean tempered--ever. He used to be all smiles and easy
going. I didn't know when he slept—seemed that he wandered
around the house most of the night.

I noticed Grandma watching Grandpa all the time. If she
didn't know where he was, she got concerned until she located
him. One day, she asked me to walk with her and she'd help me
gather the eggs.

"Sarah, your grandpa isn't in his right mind, and he's
getting worse and worse. This morning, I caught him sharpening
all the knives and threatening to kill us both. When, and If I tell

you to, I want you to run as fast as you can to get your Uncle Ronald."

I sucked in my breath, "No, I can't leave you here to get hurt."

"Child, I can't run with my bad hip, and if you don't get help, neither of us stands a chance. I know he's hurt your feelings by things he's said, but he doesn't mean it. That's not your grandpa talking. Something bad has gotten into his head."

Four months passed without incident and it seemed that Grandpa wasn't wandering around so much at night. I thought maybe he was getting better.

I came home from school one day to find the front porch and living room crowded with people. I recognized some as neighbors. Fear squeezed my heart.

"Grandma!"

There was no answer, but all went quiet on the porch, and all eyes looked my way with sympathy.

"Grandma," I called again louder.

"Your Uncle Ronald's in the kitchen," someone said.

I raced to the kitchen my mouth dry and my heart pounding from fear. He wrapped me in his arms while assuring me that Grandma was going to be okay.

"She's in the hospital—broke the same hip that she'd broken years ago—it's a bad break and she's in a lot of pain, but the doctor says she'll be all right. She was trying to get away from your grandpa. He was throwing knives at her and making threats. Had no choice but to call the sheriff. Took two deputies to subdue him. They had him locked up in jail for awhile until they realized he didn't even know his own name. I called around and found a nursing home that took him as an emergency, but I have to find a more suitable permanent place tomorrow."

Uncle Ronald and I sat together for awhile staring into the past remembering a gentle man who loved nothing more than to make people laugh. Something had crawled into his head and eaten away who he was. Today, what was left of my grandpa had died.

I thought I would stay with Uncle Ronald and Ruby until Grandma got out of the hospital, but the doctors wouldn't release her unless she had a grownup around all the time. Ruby, reluctantly agreed for Grandma to move in with them, but she didn't want me. They decided they'd let Grandma tell me when we went for a visit.

"Sarah, Diane Greer has agreed for you to live with her just until you graduate high school. You'll be real close by so we can keep an eye on each other."

"Miss Greer isn't even family—she's a social worker--why would she want to take me in?"

"She's kinda like family. I guess she feels she owes our family a debt. You know that piece of property across the river that we always called the old Greer place? That belonged to Diane's parents. They hit on hard times when she was just a little thing, and offered for your grandpa to buy it. Since they didn't have anywhere else to go, we told them to stay on and do as usual. We didn't need the land for anything, but there was a real nice piece of bottom land beside the river that they never used. Your grandpa cleared it out and plowed it up for my garden—it's been my garden since."

"What happened to her parents—when did she move?"

"Her parents moved away when she went off to college. I didn't see her again until she showed up as your social worker when your daddy died."

Things seemed to work out with me and Miss Greer. I tried not to make any unnecessary noise, and to clean up after myself. I could walk to Uncle Ronald's from her house. It was only about two miles away so I went to see Grandma every day after school. I could take the same bus to school from Miss Greer's house that I always rode from Grandma's.

Ruby didn't even try to hide her dislike for having me or Grandma around. It didn't bother me when she made snide comments about me, but when she grumbled about Grandma, I felt like socking her real hard. Once I told Grandma, "I'm gonna give her a piece of my mind." Grandma put her hand over mine and said, "Don't you go sassing a grownup child, I'll handle this."

On days when Grandma's hip wasn't hurting, she insisted she was able to walk the short distance to her own home if she walked slowly. We would sit in the rockers on her front porch. Sometimes we just rocked in silence staring at Grandfather Mountain. Sometimes I would read my homework assignments to her while she rocked with her eyes closed listening. This helped me do better in school especially when she asked me questions that I had to look up.

I didn't think too much about what I would do when I graduated from high school. The time seemed so far away, but that all changed the day the homeroom teacher announced it was time to sign up to take the SATs. Most of the girls said they would not take them because they couldn't go to college. If there was any college money then it was to send the boys to college. Girls were expected to get married and let their husband's take care of them. If the family was wealthy, then the girl could go for two years, just long enough to find a college educated husband.

For as long as I could remember, I had wanted to go college. All my life I had heard people say the key to a good life was a good education, but now I realized that was just a futile pipe dream. I told myself, "Why bother, there's no way that could happen. Besides, where would I get the money for the exam? After I graduate, in June, I won't even have a home.

My grandpa's words still rang in my mind, "When she turns 18, we're kicking her out." Grandma had said, "Stay with Miss Greer just until you finish high school." None of the grownups in my life had offered any direction or options. I think Miss Greer started to one day. She opened a conversation by asking me if I had any thoughts about what I would do with my future, but she was interrupted by a phone call. She never brought it up again. I had felt alone and frightened many times in my life, but I was a child and not expected to take care of myself. When I graduated, I was supposed to magically be an adult and self sufficient. Well, I felt ill-prepared to be an adult. I had never had a real job. A couple of times someone had asked me to babysit, and they paid me with a little change. I began praying for some divine guidance or a guardian angel.

My guardian angel came to school toward the end of April in the form of an Air Force recruiter. Sergeant Hobbs gave the class a talk about the benefits of enlisting and said he would be in the back of the library to talk to us privately if anyone had questions.

My heart beat a little faster as I made my way to the back of the library.

"Does the Air Force take girls?"

Sergeant Hobbs looked up startled, "yes, yes it does."

"Well then, I'd like to enlist now."

I had to be eighteen which I wouldn't be until October sixth, but Sgt Hobbs made a phone call and got an appointment for me to take the physical exam the following week. "Come to my office after the physical to fill in all the paperwork. We'll do a background check which I'm sure will be no problem, then you go have yourself a good summer and come back here on the seventh of October. I'll administer the oath of office and send you to basic training down in San Antonio, Texas."

Grandma wasn't as excited as I was. She said the Air Force would be too hard on me, and she didn't like the idea of me being so far from home. She had never been out of the county so Texas seemed like the end of the world to her. Miss Greer thought it wonderful. "You just be sure you take advantage of the education."

After I graduated in May, I went down to stay with Aunt Mary until I could join the air force. Miss Greer had not said I had to move out right away, but I felt it would be an imposition if I stayed longer. I told her I'd be back the week before going away for basic training to pack up all my stuff and say goodbye to everyone.

Betty Downey, who lived next door to Aunt Mary, was sitting with her watching for my arrival. We hugged and kept interrupting each other eager to fill the other in on our plans for our future. Over the years, Betty and I had become friends hanging out together each time I visited Marion. She told me she'd gotten engaged to Butch Ross since we last saw each other. "You can meet him tonight—some kids are having a party down by the lake—come go with me."

I met Frank Honley at the party. He was sitting away from everyone else and appeared to be brooding over something. Butch pulled me over to meet him saying Frank was just there for the weekend—up from Fort Bragg. He had a terrible body odor and spoke to me in a clipped almost insolent way. Determined to be civil, I sat down far enough away not to smell his odor, but close enough to make conversation.

"If you're stationed at Fort Bragg, what are you doing up here?"

"I live here—or at least I did live here. My mama still lives here--I'm just visiting her for the weekend."

"What do you do in the army?"

Frank sat up straighter and adopted an arrogant expression, "I'm in Army Security. They only take cream of the crop. You have to have superior intelligence to be in that group. I have a top-secret clearance."

I didn't know if I believed him. He didn't look or talk like cream of the crop, and besides, Grandma always said, "A braggart just shows his hinny." I was thinking about how I could excuse myself when he said, "Your turn. What are you doing here? Do you live here--what do you do--are you still in school?"

I told him I had joined the Air Force, but had to wait until I was eighteen to go to basic training, and that wouldn't be for several months.

Frank gave me a look of disapproval and sneered, "That was a mistake, those girls have a horrible reputation. Everyone knows they have loose morals. Your reputation will be ruined."

I told myself that his opinion didn't matter, but felt really bummed out by his comments, and was relieved when Betty came looking for me to go home. Determined to be polite, I nodded to Frank, "Nice to meet you—hope you have a good trip back to your base."

"Whew, I'm glad that's over," I whispered to Betty when we were out of ear shot. "He had an opinion on everything and insisted on telling me. Sometimes he hurt my feelings, and not only that, I don't think he's had a bath in a year."

"I'm sorry you didn't have a good time. I don't know who invited him. He was two grades ahead of me in school so I didn't really know him, but you know how people talk. Seems like nobody liked him. They said he was rude and acted like he knew everything. If someone got something they were happy with, Frank always had something better. Even all the years in school, everyone—even me in a lower grade—thought he was allergic to soap and water. We're planning these lake parties every weekend this summer—maybe next weekend you'll meet someone nice."

The following Saturday, I went to the lake with Betty and Butch hoping to meet nice people and have a good time. I was sitting near them and eating a hot dog when Frank Honley showed up and headed my way. "Oh no," I thought, Another Saturday ruined. Betty had said she didn't think he'd be around."

I moved onto the edge of the blanket, we were sitting on, putting a girl I had just met between me and Frank. He sat down beside the girl. I thought I had heard her name was Sue. He pulled a mason jar that was filled with a clear liquid from a brown paper sack, and unscrewed the cap. "Here," offering the jar to Butch, "Have a swig."

Butch took a large gulp, and handed it back to Frank, "Where in the world did you get a half gallon of white lightning?"

"Oh, I have my sources."

Frank leaned over Sue and thrust the jar toward me. "No thanks." I had never had any kind of alcoholic drink. I had seen what bad things it did to people.

"If you're gonna be in the WACs you have to learn to drink."

"What's the WAC's?"

"You don't even know that it's the Women's Air Corp?" He said this with a put-down tone in his voice.

I felt ashamed and intimidated. "Mix it in a glass with some coke," I insisted.

All the guys hooted with laughter. "We don't have any glasses here. All we have is a paper cup--It'll eat a hole in it."

"I don't care—mix it."

Frank thrust the paper cup at me, "Drink it fast before it eats through."

The drink burned like the dickens going down, but after a couple of drinks, I could feel the warmth spread throughout my belly and move into my limbs.

Frank asked Sue to trade places, and he plopped down next to me, "Come on, drink up," Frank urged me as he brought the cup to touch my lips.

I took another gulp and leaned back on the blanket we were sharing with Betty and Butch. Everything was out of focus and began to slowly whirl.

I heard Betty say, "Leave her alone Frank. We can't take her back to her aunts in that condition."

Frank said, "I'll take her to get some coffee somewhere and sober her up. Don't worry about her, I'll get her home."

I was vaguely aware of Frank holding me up and walking me to his car where he put me in the back seat. I slumped over into a sleep or passed out. One minute he was driving and it seemed the next minute he had parked the car, and was on top of me pinning me down and pawing all over me. Through a fog, I was aware that he had removed my panties, but I felt helpless and too weak to protest. When he penetrated me, my screams were silent. I tried to move away, but I was paralyzed. Old Al's face swam above me, and I could smell his nicotine and boozy breath. I was that little girl again on that dark road in Vermont. Only pain reached me through the fog. All I could do was lay there with my silent screams while he raped me repeatedly. Panic struggled to pull me back from the blackness that threatened to suck me in, but I kept losing the battle. When the alcohol began wearing off, and the fog began to lift, I smelled the reek of his body odor, and realized that I could move again. My screams echoed off the darkness while I pounded him with my fists. He didn't hit back or say a word. Even when he let me out at my aunt's, he didn't speak.

The next morning, I was raw, my body hurt all over, and I felt dirty. I went into the bathroom to bathe. I scrubbed until my skin stung in an effort to wash the crusted blood and semen from my thighs.

Betty came from next door to check on me. She closed the bedroom door behind her and sat on the bed. I started crying and told her everything that I could remember. "I felt so strange and tingling, like I was paralyzed and couldn't move."

"The bastard, Butch said he thought he saw him put something in your drink, but decided to mind his own business because he wasn't certain just what he saw."

"You think he drugged me?" I just thought I was drunk. I'd never been drunk before-- just thought that was what it felt like." Betty, what if I'm pregnant--I'm so scared."

"You have a while left here before you have to leave for basic training. You'll know by then, and there are things you can do. Don't borrow trouble—it might not ever happen."

When my period didn't start on time, I began to panic and with each passing day, the panic grew. A couple of weeks later, I knew with certainty that I was pregnant. I don't know why it's called morning sickness because I was sick morning and night. Every smell made me want to puke.

Betty tried to give me helpful advice. "You can do something about it, but you have to do it now. I know about this old woman out in Johnson Holler—several girls told me they had miscarriages after drinking some stuff she gave them. Everyone calls her the root doctor."

"I don't have any money, Betty. Tomorrow is Saturday. Frank said he comes home just about every weekend, would you tell him that I want to see him? What I do, depends on whether he gives me enough money for that old woman, or if he gives me any money. Don't tell him why I want to see him."

"Sarah, if he doesn't help you, then I'll take you to see his mother. She'll knock some sense into him."

I had nightmares all night. An old witch was standing over me. She had tied me to the bed, and was laughing and laughing. She held a small bloody baby over me while her cackling laughter bounced off the walls. She screeched, "I've fixed you up real good girlie-–if you live, you won't have any more of these." Each time the dreams woke me up, I went to the bathroom and walked around before returning to bed and sleep, but could not shake the dream. Around 3 a.m., unable to sleep any longer, I sat on the edge of the bed cradling my stomach. Although I hated Frank Honley, and didn't want any part of him, I knew that I could not go to that old woman in the holler. I thought about my grandma, and how much I needed her now. She would know what to do. She would know what I should think. I was dressed and ready to go before I heard Aunt Mary stirring in the kitchen. After a quick cup of coffee, I went next door.

"Betty, could you please take me to see my grandma?" When she dropped me off in front of my Uncle Ronald's house, she agreed to pick me up in two days.

Uncle Ronald met me in the yard before I could step onto the porch. I could see Ruby peeking out. She probably thought I couldn't see her. Uncle Ronald said, "Your grandma moved back home. She says her hip is fine and she can take care of herself. I tried to get her to stay, but she wouldn't be put off."

He said he was glad to see me, but he didn't invite me in. I was glad that I could be alone with Grandma because we had to do some serious talking.

Grandma said, "Sarah, I haven't had breakfast yet, and I'm sure that you haven't either. We can talk so much better with a belly full."

I helped her clean the breakfast plates, and then we dragged a couple of rockers onto the porch where we could see Grandfather Mountain clearly. After a few minutes of silent rocking, she asked, "What's got you so bothered, child?"

I blurted it out, "Grandma, I'm pregnant please tell me what to do."

"Sarah, tell me what happened. Who's the daddy?"

"I went to a party out by Lake James. Betty took me. You remember her, she brought me to see you. Well, there was this guy there, name of Frank Honley. He's stationed at Fort Bragg, but was there to visit his ma. He kept handing me drinks, and I drank too much. He told Betty he would take me to get coffee to sober up and then he'd take me back to Aunt Mary's, but instead, he parked in some dark place and raped me. I felt like I was paralyzed—couldn't move. It was like a dream. Honestly,

Grandma, I couldn't fight back. He hurt me real bad. I was bleeding and bruised. Betty said her boyfriend saw him put something in my drink. He drugged me with something."

Grandma was angry, "Why in the dickens didn't her boyfriend say something then and there?"

"I don't know, makes me mad too, don't know who to be mad about, Butch or Betty. Just my luck from that one night, I got pregnant. Betty tried to get me to go to some old root doctor she knows over in Johnson holler, but I don't want to go. I've heard rumors that she's really a witch, and sometimes girls die after going to her. I've thought and thought about it, and want to ask you if I can move back here to have the baby. I could plant a garden, and you could teach me what I need to know to live here. I could learn to take care of the three of us."

Grandma didn't answer me for a long time. I saw the tears wetting her face. I felt sorry that I had made her cry.

"Sarah, you're just a baby yourself. You haven't had a daddy to watch over you, and you haven't had a proper mother to teach you the ways of the world. I'm just an old mountain woman with no education, and no money, but I've done the best I know how. I don't see how you can move in here, or keep the baby. Folks around here would shun you. No respectable man would ever marry you. Your baby would forever be called a bastard. It'd ruin your life and the child's life. I know it's not fair, and it don't seem Christian to me, but that's just how the world is. I know his family—have known them most of my life. His dad was real bad for drinking, and couldn't hold a job. I remember when he got married to Maude. His grandma and aunt moved to Winston Salem to let them have that old house in Marion. His drinking got worse and worse where it seemed he was drunk all the time. There were rumors that he had a mean streak, that he stole for a living, and that he beat Maude. I don't know if he hit his kids or not. Sounds like the apple doesn't fall far from the tree."

"I don't want to see you go to a root doctor. Those aren't rumors but true stories. She does more than just roots. I've known many a girl who died after going down there. Sometimes, if you take the roots soon enough it can cause you to lose the baby, but what if you just lost part of it?"

She didn't say anything for a long time--just rocked and watched the sun rise higher over the Grandfather. Sometimes her thoughts caused her to sigh, and I could see the tears on her cheeks.

"Grandma, I'm so sorry that I've hurt you. Please don't cry."

She reached for my hand, "Oh, my dear child, you don't make me cry. I'm crying and heartbroken because you deserve better. You can't seem to get a break in this life, and it just seems to keep on coming. I've been thinking and trying to sort out everything, trying to make sense of the situation. I know you won't like what I have to say, and I don't like saying it, but I can only see three outcomes. You stay around here and have the baby, and its ruination for both you and the child, or you go to the holler and maybe you are killed or worse. I think the third option is the best for you and the child. You should marry that feller. It'd give you respect, and the child a name. He should take you down to Fort Bragg where you can get doctoring for you and the baby."

I started to protest, but she held up her hand to motion me to silence. "You don't have to stay with him, just long enough to have the baby and get some training for a job, then you and the baby can strike out on your own. There's bound to be a place down there where you can get a secretarial course, or I hear tell you can get some kind of a nursing diploma in a year. You could even come back here then. You'd be a married woman with a child who has the name of his daddy."

"Grandma, I don't want to be a secretary or a nurse, I want to be a doctor, or a lawyer."

"Oh Lord Child, it's a poor row to hoe if you're a woman in this world. The world just won't accept that women can do those things, but at least if you can type, you can get a job. There're probably jobs over in Boone that you could get then, if you still wanted to move back in with me. I would sure love your company. You were always feisty. That can serve you well, but don't let it be your undoing. I won't always be here to watch over you so listen carefully to what I'm telling you. Don't lose that feistiness, but think about when it's called for. Remember, don't pull out the vinegar until you've tried the honey. Now, what's called for is marrying that feller, and getting the care you and that baby need."

"Granny, he's not gonna marry me. He's down there at Fort Bragg and I probably won't see him again. Besides, I don't want to marry him. He's mean. What if he beats me?"

"You just get word to him that your granny knows his granny, and if he doesn't do right by you, then your granny will be talking to his granny. I happen to know that his grandma Honley rules the roost--don't nobody cross her. She's always been able to straighten him out. He was always getting in trouble before she stepped in and made him join the army. She said the army straightens out anybody. If he lays a mean finger on you, you just go to the army police and have them throw his ass in jail. I hear tell they will do it too. If they won't take up for you, then grab your youngun and hightail it on back here."

I didn't like what I was hearing, but I rocked in silence for awhile thinking it over, and then remembered that I wanted to ask grandma about Ruby. "Why did you leave Uncle Ronald's--where did Ruby come from? She doesn't like me much."

"She doesn't like any of us--especially me--cause I put up a stink when Ronald said he was marrying her. You're old enough now to hear what happened. Seems like nobody around here had ever heard of her until one day she just showed up at old Ike Andrew's place. Well, she took up with him and just stayed on. They had a couple of kids together--they're grown up now. Rumor has it that Ike would not marry her, and had been threatening to kick her out. Well, she started showing up where she knew Ronald to be, and flirting with him to beat the band. She got him off in the barn one day and went at him like a bitch in heat. Little did he know that she had one of her kids sitting in the hay loft watching with one of those newfangled Polaroid cameras. He took pictures of the hanky panky. Imagine letting one of your kids watch something like that! Well, she took those pictures to Ronald, said she was pregnant and he'd have to marry her. I was madder than a hornet and told her so. She was a fifty-seven-year-old woman with grown kids claiming to be pregnant-—a regular hussy."

"Grandma, did you call her that to her face?"

"Yes, and some other choice names too. Anyhow, she convinced him to marry her. She didn't want me there when I broke my hip, and was hateful to me when your uncle wasn't around. I finally had enough and moved back home. I don't need her or anyone else to take care of me."

On the ride back to Marion, I told Betty what Grandma advised, and asked, "Betty, he said he would be up here again

Friday night, would you tell him I want to see him? Don't tell him what I want."

"Okay, but I don't like this at all. How can you marry someone who slipped you drugs and then raped you? Besides that, you don't even know him. Wouldn't it be better if you'd just do something about the pregnancy?"

"Betty, I don't know what else to do. I don't want to go to that old woman. The thought of her terrifies me. I've heard stories. Grandma said she's rumored to have killed several girls. If I don't go to her, then that means having the baby, and I don't want it to be called a bastard. Grandma said I should stay married to Frank just long enough to have the baby and get some kind of education. I'll make it work, you'll see."

Betty said, "I think you're making a big mistake. The way he treated you and you weren't even married, imagine how he'll treat you after? Honey, you were bruised and bloody—he did a number on you. Seems to me that going to see that old woman is a better choice than marrying him."

"I'm only staying at Fort Bragg until the baby is born, and then I'm going to grandma's. I asked around before joining the Air Force--found out the hospital in Banner Elk has a free eight-week course for nurse aides. If you pass the test and get the certificate, you have a job with them. I know its low pay, but it's something to give me a start. Betty, I feel trapped and scared—I don't know of any other way. Honestly, it's just for a few months."

Frank sent word that he would pick me up after supper Friday. I changed my mind, and back again several times about telling him I was pregnant or giving him an ultimatum, but fear and desperation were pulling me. He didn't ask me where I wanted to go but drove straight to the lover's lane parking area. He pulled the car under a canopy of trees, shut the engine and twisting around to face me said, "I knew you couldn't stay away from me for too long."

His insolence loosened my tongue, and everything I had practiced saying just spilled out. I even told him about our grannies knowing each other. That seemed to take some of the swagger out of him.

His immediate answer took me by surprise, "Okay, I'm going to marry you."

I had anticipated anger, recriminations, denial, but this reaction was stunning. I didn't even have to threaten him that I'd sic the grannies on him. Maybe just mentioning his grandma had been enough. Still, I had to know why he didn't push back.

Frank answered, "Let's say it's like a business deal. Soldiers with wives get a housing allowance and don't have to live in the barracks, and another bonus is I'll have someone to do my laundry, cook my meals, and you'd have to spread your legs when I wanted it. Another bonus is that soldiers who are married get faster promotions. You need a father for the baby and a roof over your head. So, we're both getting what we want."

My reaction was a combination of shame and indignation. I felt cowered and trapped with an urge to slam out of the car, but sat still listening to him and remembering my granny's warning not to let my feistiness get away with me. I needed to go to Fort Bragg with him, register his name on the baby's birth certificate and head back to my grandma.

Frank said, "There's no need to be talking to my grandma, I'll call into the Base and ask for a couple of day's emergency leave. We'll go Monday morning to get a marriage license, and whatever else we have to do."

Frank rushed me through getting the license, and the blood test. Two days later, we were standing before a justice of the peace saying our vows. Afterward, Frank drove me back to Aunt Mary's. He said he had to get on the road and get back to Fort Bragg. I was stunned and said, "I thought you would take me with you so I could get a doctor. I can pack my few clothes in five minutes if you'd just wait."

Frank's tone was cryptic, "Where do you think I could put you––in the barracks? I have to find us a place off base. I'll be back next weekend to get you."

Aunt Mary was fixing dinner when I entered the kitchen. I sat at the kitchen table and told her that I had just married Frank Honley and would move to Fort Bragg next weekend. Then I broke down and told her the whole sordid story. Her reaction was just as alarmed as Betty's. "Oh, honey, not to him. Isn't there something else you could do? I've heard of far-off places where nobody would know you. I hear tell they will take care of you until the baby is born, adopt the baby out to a good home, and you could go on as usual with your life."

"Aunt Mary, I don't know anything about those places, or where they are. I don't even know where to find out. I'd like to think this baby is mine—not his. Maybe it won't take after him at all. I have to give the baby a name, and I'm just going down to Fort Bragg long enough to get a doctor for us, and some kind of job training. Grandma said to get some kind of education and a job, then I could leave him. As soon as the baby is born, I'm planning on getting back to Grandma's, and applying for the nurse aide training at Banner Elk Hospital."

She put her arms around me, "I sure hope you're right. I pray that it'll work out."

When Frank didn't show up by dinner time Sunday, I had a sinking feeling that I'd been abandoned. Why did he say he was coming back for me if he didn't mean it? I tried to take comfort in his comments that having a wife would be a positive thing for him, and that we understood we both were benefiting, but the memory of the toneless voice and eyes taunted me. Well, I thought, I'll wait another week—I'm sure he'll be here next weekend. He's probably having trouble finding somewhere for us to live.

Another weekend came and there was no sign of Frank. I reminded Betty that Frank was supposed to take me back to Fort Brag with him two weeks ago, but he hadn't come back. Grandma said if he didn't do right by me to let her know and she would talk to his grandma—I don't know what else to do."

"Sarah, Frank has been here in Marion—both weekends. Butch ran into him at the auto supply store. He said he was fixing something on his mama's car. I think you should go see her, after all he did marry you. Legally he's responsible for you. If you don't have any luck with her, I'll take you and your grandma down to Winston Salem to see Mrs. Honley. I heard the same thing—that she would make him marry you and take care of the baby. Butch said he knew her and she was hell on wheels, that nobody crossed her, especially not Frank.

"You said that you knew his mom. Would you go with me?"

"Let's go right now before you chicken out."

Although it was only mid-morning, Maude Honley smelled boozy. Her face, a roadmap of broken veins and her reddened nose told me that she'd been hitting the bottle for a long time. She kept looking around as if to find somewhere to hide.

"Frank told me about you. Told me to come fetch you. I was planning on it sometime this week or next."

"Where's Frank? He said he was coming to take me to Fort Bragg? Why didn't he come back for me?"

"He couldn't. He was getting ready to go to the Philippines. He's probably over there by now."

I gasped. "Why? Why did he go to the Philippines? Why didn't he tell me he was going?"

"He asked to go. He said you were to stay with me until he could get the Army to send for you. Said things would work out better that way—said he was promised a promotion if he would go. He's gonna need the extra money now to support a kid. He told me he would have the army send for you in about a month."

I knew Maude didn't want me to move in, but she seemed unable to deny Frank. I briefly wondered why she allowed her son to give her orders. I didn't want to move in with her either, so I said, "If it's only a month, I'll just go back to Aunt Mary's or up to my grandma's. When the Army sends for me, you can let me know."

Maude seemed irritated, "That ain't gonna work. They have my address, and I can't be sure to get the word to you in time. I'd

have to drive you either to Asheville or most likely down to
Charlotte in a big hurry."

Betty and I headed back to get my few belongings from
Aunt Mary's house. I had already been there too long. My cousin,
Robert, would welcome his bedroom back. He had slept on the
sofa in the living room most of the summer.

Maude showed me to a bedroom that was so piled with
clothing, rags, and stacks of paper that it was hard to find the old
broken-down bed. Next morning, I awoke to an empty house.
Maude had already left for her factory job. I prowled the kitchen
for something to eat, but could find nothing. I waited all day for her
return. Surely, I thought, she isn't going to let me starve.

She brought home a small ball of hamburger and a can of
pork and beans. When the hamburger was fried, it rendered so
much fat that we were left a small patty not much bigger than my
thumb. While I washed our plates, my stomach continued to
growl, and Maude smoked out on the front porch. This day set the
pattern for the many days to come. I would awake each morning
to an empty house with empty cupboards. I walked repeatedly to
the mailbox praying there would be a letter from Frank or some
word from someone who would deliver me from the hell I found
myself. I couldn't write to Frank because he had not given his
mother or me his address. Maude lived several miles from town. It
was too far to walk. There was no telephone or television in the

house-—only an old radio that received a scratchy, barely audible station. My waist expanded so that I could no longer button my clothes, and without any money, I had to just let the gap get larger and larger. I interspersed trips to the mailbox with fits of crying and vomiting. The nausea seemed to get worse. I considered begging Maude to take me to my grandma's or to my aunt Mary's, but she had told me pointedly that the tickets and orders for me to travel would come to her address, and she couldn't guarantee getting word to me in time. I knew that to be true because when she was drinking, mail would have sat in the box for days if I didn't get it. Sometimes I watched the road leading to the house hoping someone would come to visit or check up on me. But no one ever came. Not even Betty.

Days faded into weeks and weeks faded into months until I figured I was about six months pregnant. Gnawing hunger shadowed me night and day, and I was passing out or feeling faint much of the time which seemed to worry Maude more than anything. She looked at my expanding belly and sighed, "what am I to do with you-—what are we going to do? Several people at work told me that the Army won't let you fly when you're seven months along. Frank hasn't written not even a line since he left, and I don't know how to get in touch with him. Tomorrow morning, we're going to Winston Salem to see his grandma. I know that Frank went to see her from Fort Bragg lots of times-—maybe she knows how to get in touch—even better, maybe she and Frank's aunt can find a way to get the army to send you a plane ticket. His aunt has an education and a good job. She probably knows who to talk to, or maybe she can go with us to the Red Cross. I've heard they'll help servicemen and families."

Frank's Grandma and Aunt Marge were sympathetic and civil. Aunt Marge said, "Mom, get one of those envelopes from the letters he wrote you from Fort Bragg. Let's take that address with us to the Red Cross Office, and see if they can track him down. They should be able to contact his old unit."

When Mrs. Carter in the Red Cross office heard my story, she was determined to get me to the Philippines as quick as the army could arrange it. Grandma Honley kept muttering, "No grandson of mine is going to get away with treating a girl so shabby and abandoning my great grandchild."

Maude just wanted to pass me off before the baby popped.

Mrs. Carter took the address from Grandma Honley, and after much searching and some phone calls tracked down the First Sergeant in Frank's old unit. Mrs. Carter told him an abbreviated story of my plight and asked how to get in touch with him in the Philippines. The First Sergeant verified that Frank had been stationed there and said we needed to speak to his old commanding officer. That turned out to be a long conversation because Granny Honley had taken over the phone. She made him promise to have the army send me a plane ticket right away, and to alert Frank when I would be there. She told the commander that she would sit there and wait for him to get Frank on the phone. The commander seemed amused by granny but he was being patient. "I can't talk to anyone over there right now because they're in bed. It's the wee hours of the morning over there. I promise that early tomorrow morning I'll take care of everything. The young lady should get what she needs to travel in a couple of days. I'll ask his new commander to talk to frank."

After the phone call, Granny Honley seemed quite pleased with herself. "I'm sure you'll be on a plane before the week is up."

On the way back to their house, Aunt Marge said, "It's getting late, you might as well stay for dinner. I have to warn you Maude, that Dick is staying with us. He went on a drunk and lost another job so he moved back in. We go through this back and forth. He'll straighten out, get another job painting someone's house, and move to some cheap room. Then he'll get on a drunk and lose the job. If you don't want to see him, I'd understand, but it looks like Sarah could use some food, and a rest before heading back to Marion."

At the prospect of getting a meal, I crossed all my fingers that she would consent, and that the meal wouldn't be hot dogs and beans or hamburger and beans.

Dick was there when we returned, and when introduced to me, he said, "What a cutie you are," and he put an arm around me and kissed me. I turned my face before his kiss landed on my lips. He smelled of booze and cigarettes which made my stomach turn with nausea. I ran to the closest bathroom just off the kitchen, and puked into the toilet. What a disgusting man, I could hear that all three women had moved to the kitchen and were preparing supper. I could hear clearly what they said.

Aunt Marge said, "I hate to say this, Mama but I do believe Frank intended to abandon that poor girl. She seems very frail and so young. Do you think she can make it all the way over there by herself?"

Maude spoke up, "She has no choice. She hasn't been to a doctor yet, but she needs to see one before that baby comes. What do we do if she doesn't get that plane ticket?"

Aunt Marge spoke up, "We'll sic mama on them. She doesn't take any guff from anybody."

I didn't want to go back into the living room because I wanted to avoid Dick, but I was feeling really dizzy and needed to sit down. The minute I entered the room, Dick grabbed me and planted a kiss on my lips. I pushed him away, but he held me to him. He let go in a hurry when Granny came in to ask what I wanted to drink. She gave him the evil eye and asked if I would help set the table.

It was a wonderful meal, with fried chicken, mashed potatoes, fresh green beans, and other food. I ate so much that I had trouble getting up from the table. I thanked them for the meal and the help, and then Maude and I headed back to Marion.

Maude and I were silent until we passed Hickory. She asked me what I thought of Frank's aunt, granny and dad. I answered honestly. "I liked his aunt and granny, but I thought his dad was disgusting."

I had not seen Maude laugh so much. There was an easy silence between us for the rest of the trip.

I checked the mail each day with new anticipation, praying for some news, and each day when there was nothing for me, I felt despair and climbed back into my black hole. Ten days had passed when I was yanked suddenly out of the hole by a special delivery. I signed for a thick legal sized envelope and assuming it was from Frank, I tore it open to find military orders and instructions telling me that I had a flight from the Charlotte airport two days later. I would fly to San Francisco, and then take a bus to Travis Air Force Base where I had a seat on a chartered Pan Am flight to the Philippines.

It took about three minutes to pack my ratty old suitcase with the few dresses I owned but could no longer wear. I kept out my only dress with a full skirt to wear on the trip. It did a fair job of hiding my stomach, but it gaped and showed at least three inches of skin at the waist. Marge was overjoyed to have me go. She flitted around rooting through all the piles of clothing and rags lying around the house. She came up with a very wide belt that she asked me to try. It was uncomfortable but it did the job of hiding the gap.

When the plane landed in San Francisco, I reread travel instructions the Army had mailed. I was to take a bus to Travis Air Force Base, and report to the terminal for a chartered Pan Am flight to the Philippines. I claimed my suitcase and began walking around the terminal looking for signs for the bus. Everyone I asked said they had no idea about a bus. In desperation, I left the building and started walking outside looking at signs and asking. I had to set the suitcase down every few yards to rest my aching arms and back. A man's voice called from behind, and I turned around to see an older soldier in army fatigues. His sleeves were covered in stripes, and behind him stood a whole crew of GI's. He said, "I overheard you asking about a bus to Travis. Why do you want to go out there?"

"I'm supposed to get a plane to go to the Philippines--my husband is stationed there, and the army sent me these orders." I held out the papers in my hand.

He took them, read through the first page, and handed them back.

"Ma'am the army takes care of its own. We'll make sure you get on that plane."

He motioned to one of the GI's, "You carry her suitcase, and make sure it gets on that plane."

I noticed his name tag said Buzelle, but he introduced himself anyhow with a salute. "Sgt. Buzelle at your service ma'am. I'm taking my whole squadron to Guam, so we'll be on the same airplane until we get there. You won't have to get off. There'll be some others getting off besides my crew, and after refueling, you'll be on your way to your husband. Follow me—I want you to sit down at one of the tables in this bar to wait. I'll send one of my guys to get you when the bus arrives. Can I get you something to drink?"

"Could I have a glass of milk?"

Sgt. Buzelle looked amused and said, "Sure, I'll find you a nice tall glass."

He put a large glass of milk in front of me, and went back to his men.

That milk tasted better than cake. It was the first nourishment I had since leaving Marion, and that had been only a biscuit and cup of weak coffee.

As promised, Sgt. Buzelle sent for me to board the bus, and when we arrived at Travis, escorted me to the check-in counter.

He checked in my suitcase, and again gave me that quick salute, "Young lady, have a wonderful time in the Philippines. It's been a pleasure."

I had tears of gratitude trying to adequately express my thanks. "I don't know what I'd have done if you hadn't helped me. Thank you so much."

He patted me on the back, "Maam, we take care of our own in this man's army. I hope someone is kind to my wife or daughters if they are ever in need of help. I always say to pass along kindness, and it will be returned to you."

The person at the check-in counter said they were collecting three dollars for the food and drink on board the plane. I was too ashamed to admit that I had no money, so I quickly said that I felt too sick to eat anything, and that I'd wait till I got there. She shrugged and pointed out that it was an eighteen-hour flight, then finished checking me in. Later when I got a whiff of the meal they were serving, I thought I'd pass out from hunger, but pretended to be asleep.

Throughout the long plane ride to San Francisco, and then the two hours wait for a bus to Travis Air Force, I had moved as if in a trance without much thought, but once on the airplane heading to the Philippines, uncertainty and fear began to replace the numbness that had gotten me this far. I didn't know if Frank's commanding officer had actually talked to him, and I had not heard from Frank at all. What if he doesn't know I'm coming? What if he doesn't come to the airport to pick me up? What if he doesn't want me there?"

As we prepared for landing, the pilot informed the passengers that it was eighty-nine degrees at Clark Air Force Base, and the humidity was ninety eight percent. When I stepped off the plane, I was immediately bathed in sweat. It dripped from my forehead and ran into my eyes stinging and blinding me. Someone handed me a tissue and said, "It's the humidity. I'd like to say you'll get used to it, but you won't."

I was weak with relief when I saw Frank making his way to me. He gave a quick jerk of my hand and asked me to follow him, but I kept lagging behind forcing him to turn back for me. After a couple of times, he took the suitcase which helped me move faster. I thought, it's about time, it's the least he could do, but I forced any negative thoughts from my mind and kept my mouth shut.

Frank said he'd rented a small house from a Filipino carpenter and we'd take a jeepney to get there. He helped me step up into one of the most garishly decorated vehicles I'd ever seen. The Virgin Mary swung from the middle of the windshield, and something in red or gold danced from every surface. There were tassels and mottos and all types of religious icons.

The jeepney stopped in front of a small cinderblock house. Like all the other houses we had passed, it only had wooden shutters, and no glass in the windows. There was a tall fence surrounding the house. Frank saw me staring at the pieces of broken glass shards stuck in the top of the whole perimeter of the fence. "It's for security. There's lots of theft here."

Inside, there were two rooms and a bath. There was a bedroom, and a combination living room and kitchen. The floors were red concrete. The only furniture was a small sofa made of rattan with loose cushions, a matching chair, and an end table in the living room. There was a small table for two on one end of the kitchen with two straight chairs, and in the bedroom, was a bed with a night stand, and a small dresser. It was a very simple house, but it appeared to be in good repair and clean. There was no telephone or television, but the landlord, a talented carpenter, had carved an elaborate case for a radio which he had loaned Frank. The house felt like a mansion. I dumped the contents of the suitcase into one of the three drawers of the dresser. Frank stood in the doorway giving me orders and criticizing how I dumped my clothing in the drawer. "Why don't you hang up your dresses--there's the closet with hangers."

I had promised my grandma not to make trouble if it wasn't called for, but I was so tired and hungry that I couldn't hold my tongue any longer. "Why didn't you write? Not one word from you all these months. Your mama said she suspected you had second thoughts, and your grandma thought maybe you had abandoned me."

Frank's demeanor suddenly changed. He became a whimpering, and defensive victim. "I have a job you know. I spent any time off looking for something to rent that I could afford. They refused to cut orders for you until I could prove I had a house. I did the best I could."

The rape and his brutality that summer night was the white elephant in the room. Neither of us brought it up.

I felt too tired, too hungry and sick to even consider the lack of logic in his excuse, and I was confused by his reaction, but told myself this was something to think about after eating and resting. The belt hiding the gap in my dress was causing pain and had to come off. As I pulled the belt away from me, I was overcome with dizziness and fell across the bed. Frank stared at my exposed middle and looked alarmed. "What's wrong with you?"

"You didn't send me a dime--I didn't have any money at all so I couldn't buy maternity clothes. The only food that was ever in the house was when Maude brought home a little something for supper which was never enough, and a lot of times, she didn't come home until late without any food--I guess she ate out somewhere--I know she boozed because I could smell it on her across the room. You ask what's wrong with me Frank? Everything. I'm sick. I keep passing out. I didn't have any money for a doctor. Everyone said I should be taking vitamins and iron, but I didn't have the money, and I didn't have any way to get to the doctor anyhow, and I haven't eaten in eighteen hours of the flight because I didn't have the measly three dollars they wanted for the food on that plane. You ask me what's wrong with me? I'm exhausted, I'm sick, and I'm starving."

Frank said, "Tomorrow, I'll take you to sick call. Then we'll go find you one of those Filipino mumu dresses. They're loose enough to be maternity. That's all the women here wear because it's so hot, that and those rubber shower clogs for shoes. There's some eggs and bread in the refrigerator for breakfast--we'll go to the commissary for some food before we come home tomorrow."

"I'm hungry now, I want to eat now."

Frank gestured toward the stove, "I don't know if the broiler in the stove works for you to get toast, but the frying pans in that drawer."

I scrambled half of the eggs, and managed to get half the loaf of bread unevenly toasted. I made myself sick by eating so much so quickly. It was the most food that I'd eaten in one meal in all the time I lived with Maude except for the one meal at his grandma's house. I wished I'd had jelly to put on the toast. I was craving jelly. Tomorrow, tomorrow, I'll get jelly.

I lay beside Frank in the double bed while he read. He hadn't made any move to have sex, and I remembered that he told me it would be my duty to have sex whenever he wanted it, but I was desperate for sleep. He was in the middle of a book, and his lamp was too bright. I turned my back to the light and tried to count how long it had been before I'd slept. I had been up at 5am to get to the airport, then four hours to get to San Francisco, then I had waited at least two hours before the bus ride to Travis Air Force Base, then there had been a couple of hours before the plane had left Travis for the Philippines. Someone had said that it was an eighteen-hour flight, I didn't know if that included the time and date change. Before I lost my battle to stay awake, I wondered if I had added the hours it took to get to the plane. My mind kept wandering into sleep, and I'd pull back trying so hard to stay awake until finally I lost the fight and fell sound asleep. Sometime during the night, I woke up with Frank groping me. He'd finished his book. After he had his way with me, I went to the bathroom without turning on the light, and felt something scurrying down my arm. I fumbled for the lights while shrieking loudly and saw a little green lizard running up the wall. Frank thought it hilarious and explained that geckos live in the house with us which is a good thing-—they eat lots of insects. The overflowing clothes hamper, in the corner of the bathroom, disturbed me. What was it that bothered me so much by that sight? I returned to the bed, looked up to the ceiling and saw a couple of geckos staring down at me. It was hard to get back to sleep. Frank barked at me, "Turn off the light and you won't see them."

In the darkness, I lay there puzzling over the clothes hamper until finally, I rose up on my elbow and asked, "Frank, how long have you lived here?"

"I've lived here for about three months. Remember that I told you married fellows get a housing allowance and aren't expected to live in the barracks."

"You told me that you had to have a house before I could come over. I could have come over three months ago."

His response was a dismissive, "What difference does it make? You're here now."

An unfamiliar sound outside the window awoke me, and I sat up and looked out to see a large creature grazing just a couple of feet from the window. It looked like an ox, but much larger. A half-dressed boy of around eight was talking to the obviously stubborn animal. In exasperation, he grabbed the creature by its huge horns to encourage it to move. Frank was amused by my reaction, "It's a water buffalo or caribou. They wander all over the place here. They won't hurt you."

Sick call was held every morning on the base. If you wanted to see the doctor for something that couldn't wait for an appointment, you just showed up, put your name on a list, and waited to be called. I had to write a sentence telling why I want to see the doctor. I wrote, "I'm pregnant and I keep passing out." This must have pushed me to the top of the list because I didn't have to wait more than half an hour. I answered all the questions, and the medic took some blood telling me that I should go to the end of the hall to wait outside the OB-GYN clinic while they ran the blood test in the lab, and I would be worked in around the scheduled appointments.

The OB doctor expressed alarm that I hadn't seen a doctor, and said my blood test indicated I was severely anemic. "I'm sure that's why you're passing out. You should have been taking vitamins and iron supplements from the beginning." He handed me a paper bag with prenatal vitamins and a bottle of iron with instructions to make an appointment for the following week.

Frank took me to the cafeteria next to the PX for a sandwich before we went into the PX to buy me a mumu. It was a cheap dress that was gathered at the neck to flow loosely out. It was a relief to have something to wear that covered my stomach and didn't bind. Our last stop for the day was the commissary to buy groceries. I was giddy to see so much food everywhere, and busied myself filling up the buggy, but Frank was busy putting things back on the shelf. "Stop it. I don't have much money to last until payday, are you trying to embarrass me? I'm gonna pick out what to buy," he growled at me.

There was no way He could ruin my day, there was still plenty of food left in the buggy. I had seen a doctor and received long due medical care, I had a dress that covered my expanding belly, I had food in my belly, and the food in the cart was not hamburger, or pork and beans, or hotdogs. This was the best day since moving into Maude's house which already seemed in the distant past.

Emboldened by the success of the day, I said, "Frank, we need to buy a crib and baby clothes."

I thought he was going to slap me the way his face glowered. "Don't you listen to anything people say to you? I just told you we can't afford to spend any more money till payday, and you're not due for another two to three months."

For a second, I thought He might apologize because the red left his face, and in a second, he changed into the whinny victim that had startled and confused me the night before. "As soon as I get my next pay check, we'll find a used crib and some baby clothes. The wives around here always have them posted on the bulletin board outside the PX. Can't you see I'm doing the best I can?"

We had ham and cheese sandwiches for dinner. I planned to cook the chicken, open a can of green beans, and bake a potato for dinner the next day if I could figure out how to cook. Frank assumed I did, and that I would be his cook. No one had ever taught me how, but I had watched plenty of times, surely, I could figure it out. The meal was barely edible. I was surprised that Frank didn't say anything, but ate everything on his plate.

The next couple of days, I was alone in the little house with nothing to do, which gave me plenty of time to think. The only sound was the occasional buzz of a saw next door in my landlord's wood shop. I found the sound comforting to know another person was nearby. Frank's stash of paperbacks held no interest. They were all science fiction or conspiracy theories which he read constantly.

One morning after Frank had gone to work, I heard someone rattling and determinedly knocking on the gate, and when I stepped outside, a man explained he was there to collect for the security.

"What security?"

"We guard your house––lots of thief's here––I guard your house. You pay me ten pesos every month."

I shooed him away saying I didn't need a guard and that I had no money. The look on his face when he turned away sent shivers up my spine. I had second thoughts, maybe I'd made a mistake.

Just two days later, I found out that I *had* made a mistake. Frank received his paycheck, and took me to the commissary to get a few groceries. We returned to the little house to find it empty except for our clothes. They even took the brass that Frank pinned on his uniform. I cried over the loss because all was borrowed from the nice Filipino carpenter. They even stole the pretty radio. When I went to him to apologize, and ask how I could repay him, he said, "No, no, I'm sorry for you. You don't pay me, I'm the landlord. I'm sorry."

Frank found a jeepney to take us to the entrance of the base, and from there, we took a bus to the NCO club where he left me to sip a glass of ice tea while he visited his first sergeant to ask for help. The next couple of hours were a whirlwind. We were in luck. There were no houses available on base, but there was one closer to the base, and in a neighborhood where most of the married soldiers lived. It had just been vacated, and was already furnished with items from the base supply. We fetched our meager clothes from the carpenter's house, and moved into our new home within two hours. I was busy making the bed with sheets borrowed from base supply when I heard someone knocking on the gate. Frank said he would answer, and if it was the Filipino security, he would pay them so we didn't have a repeat break in. But he returned quickly saying there were three women waiting to meet me.

My welcoming committee introduced themselves. Virginia lived opposite me, Joyce lived next door on one side, and Lillian lived on the other side of me. They said if I needed anything to just yell, and they got together every morning around nine for coffee and gossip. I was welcome to join them.

I went to bed that evening in my new house with a feeling of optimism. Maybe things wouldn't be so bad after all. The proffered friendship from my three neighbors promised to lift the loneliness that I had felt longer than I could remember.

My beautiful baby girl didn't wait--she was born the following week, even before my first OB appointment. I went into labor after dinner, but didn't realize it was labor because I was less than seven months pregnant. As I paced back and forth the pain in my back became stronger and felt as if something was pulling me into. Frank called for an ambulance when I was in so much pain that I couldn't walk. When we arrived at the hospital, a nurse greeted us and said the delivery room was in use so she helped me into a bed in a labor room. While the nurse donned gloves to examine me, she told Frank to wait outside in the hallway, and she would keep him informed.

When the nurse saw that my contractions were not spaced apart but continuous, and that I was bleeding badly, she called for a doctor and more nurses who rushed in immediately. The doctor delivered my baby and lifted her up to hand to a waiting nurse. My baby did not cry. The doctor and two of the nurses abandoned me, and went to help my tiny little girl who was in trouble. I sat up in the bed and begged aloud, "Please breathe baby, breathe please."

All was silent except for sounds of resuscitating my baby girl. After what seemed an eternity, there was a faint cry, and then another louder cry. The medical team sighed loudly as if they had been holding their breath the whole time. I reached to hold her, but the nurse, who had first attended me, said she was too small to handle and she was placing her into an isolette with some oxygen. Another nurse wheeled the isolette to the nursery where she could be monitored full time.

The doctor checked me and ordered a unit of blood. I had the blood seeping into my veins when I was wheeled to a bed in another room. I asked about Frank. Someone said he had gone home, and did not answer the telephone. The medic said she would keep calling. Afterward, the nurse held my hand and smoothed my hair. She told me that I could hold my baby when she weighed 5 pounds, and that I could even take her home then if the doctor approved. Without consulting Frank, I named her Ada after my grandmother. One of the nurses said, "I've gotten in touch with your husband, and he said he'd be here soon." But he didn't come for three days until he was informed I could go home. It was painful to leave Ada in the hospital when I was discharged, but I vowed to visit her every day.

All the military wives on our street were at my house to greet me. They had furnished the extra room with a crib, changing table, diaper pail and rocking chair. There were stacks of diapers, night gowns, and all things needed for a newborn. I was overwhelmed by such kindness.

Lillian seemed to be the ring leader and coordinator of the group. She told me that I also had a house girl, a live-in housekeeper and baby sitter. She said they had convinced Frank to hire her by explaining it was an unwritten obligation just like paying security and hiring the jeepneys. Frank, who was standing beside me, didn't object or comment. Virginia said Marie had already moved in and had been taking care of my house and helping them stock the nursery. I looked at Frank, and he just nodded. He had not said a word to me about it.

Each morning before joining the women for coffee and gossip, I called the hospital to inquire on Ada's weight, and condition. Every morning there was a slight improvement. She might have gained an ounce or two. Around four o'clock, I visited Ada. Standing outside the nursery window watching a nurse hold my baby, my arms ached to hold her.

I thought of my grandma, and the need to write her about her new great grandchild. I had written only one letter to her while living at Maude's, and that was to tell her that I had married

Frank, and I would be going to the Philippines. I didn't have the words to tell her how miserable and needy I was.

Dear Grandma,

I named my baby girl Ada after you. She was born too early and didn't weigh enough so the doctor put her in one of those incubators. They call them something different, but I can't remember now. She is beautiful and gaining weight every day. I can bring her home when she weighs five pounds. Grandma, you were right about getting married. Even though married to Frank is no picnic, my baby has the best of medical care. Don't worry, he doesn't beat me or anything like that. He doesn't pay much attention to me so I'm left to do mostly as I please as long as I make sure his clothes are clean, and I put food on the table, and I don't try to talk to him. If I had stayed there, little Ada would not have lived. She has what she needs for now. We have a roof over our head and enough food. Another good thing is I have several new friends who are so much help to me—they are teaching me how to care for a baby. We have to stay here until the two- or three-year assignment is up, but as soon as I can, I plan to come back to the mountains to be with you. I have asked around and found that there are no schools of any kind here for adults-- or jobs. I don't know where Frank will be stationed next in

What I didn't put in the letter was that I really
needed to talk to her. She always knew what to do, or if my
head needed to be set straight, she could point out how to
think about things. What I needed to talk about required
sitting in rockers on her front porch, talking and rocking
until grandfather mountain cast shadows on the porch.
Then she would always say, "well, we best be getting in."

I needed her to tell me how to think about Frank. I
didn't know him at all, and he frightened me. Based on that
one night of evil, I thought he would be mean tempered
and knock me around, but he had many faces. His mood
could change in a flash. There was no subject that he was
not an expert. When we were around other people he
talked and bragged nonstop about his superior knowledge,
and loudly gave his opinion on every subject. I saw the

look of trapped desperation in whoever happened to be unfortunate enough to be the recipient of his superior knowledge. When at home, the personality I saw most often was the poor old me. "See what you made me do, can't you see I'm doing the best I can." He was a whiner, and he played on making me feel guilty, which destroyed any confidence in myself. He made me feel that I did not see what I saw, or hear what I heard. Most of the time he was silent and brooding around the house with his nose stuck in a science fiction or a book about conspiracy. He convinced me to read one of the books about how the United States was really an evil empire and we were all a nation of sheep. It was at the end of conversation about the book that he commented, "If I had the power to press a button to blow up the world, I would do it in a heartbeat." My blood froze. The tone in his voice was the same that I heard that horrible night, and I knew he meant what he said. He quickly hid that face.

But what I really wanted to discuss with grandma was the gut feeling there was something sinister about him--that beneath the arrogance, the pontificating, beneath the whinny victim was something evil. There was a rage in him that he kept out of sight, but I felt it and knew it was there. It was in the lifeless coldness of his eyes. It was in the clipped tone of his voice. I found that I was always on edge waiting for something evil. If I had to choose which Frank, I would probably choose the outwardly angry Frank and being punched. At least, I could honestly react with anger. I didn't know how to think about this Frank or trust any of my feelings.

Grandma's words of caution were never far from my mind, "Trust your gut. If something doesn't seem right, then it isn't."

Only a week and a half passed before I received an answer from her.

My dear Sarah,

"I'd love to see you and my new grandchild, and I'd love for you to come back home, but I fear I won't live much longer. Please, please remember, before you leave the marriage, get some kind of training so that you can support yourself and your little one. I wouldn't put too much stock in him supporting you if you leave him. I know you will come out ahead. You have a stubborn streak that doesn't give up on anything. I've seen your fierceness and bravery time and time again. Dear child, you have always been a blessing to me.

Grandma

I dismissed this because it was common for old folks in the mountains to talk like that. They were always saying things like, "This thing paining me is gonna be the death of me. I'm afraid my time on this earth is coming to an end." Most of these folks seemed quite hardy and lived for another twenty or so years. But grandma never said such things. I felt a chill--was her letter a premonition?

Two weeks later I received a letter from my Uncle Ronald telling me of my grandma's death. I found the letter, my granny had written, to check the postmark, and saw that she must have died just a day or two after she mailed it. Uncle Ronald wrote, "She's buried on the hill above the house where your daddy and Uncle Blaine are buried. We sold the land and house to a feller from Florida. He plans to tear down the old house and build several houses on the land."

It was so final. He must have sold the house right after her death. Why so quick? I read between the lines, Ruby hoped to close the possibility of me returning. She had never wanted me around, and always treated me like I did not belong there, but grandma had held on to me and kept her at bay. Ruby must have been pushing him to sell quickly. I just did not want to think badly of my uncle. There was nothing to go back to. My grandma was my home.

My grief was overwhelming and twofold. Not only had I lost my beloved grandma, but I had lost the only place that ever felt like home. The house was old, and didn't have modern conveniences, but it was comfort. It was home. The grief was almost more than I could bear, but I was determined not to share it with Frank. He would not give me any comfort, and would find a way to use it against me. Virginia sensed my loss, and in an attempt to lift my spirits suggested that we gather a group to go downtown Angeles for the Easter parade.

"They have an Easter parade? I heard that they march along whipping themselves until they're bloody."

Virginia answered, "It's a religious ritual. They can sin all year long, but if they do this whipping thing, they call flagellation, they're washed clean of sin. I read that they also reenact the crucifixion. I'm pretty sure they're tied to the cross, and not actually nailed. Anyway, it's a religious thing, but Claude said that although they're Catholic, the Catholic Church frowns on this practice. Let's go."

There were four of us. We found a good vantage point where we could see the men marching with whips and those carrying crosses. We were close enough to the hill at end of the street where the crosses would be erected to see everything. The men were barefoot and shirtless with deep gashes on their backs which were bleeding badly. When one of the men passed by just three feet away, I could see that the gashes appeared to be deep knife cuts and not just from the whips. The whip landed on his mangled back and splattered blood across my dress and feet. The sight of their mangled and bloody backs seemed to excite the observers lining both sides of the street. My little group had ceased all chatter as we gazed at the horrible scene. I wanted to turn away but was riveted in place. The men carrying crosses followed the ones with whips. They were dressed in robes and were also barefoot. It was a sweltering hot day, and the crosses appeared to be heavy wood. Someone darted out of the crowd and shoved a crown of thorns on the head of one cross bearer. Droplets of blood mingled with sweat dripped down his face. When they arrived at the foot of the hill, they dropped their crosses on the ground and lay down on top of them. The man with the thorns was to be crucified first. I had assumed he would be tied to the cross to mimic the crucifixion, but someone began driving nails into his hands. The crowd was driven to a fury of emotion.

Joyce was whimpering and saying over and over, "No, oh God, no."

I grabbed her hand and motioned to the others to leave. Neither of us said a word until we reached the bus stop. Then Lillian said what we were all thinking, "That was not a good idea. I could have lived without seeing that."

I tried to tell Frank about my experience. It had left me so shaken that I felt the need to talk about it, but he cut me off in mid sentence to get back to his science fiction paperback. I don't know how many men were crucified, but the next day, word was that one of the men died on the cross.

I found Marie to be a godsend since I couldn't seem to muster the energy to do much of anything except gossip with the women, and drink iced drinks. My body wasn't adjusting too well to the tropical heat and humidity. Our conversation wasn't all just idle gossip. I confessed that I was ignorant about raising a child--that I was terrified because I knew nothing about what babies needed. Although Virginia, Lillian, and Joyce continued to tell me I should not worry because it would come naturally, they still spent hours educating me. I learned how babies should be bathed, what type of lotions and powders to put on their bodies and bottom, how to fold a diaper, how to pin it, and many other lessons that I would forget and then be reminded over and over.

One morning, Virginia, who was usually the first one there for our morning coffee klatch, was late. Joyce and Lillian seemed stressed, and I had the feeling they were trying to hide something. We heard a terrible commotion coming from Virginia's house, and we heard her sobbing and begging Claude to stop hitting her. It sounded as if she was being thrown against something solid, and we could hear the smack of Claude's fists. Virginia howled in pain, and begged him to stop. I stood up and headed for the door intending to go to her aid. Joyce and Lillian pulled me back. Lillian said, "We've been through this many times before. Claude gives her a terrible beating almost every two weeks. This time he went a little longer. Each time, we have begged her to call MPs and leave him, but she always makes excuses for him because he says that he is sorry and promises not to do it again, but two or three weeks later, he gives her another beating."

Lillian chimed in, "Last time he broke her jaw. I'm afraid one of these days that he'll kill her. She told us that if we report him, she'll not tell the MPs anything."

After Claude slammed out of the house, I thought we should go see what we could do for her, but Virginia wouldn't let us in. She talked through the door, and begged us to go away because if Claude came back and found us there, it would be worse for her. She assured us she would be okay and would be over for coffee the following morning.

We didn't see Virginia for two days, and when she joined us on the third morning, we could see that she had tried to cover up facial bruising with makeup, but not really successfully. It was obvious that both eyes were blackened.

I couldn't keep quiet. "Virginia, no one should put up with that. One day, he's going to kill you if you don't get away from him. If you need someone to testify to the MPs, I'll tell them what I heard."

She sighed and looked defeated, "Sarah, I don't have anywhere to go. I don't have any family, and I don't have any skills to earn a living. The most important reason is little Carly. I can't feed him or put a roof over his head, and Claude says if I ever leave him, he'll find me and take him from me."

"Virginia, how do you know that he won't start beating on Carly? Besides what kind of lesson is he learning?"

Virginia waved her hand in dismissal. Someday, when he gets older maybe it will be easier. Maybe we'll be in an easier place, and I can find some way to earn some money."

Lillian spoke up, "I know how we can earn money now. We can sell on the black market. I know several wives who claim to make a lot of money. If any of you are interested, I can get details from this woman I know at the end of the street."

We looked at each other quizzically, gave it some thought for a few minutes, then all said in unison, "Yes."

Lillian called us over late that afternoon to explain how it worked. She also had a list for each of us with the items the buyers would pay for. She explained, "If we have items for sale, we tie a green ribbon or string on the gate, and the buyer will let himself inside the gate. I think he always comes after dark."

We unfolded our list and read aloud, boxes of Velveeta cheese, Kool cigarettes, Folgers coffee, etc. Our profit would come from the difference we paid at the commissary, and what the buyer paid us.

Virginia said, "Please don't any of you tell Claude, he would kill me if he found out." We assured her we were in the same boat, and we were all in agreement that the safest time for the buyer to come to our houses was when the guys were on swing shift because not only would the husbands be at work, but most of the time, it would be dark.

The military was paid once a month, and Frank gave me what he called my monthly food allowance so I tried to buy enough to last the whole month. Once I spent only half of the money so I could go again in two weeks, but Frank took it away from me saying since I had money left over, obviously I didn't need all that he had given me.

I sheepishly told Lillian my dilemma, "I don't have any money until payday and that's not for another week. Even then, I'll have to really plan to buy even a few of the items, but it sounds like we need to do this more often. Something we didn't think about is swing shift only happens every third week of the month."

Lillian was thoughtful for a few minutes, "What if I can get the buyer to come once when they work days, and once when they work the swing shift, and what if I loan you a bit of money for the first purchase--you can pay me back with your profits later on?"

The rest of us agreed that if she could arrange it, then it might work. She was the only one who had a car, so she volunteered to take us all to the commissary on regular buying trips.

The first time the buyer came to the house, I felt guilty like I was committing the worst sin in the world, but when I stashed my profit in a mayonnaise jar carefully hidden in my underwear drawer, the guilt lessened.

I hadn't had a chance to read the base newspaper that I'd picked up earlier and thought it a perfect time to catch up on base happenings. Two stories caught my attention. The first one about black market made my heart race, and I felt fearful for what I was doing. The story said that black market had become a huge problem on Clark Air Force base claiming that thousands of dollars were lost daily. It further claimed that the commissary and PX received a set inventory, and black-market reduced supplies and raised prices for everyone who depended on shopping there for tax free goods. The story went on to say that undercover police would be watching the checkout registers, and if someone bought much more than they could possibly use, then they would be stopped. The article gave an example that if someone bought one hundred bars of soap each month, they would be nabbed because nobody needed to take that many baths. They had the same logic for cigarette sales saying no one could smoke a hundred cartons of cigarettes in a month. There were other rationed purchases like alcohol and sodas. Anyone caught black marketing would be deprived of commissary and PX privileges. I folded the paper open to the story about black market as I rushed over to Lillian's house. She read the story and snorted. "Sarah, no one is looking for us with our onesie twosie purchases. They're watching for the person who buys a hundred cartons of cigarettes, or a hundred bars of soap like the article says. No one is that clean. Stop worrying."

One morning, three months later, I made my daily call to the hospital. The nurse told me Ada had just been weighed, and at four pounds and thirteen ounces, the doctor believed she was strong enough to go home.

As I hung up the phone, Frank walked in just having finished a night shift. I was so excited that I almost knocked him down when he came through the door. "We can pick up Ada now. I just called and they said she could come home."

Frank kept moving toward the bedroom while unbuttoning his shirt. "I'm not going anywhere. I'm tired and going to sleep now. You'll have to either wait or go get her yourself."

I could hardly believe that he meant it, no one could be that cold, but he finished undressing and climbed into bed.

I thought about going alone, but dismissed the idea because I had to walk about three fourths of a mile to get a jeepney. After thinking about my options, I decided to ask Lillian to drive me. She said she would love to go fetch a new baby.

I carried Ada as if she would break although the nurse insisted she wasn't that fragile. Lillian opened all doors for me then helped me into her car.

After Lillian had seen me safely into the house, I took Ada immediately into the bedroom so Frank could hold his daughter for the first time. He sat up in the bed and screamed, "Get her out of here!"

I quickly closed the door behind me, and shaking with emotion, fell into a chair. I wasn't sure if I was frightened, or just angry. Frank confused me. His reactions, his conversation, his moods were strange. I had stopped being so watchful and tense around him, probably because I had been occupied with my new friends, and preparations to bring Ada home. He never took an interest in any of my activities nor did he seem to care as long as his needs were filled. But I had thought he would show some care for his own child. Sometimes, I felt remorseful for judging Virginia, because I was no better. Frank didn't physically beat me, but his words and body language felt like a hard punch, and our marriage wasn't based on love or respect, but out of need. My need. Virginia and I both took whatever was dished out because we felt we had no other choice. We both had a child that needed food and shoes which we could not provide, and neither of us had any marketable skills. I felt even more determined to find a way to get those marketable skills.

I held my baby girl close to my heart and breathed deeply the sweet baby smell, and stroking her tiny head made a vow to her, "I will protect you and never let you be hungry. As long as I live, you will never be in rags, and you will always have a clean, comfortable bed."

Once, I saw a lizard that changed colors. Frank was like that lizard. His mood could change in a heartbeat. He would go from scathingly arrogant to a whiny victim in a flash. I hated the whinny victim the most. His body and face drooped in a hang dog expression. He would pile on the 'pitiful me' talk, and imply that I was treating him badly. After all he was doing the best he could. On the surface, his mood appeared to be the whinny victim, but there was a rage just beneath the surface which he managed to hide from everyone. At times, I saw flashes of the rage, and it chilled me to my core.

He usually did make me feel guilty and stupid about everything I said or did, but mostly totally and absolutely bewildered. I could not justify that brutal man who raped me with this weak and whiny person. He was also secretive. He had managed to find an extra long telephone cord somewhere, and when he came home after a day shift, he'd receive phone calls that he'd take into the bathroom where I couldn't hear his side of the conversation. I answered the phone a couple of times, and a man asked to talk to him, but wouldn't give me his name. Shortly after hanging up, someone knocked on the gate. Frank went out to talk to them. It was always after dark so I couldn't see who was there, but I heard a man's voice. They would talk for about half an hour. Once I asked Frank who was on the phone and who was he talking to at the gate. He put on his victim face, "Are you accusing me of something? It's just about something going on at work." I didn't have to be Einstein to know that wasn't true.

Then there were the times when he didn't come home from his swing shift. The shift ended at eleven. I usually went to bed early and got up early. Many times, I'd find his side of the bed not slept in, and he was nowhere in the house. He seemed to sneak up on me when I was getting dressed. The first couple of times this happened I asked him why he didn't come home, and he said, "Why, are you accusing me of something? We get problems at work that need to be solved before we can leave. After all, you know that I handle top secret information, and my job is important, don't you? What are you accusing me of now?" The second and last time this happened, I commented about his absence, "You must have had a busy night at work." He insisted he had slept on the couch and was there the whole time. I knew he was not there and did not sleep on the couch, but kept my mouth shut to avoid another put-down. I never mentioned his absences or secretive phone calls again. Actually, I preferred his absence from the bed. He had rarely demanded sex since Ada was born, and the times he did were rough and left me in pain. But even with rare sex, I needed a way to prevent another pregnancy.

I listened intently when my new friends talked about birth control. They were excited because there was a new and more reliable birth control available—pills that you took every day. They were all going to get pills and get rid of the messy diaphragms that weren't totally effective.

I didn't have the chance to get pills before discovering I was pregnant again. Ada was only two months old, and visions of near-starvation, isolation, and sickness flooded over me. When I called to make an appointment with the OB/GYN clinic, I was informed the earliest appointment was almost three weeks away. The scheduling medic suggested I come in to see a doctor on sick call who could do a rabbit test. Two days later, I went back to the clinic for the results, and was crushed to find it was positive. I hurried home so I could be alone for awhile to think. Fate had dealt me a losing hand. What do I do now? I had not planned on another child. Becoming independent with one child was going to be hard, now I had to plan for two children.

When I told Frank, he just shrugged. I don't know what reaction I had expected, but one would think when told of a new baby that you'd express some emotion whether it be anger or happiness.

Three weeks later, I saw the doctor who had delivered Ada, and tearfully confessed my fears of passing out all the time, and the horrible pain I'd had to endure during labor. He tried to calm my fears by explaining, "Your other baby was just too small for me to give you any pain meds--it would have put her to sleep. I knew you'd thank me later. We'll get you to full term and you'll have options for several pain medications."

Sometimes, we got together with the other young families around us. It was during those times that I noticed Frank stretched the truth, and even sometimes appeared to fantasize about a lot of things. He began telling the group about how we were such close friends with the Kieths. Sgt Kieth was Frank's first sergeant, and in reality, I had never met them, and I'd never been to their home. When I questioned Frank about this claim he answered, "Well, I haven't seen them much since you got here, but before you came, I used to baby sit for their two little girls and they'd invite me for dinner lots of times."

A couple of weeks later, Lillian, Joyce and I were having lunch at the NCO club. We had just finished our black-market shopping and were spending some of our earlier profits for lunch.

A very pretty woman came over to say hello and asked if she could sit with us. She was introduced as Jane Cantlin, who lived on base near the Kieth's. Jane told me that Laura Kieth was her best friend. A little voice inside told me to keep quiet but I asked anyhow, "You probably know my husband, Frank Honley. He says he babysat for the Kieths before I got here and that he spent a lot of time at their house."

I could sense a negative reaction. "He did volunteer to babysit a couple of times when Laura asked the GIs in the squadron if their wives or daughters wanted a babysitter's job. But I don't think he spent any other time there. I heard that he was bosom buddies with that young kid-oh-what's his name--John Brownlee or something like that. I think they spent most of their spare time downtown Papanya at the topless bar."

She was very cool toward me the rest of the lunch, but my curiosity was roused. Obviously, Frank had said or done something to anger her and the Kieths because Jane said, "They learned a lesson and would never have a GI babysit for them again."

That evening, I asked Frank about John Brownlee. "Why haven't I heard about him or met him if you were such great friends?"

Maybe it was my imagination but it seemed he turned red and was flustered.

"Who've you been talking to? He and I spent some time together just to have company before you came. No big deal. I don't need to answer to you about what I do or who I pal around with."

By his reaction, I knew not to say anymore, and not to bring up questions about the Kieths or John Brownlee.

There were no jobs or colleges for military wives, so we had endless days to fill. We played the nickel slot machines at the NCO club when we had an extra dollar. That always provided a nice break because the NCO club was air conditioned. But most of the time, flattened by the tropical heat and humidity, we sat around in our non-air-conditioned homes sipping iced tea, fanning ourselves and gossiping. As my belly expanded, I especially felt discomfort from the heat and humidity.

I was about eight months pregnant when Frank said he was taking me on a day trip to the mountains for some cool breezes and a change of scenery.

I was amazed by this, "I didn't think there were any mountains in the Philippines, just flat islands."

It seemed out of character for Frank to be so eager to take me on an outing for just the two of us. "There are plenty of mountains. The one we are going to today is called Tagaytay. It looks out over the Taal volcano--quite a sight. Wait until we get up there and you feel the cool breezes, you'll want to stay."

This was obviously somewhere that Frank had visited before. He always talked down to me when we were alone, but today, he talked non-stop in a normal conversational tone, and instead of putting me at ease, it set off alarm bells. We wound our way up the mountain and parked in a restaurant parking lot. Frank had recently purchased an old clunker, and was eager to find excuses to drive. He led me onto an outdoor terrace which was part of the restaurant. When we were seated, he ordered for each of us a green coconut filled with vanilla ice cream. He looked rather smug when he said, "this is the specialty here and a real treat, the view doesn't hurt either does it?"

I looked at the beauty all around me and thought of the grime near the base, and what most American military would always associate with the Philippines because they never left the area of the base.

Frank urged me to move to the edge of the patio where I saw it was a sharp drop to the canyon below. I looked down and across to the mountains beyond admiring the view. Some movement made me look sideways at Frank. His facial expression and the look in his eyes gave me a chill. Suddenly I knew he intended to push me over the edge to my death and the death of my unborn child. Quickly, I stepped back and returned to my seat at the table while managing not to show Frank I knew the danger I was in. I shoved my hands into the pockets of my mumu until they stopped shaking. Frank stood where he was near the edge and called out to me, "You need to see the rest of the view."

I told him I was not feeling well and needed to sit. We headed back to the base and neither of us said anything except that it had been a nice trip. On the ride back, I tried to convince myself that Frank did not have bad motives for taking me there, and that I was just being overly dramatic. I always did have an active imagination.

I was grateful that Marie had fed Ada and put her to bed because I was feeling nauseated with a crampy feeling in my gut. I wondered if the green coconut was making me sick. But when the pain moved to my back and became intense, I realized I was in labor.

The nurses helped me undress and get into bed in one of the labor rooms. After examining me, the doctor said, "It's going to be awhile so try to get some sleep." I was in too much pain to sleep but he refused to give me anything for pain until I'd dilated more, so I lay awake listening to the strange sounds around me. The strangest being the sounds of the fighter jets revving up and taking off in the middle of the night. The roar was almost deafening since the flight line was next door. I heard the nurses talking at the nurse's station. It sounded as if they were saying the governor of Texas had just shot President Kennedy. Surely, I was hallucinating from the pain, and rang to fetch a nurse. She said,

"No, someone else shot the President, but the governor of Texas was riding in the car with him at the time. President Kennedy's been taken to the hospital and everyone is waiting to find out how badly he's hurt. The roar you're hearing is the scrambling of the jets—everyone's on alert."

She examined me again to see how much closer I was. "I'm going to recommend you go home and rest there because you haven't progressed at all. You're in labor but it's being so slow, you'd be more comfortable at home. The doctor will be in a minute to check you and confirm."

The doctor cautioned, "Don't go far because you'll be back soon--I just can't tell how long it'll be. Everyone is different."

Fortunately, someone had stopped Frank before he could leave, and asked that he stick around a little longer. He suggested that we go to the NCO club where we could get breakfast, and see if there was any news on the TV in the lobby. The television station at Clark Air Force Base was operated by the Air Force and came on at 4pm for about four hours daily, but when there was something big going on in the world, they had earlier broadcasts. A crowd was huddled around the television watching still pictures of President Kennedy accompanied by dirgey sounding music. I found a seat away from the crowd but still within view of the TV screen. Frank and I sat there for over three hours with me dozing off and on while the pain in my back became stronger and stronger. I was jolted fully alert by the sudden increase of noise from the gathered crowd. People seemed to be talking at once, and Frank said, "They just announced that President Kennedy has died."

I must have sat up too quickly because a pain ripped through my back and abdomen which took my breath away. I sat very still hoping it wouldn't come back, but a couple of minutes later, waves of pain washed through me.

Frank had not noticed my pain. He stood up, stretched and said, "We probably should just go ahead home--it's not really that far off base."

"No," I whispered, "I need to go back--it's that time."

My beautiful Amy was born shortly after arriving at the hospital. I just had enough time to get undressed and another exam.

She rarely cried, and after the first week, usually slept through the night. When she was just three or four months old, I would awaken each morning to hear her cooing and trying to talk to her toes or the toys just out of her reach. I began associating the sunrays dancing off my bedroom walls with Amy's delightful gurgles.

As much as I loved both my babies, I did not want to get pregnant again. I had two babies just a year apart, and I was barely nineteen. Frank had not touched me for sex for the nine months I was pregnant with Amy. The last time he had demanded sex was the night Amy was conceived. It was not normal sex nor was it love of any kind. Instead, it was a violent depraved rape. Frank hurt me so badly that I rolled away when he was through with me, hastened to the bathroom, and threw up. What a relief these months had been, but now, what would he demand? When I went for my first post partum check up, I requested a prescription for the new birth control pills which the doctor willingly gave me. This turned out to be unnecessary because Frank never touched me again. I felt relieved, but also wary because I didn't know what he would do if he decided he didn't need me for anything before I was prepared to support two babies. I assumed he was having affairs. Many times, I saw him making eyes at a woman and mouthing something, and many times, she ogled and mouthed back. I was careful to never let on that I had seen them.

I took a two month break before continuing with my black-market career. Before Amy was born, my mayonnaise jar was stuffed with bills, but I was far from having enough to buy our freedom. I saw a Fisher Price toy in the PX for Ada and a mobile of butterflies for Amy—perfect for Christmas. If I took just enough for those and splurged a bit for a small tree and a string of lights, I could sell a little extra and, wouldn't have to deplete my savings by too much, but my sales career came to an end when Frank returned home unexpectedly one evening, and saw the buyer leaving the house carrying a sack of goodies. I was putting my money away in the mayonnaise jar when he stormed into the bedroom and caught me in the act. He grabbed the jar and the bills from my hand, and stuffed everything into his pocket.

"In order for you to have that much money stashed away, you must have been doing this under my nose for a long time. You're forbidden to ever do this again. It's illegal, and I don't want any attention thrown on me. If I catch you even thinking about it, I'll ship you back to the states where I found you."

I managed to protest feebly, "Frank, I just sold a little at a time, and saved every cent--I was hoping to give the girls a nice Christmas. Please give me the money."

Frank made a derogatory motion and stomped into the kitchen. I sat on the bed listening to him opening and shutting drawers. He must have found what he was after because he left the house and drove away.

I didn't dare dabble in the black market again. I had endured Frank's anger, and knew he was capable of much worse.

Ada was almost two and Amy was a year old when Frank received orders for Fort Lewis in Tacoma, Washington. We had been constantly reminded of the war in Viet Nam. The roar of fighter jets taking off and landing on the flight line could be heard almost twenty-four hours a day. Soldiers coming and going from Viet Nam landed at Clark Air Force Base. Whether they were coming from a year in Viet Nam or heading to Viet Nam, they usually spent a day or two before leaving Clark Air Force Base. Some of them were eager to talk. We received limited television news, and other than *The Stars and Stripes*, there were few other resources for news. These soldiers were supposed to be only going to Viet Nam as advisors, but sometimes we heard of Americans being killed.

Everyone knew that orders for Fort Lewis, Washington meant you were headed to Viet Nam after receiving training, and Frank had learned he was part of a squadron assembled from soldiers arriving from all over the world to prepare for duty in Viet Nam. But we were continually told Americans were only advisors.

When I asked Frank if we could visit family before reporting to Fort Lewis, he snapped his response, "We're not going to be anywhere near the east coast. Don't you think I would like to see my family too? I don't get any leave time, and have to report immediately to the base."

We were allowed to spend a week in the guest quarters, and spent hours each day looking for a place to rent, but couldn't afford anything close to the base, so we kept looking farther and farther away. I met several of the wives in the hallway of the guest house, and heard their frustration. We all felt as if we were in limbo not knowing if we were coming or going, and they expressed dismay at the cost of rentals.

Frank's first sergeant ordered him to teach me to drive and take me to get my license right away saying that if they shipped out suddenly, he couldn't leave me without a way to get around. Frank took me to a large empty parking lot, showed me some basics like where the accelerator and brakes were and told me to drive. I did wheelies and practiced parking while the girls rode in the back seat and squealed with laughter. They thought we were having fun. When Frank thought I'd had enough lessons, he drove to the DMV. He said he would wait on a bench inside as he placed a daughter on each side, then he told the person testing me that he was shipping out to Viet Nam and his wife had to have a way to get around.

I careened around turns, knocked down cones, and generally embarrassed myself, but the tester said that I had passed as he looked at Frank, then he turned to me, "I hope I don't meet you on the road. I suggest you have your husband or someone with a license riding with you and that you go to a back street to practice some more."

After an exhaustive search, we found a rundown house to rent twelve miles from the base, and Frank made arrangements with base housing to deliver a bed, a small table and two straight chairs. He arranged for the delivery of our belongings shipped from the Philippines. It was a meager shipment of two cribs, some basic children's items, a small stack of linens, and a few kitchen necessities.

We had just one day left in the guest quarters when the wives were notified to assemble in the theater for a briefing.

When I settled in a seat and looked around, I was surprised to see there were at least fifty other women there. There were two lieutenants and a captain on stage.

The captain spoke first, "Your husbands will not be in harm's way, they'll be going as radio relay operators, and will never be where there is combat. At this time, we are not at war, but that day may come soon and when it does, we will be prepared. Your husbands are heading to desert training on the east side of the state, and then cross training in radio relay operations. Since many of the messages they'll handle are sensitive, they already have a top security clearance which saves time. I wish to introduce Lt. Brooks who will give you some more information and answer any questions."

Many of the wives stated that they wanted to move to be near relatives. Since my grandma had died, I didn't have anywhere else to go. It seemed logical to stay at Fort Lewis where I had medical and commissary privileges. There were several wives who were staying, and I hoped to get acquainted with them.

A day later, we moved into the little rented house. Special services delivered the items requested, but our belongings had not arrived from the Philippines. We were told it may be another one to two weeks, but we could borrow a few of the basics from housing. Frank managed to borrow a bed, some linens, a pile of wool army blankets and a small box of kitchen cooking and serving items. It was crude, but I was able to make do. Fortunately, there were some built-in drawers at the end of the hall. Two of these stuffed with army blankets worked quite well as beds for the girls. They were so small they fit just fine in the drawers with room to spare. About three weeks later, we received their cribs.

Month after month passed, and still Frank had not shipped out to Viet Nam. Every day there were numerous stories about Viet Nam and what the American role was. The Newspapers were filled with suspicions that American soldiers were more than advisors. Then someone would ask, "Since the United States has not declared war, why are we sending soldiers there?" What I had seen and heard when in the Philippines, I knew that we were at war. It didn't matter what the government wanted to call it.

It was a miserable time spending the days alone with two babies, no transportation, and no friends--not even a friendly neighbor. Frank took the car to work, and there wasn't even bus service that far out. The only times I left the house were the monthly trips to the commissary. It was such a contrast from the Philippines where I had daily visits and friends. My plan had been to get a job and some schooling, but time was slipping away while all I could do was wait. Also, it was not good that the girls had no outside stimulation and no play mates. I had not felt like I was in such a dark hole since those months at Maude's home. The days crawled into weeks, and the weeks crawled into months waiting for something to happen. Frank insisted that he was still going to Viet Nam he just did not know when.

Amy had started to walk, but Ada was not walking and she was almost three years old. I called the base hospital to make an appointment with a pediatrician. Frank took time off work to take us for the appointment. After the pediatrician examined Ada, he asked two more doctors to examine her. Then the doctors began to explain that Ada had cerebral Palsy. They had read her medical history about her premature birth, and that I had bled excessively during the delivery depriving her of oxygen. She had a very mild case, and the main reason she didn't walk was that the Achilles tendon didn't keep up with her growth. They could fix the problem by performing surgery to lengthen the tendon and put her in a brace for a few weeks. She was scheduled for surgery in six weeks. A shortage of orthopedic surgeons meant the schedule was always filled. I wondered if malnutrition through most of the pregnancy had caused her to be premature, but didn't ask.

One evening when Frank was working the swing shift, I went to lower the shades in the living room. It was still twilight, and the world outside was not in focus, but I could clearly see the glow of two cigarettes across the street. Peering into the approaching darkness, I could make out two figures facing our house. They were leaning against an automobile and smoking. I closed the blinds, and went to a window in another front room where I could look without being seen. The men were definitely watching my house. Around the same time, my phone began making strange noises. There was a strange clicking sound which I thought might just be a bad connection, but when the phone noise continued for a couple of days, and the two men showed up outside for two more nights, I became alarmed and told Frank. He shrugged and said, "It's only the FBI. They run surveillance on all soldiers in the security service every year, and apparently, it's my turn."

I knew Frank had a renewed security clearance each year, but I didn't think the clearance involved surveillance.

The next day when he returned from work, he said, "You can relax now, the surveillance is over. They won't be back and the phone's been cleared."

Frank had told so many lies, that I knew to distrust anything he said, but I was puzzled. What was he up to? At least the men did not return, and the phone noise was gone.

A couple of days later, Frank came home carrying a car full of boxes and told me to start packing. "An apartment has opened up right outside the base, and my first sergeant told me to move as quickly as I can. A crew will be here tomorrow to load our stuff and move us in. The brass wants all soldiers who don't live in the barracks to live as close as possible. We live too far away."

I was ecstatic. Not until everything was packed including all clothes except what we would wear the next day, did I drop into bed exhausted. I was so tired and keyed up that I didn't fall asleep until hours later.

Several women whose husbands were in the same unit as Frank, lived in the apartment building. Two of these women lived on the same floor, and came to welcome me within two hours of moving in. Helga and Rita both had huge smiles and were very chatty. I could feel my loneliness melting away, especially when they said they had children the same age as Ada and Amy. Playmates for them. The very next morning, Helga knocked on my door and asked if Ada and Amy could come over to play with her two. Before I could answer, the four toddlers were giggling and running off to play. Ada had developed the ability to walk on her knees. When anyone stood her up to encourage that she walk upright, and on her feet, she either sat down quickly or fell over. It didn't appear to slow her down, but everyone who saw her, made comments.

The rumors of war became louder and louder. There were numerous protests, and unrest throughout the country about a war that wasn't a war. One day, a group of protesters were marching past our building, with the press not far behind. I had not dared express my disdain for sending our men to possibly die in a war we didn't understand, and that I felt no reason to get involved. It was just too easy for me to begin marching right along with these people. Someone thrust a microphone in my face and asked me to comment on why I was marching. I looked down at my two daughters, one perched on each hip, and said loudly that I was setting an example for my daughters to speak out when you see injustice. I also said something like, "This was is just wrong."

That evening Frank stormed into the apartment with his face a dark red. I thought he was going to hit me, but he stopped short, and commanded in a voice so cold and full of fury that it left me weak with fear, "My commanding officer saw your disgraceful tirade on TV. He ordered me to control my dependant wife. You've made a fool out of me."

My voice was shaky and my body trembling, but I managed to speak up, "I was just expressing my opinion—how I feel about this war or whatever you call it."

"You are not allowed to have an opinion, and if one creeps into your little pea brain, don't express it. Everything you say or do, reflects on me."

The next day, Frank called from work, "We're on alert—the the brass is making everyone create a power of attorney and an allotment to send their paychecks home each month. We're allowed to keep only fifteen dollars. The brass said that where we're going, we won't need money. After everyone has completed and signed forms, we have an hour to go home and grab the duffle bag that we packed months ago. It's in the back of the hall closet. Pull it out and put it in the living room. I'll be there in a few minutes, and you will have to drive me back to the base."

There were many wives and girl friends in front of the barracks kissing their husbands and older children hanging on to them crying. Ada and Amy sat in the back seat wide eyed not understanding what was going on. Frank had learned to put on a good show in front of people. Normally he would kiss me on the cheek and hug the kids. I had learned it was just for show so I turned my cheek to him, but he ignored it. He grabbed his duffle bag, told the girls to behave, and said he would see us again in a year, perhaps. He quickly disappeared inside the barracks not giving me a chance to express any sentiment.

I sat on the edge of the seat gripping the wheel and drove about fifteen miles an hour. People honked horns all around me and made jesters. I was not going to be bullied into going faster. I had not driven the car since taking the road test, and I had two precious little people in the back seat. As soon as I walked in the door, I turned on the TV to see if there was any news. There was a stir because an American ship had been attacked in the gulf of

Tonkin. The reporters said, surely now, we will declare war. I listened to the news as I prepared dinner for the girls and turned it off while putting them to bed.

Sitting in the dark listening to a quiet house, I imagined the walls sighed with relief that Frank was not there. I was glad he was gone, but I didn't want him to be killed in a war. I felt ashamed that I hadn't pushed back when he silenced me. Instead, I'd been reduced to shaking fear at the implied fury in his voice. He rarely showed any emotion. I always had the feeling he was forcing himself to be on guard, and there was a terrible character flaw carefully hidden, or that he harbored dark secrets that I didn't have the capacity to recognize. The only clue yesterday was the red that crept over him, and the tightness in his jaw. His eyes frightened me--that's what frightened me so much yesterday They were cold almost lifeless as if they didn't belong to the face. I could not figure out intellectually what bothered me so much-–I just had a negative visceral reaction to him.

The next day, I bought two newspapers, spread out the employment section, marked every position for which I might qualify, and carefully drew up a chart placing each job opening in order of distance from the apartment. Then I looked up day care centers, and picked the two that were closest to home. I bargained with my new friend Helga for child care for the afternoon, "If you'll watch Ada and Amy for an afternoon, I'll watch

Michael and Zoey for an afternoon." My girls got along with her two kids. They had played together every day since we moved in.

The first job was for a receptionist. All that it required was greeting people and keeping an appointment log. That sounded easy to me. The lady at the front desk handed me an application to fill out after she told me the salary was $1.15 an hour. I managed not to gasp at the low pay, but filled out the application and handed it back. After waiting for at least twenty minutes, she returned, handed back the application pointing to the area on application where there were two questions that I thought was none of their business. The first question was whether it was okay with my husband for me to work, and the second question was what does your husband do for a living? I answered truthfully that he was in the military. The interviewer, who had identified herself as Mildred, said, "We do not hire military wives because of a bad experience in the past. Also, just when they're properly trained, they move on."

All five places, where I applied, told me the same thing, and the receptionist position was the highest pay of them all. I decided to check out the day care anyhow, just in case I could lie about my husband when I applied somewhere else.

Both day care facilities handed me brochures telling me how much for each child and how they operated. For two children, the cost would be much more than I would earn in any of the five positions. I was stunned to learn that I simply could not afford to work.

I returned home from my disappointing day in a foul mood, and it was in this foul mood that I received the telephone call. When I answered, a male voice said, "I am Doris's husband, you know, I met you when you moved in. I think you're beautiful and I fell in love with you the moment I set eyes on you. You must get lonely now that Frank is gone. Can I come over and we can talk?"

I was aghast. I had heard many lame come-ons but this was the absolute worst. I took a deep breath and unleashed my anger and frustrations of the day, "I am insulted, no, I'm furious that you would even think I'm that type of woman. Don't you ever call me again. Don't you even come anywhere that I can see you." I slammed the receiver down. Too bad, I liked Doris, but now it would be too awkward to be around her.

Two days later, I received a similar call from another sleazy husband in the building. My response to him probably melted the phone in his hand. I felt so alone. Would I ever have someone put their arm around me because they loved me and just wanted me to know it?

As it turned out, I could not have managed a job and the medical needs of my child. She needed all my attention. With all the events of the past weeks, I'd forgotten about the surgery appointment for Ada until receiving a call from the Army hospital reminding me of her surgery, and pre surgery information.

There was no other choice but to take Amy with us. Helga had plans for the day, and there was no one else I felt comfortable or knew well enough to ask to care for her. We sat in the waiting room for what seemed an eternity. Amy was very restless needing food and a nap. I tried everything to distract her until the surgeon came to tell me the procedure went well. He said she was in a cast and we would return to have it removed in six weeks. For most of those six weeks, she could not put any weight on her leg so that it could heal properly. He said I could go in to see her, but Amy couldn't go into her room. He called for a medic to watch her. As I left the waiting room, I saw that the medic had magically produced some crayons and paper, and Amy was happily munching on peanut butter crackers and chattering away.

The next several weeks were exhausting. I didn't have a stroller or a wheel chair so I had to carry Ada on one hip while holding Amy's squirming hand whenever we went out. Ada and the cast were so heavy that I thought many times I would drop her. Consequently, I only went out to buy food, and to do laundry.

The day the cast came off, I was stunned to see how much her little leg had shriveled. It was half the diameter of her other leg. The doctor said it was because she hadn't used those muscles in weeks, and with some therapy, it would catch up.

The laundry room in the apartment building was in the basement. There were four washers and four dryers-—all coin operated. There were always two or three women in the room when I went down to do laundry. They gossiped about everything and compared notes about the letters from their husbands. I just nodded and smiled when they told stories because I didn't want to confess that Frank didn't write. Three months after Frank left for Viet Nam, I received a fat envelope from him, and quickly opened it. A stack of photos fell out and scattered on the floor. He had scribbled a short note that the women there looked like children they were so small-boned. The same woman appeared in every photo. She was usually riding a bike. Frank said she was a small woman, but she looked like a child to me. There were also pictures of a bar where he said the guys in his unit hung out. He told me to put them all in the wooden box he kept on the dresser. I showed the photos to Helga, and asked if she thought the person in photos was a grown woman. She answered, "Sure looks like a ten- or eleven-year-old to me." She shuffled through the stack of pictures, and then said, "But I've never been around any Vietnamese women so how would I know. That bar is the one my husband writes about, he says that all the guys hang out there all the time."

Frank sent me another letter a month before he was due to return. He had written only two letters the whole time. He had sent photographs for me to store for him with a one-line note. When I opened this letter, it was two or three pages. He wrote that he had received orders for Ankara, Turkey, and had twenty days to visit family before reporting to his new unit in Turkey. He enclosed a copy of the orders to present to transportation for packing and shipping our few belongings.

Frank wrote, "My mother married Howard Lauter last month, and moved to Detroit with him. He works at Chrysler doing something. We'll drive the northern route across the states and down into Detroit to visit with her for awhile. Then we'll drive to Winston Salem to visit with my aunt and Grandma for a week or so before going on to the New York port to ship the car. The plane to Turkey leaves from Idelwild. My aunt warned me that my pop was living with them again and drinking a lot. She didn't know if he would still be there when we arrived. Get appointments with packers for the day after I come back. Start cleaning now so we can clear the apartment and be on the road right away."

I had met Howard when I lived with Maude. He seemed like a decent fellow. Maybe they will be good for each other, but I remembered that they both drank too much. When Howard was around, they both appeared to be soused. The prospect of seeing Dick again was daunting. I shuddered at the thought of spending even one day around him.

I wrote Aunt Mary asking if I could visit with her for a couple of days, and if she knew where my mother, brother and sister were, could she arrange for me to see them. She answered, "Your brother lied about his age and joined the army. I heard he was at Fort Dix in New Jersey and had been in Viet Nam. Your sister is still at home with your mother, but Al doesn't live there anymore. I'm not sure what happened, your mother just said Barbara and Eddie ran him off."

There had to be more to the story—Barbara would tell me when I saw her. I had to find a way to convince Frank to let me go to Marion with the girls for a couple of days. I would never leave them alone in Winston Salem.

The day Frank arrived, I had arranged to pack our belongings and clear the apartment on the same day. I had scrubbed the place until my hands were red and chapped, and my nails broken into a jagged mess. If it didn't pass final inspection, I thought I'd just sit down and cry. Everything went smoothly, and we were on the road early the next morning. It was an exhausting trip, Frank stopped only when he needed gas, and when he was so tired he was weaving.

I hadn't seen Maude since leaving Marion for the Philippines, and was shocked at her appearance. She had been quite hefty, but now thin and pale, and obviously sick. She said she had cirrhosis of the liver and was on a bunch of drugs, but insisted she was getting better. Frank said, "We won't stay too long because having noisy toddlers around is too much for her."

Howard insisted she really was much better, and said her doctor thought she would be fine, but he confessed that she had been in the emergency room three times during the past month. Each time it was because blood vessels in her stomach and liver had burst. The doctors there had made her swallow a balloon which they inflated so it would put pressure on the blood vessels. It had been successful in stopping the bleeding. She seemed to enjoy seeing Frank and her grandchildren, and she was civil toward me. I pitched in with the cooking and cleaned the kitchen afterward. I also did some laundry and vacuumed the house. We spent three days with her, before heading south to Winston Salem.

Much to my relief Dick was not there when we arrived in Winston Salem. Frank's Aunt said he was in the hospital in serious condition. Along with his drinking, he had been a heavy smoker for years, and had developed cancer in one of his lungs which a surgeon had removed. She said he did not look well at all when she saw him, and that Frank should go right away to the hospital. We all piled in the car and went to the hospital. When we entered his room, he was trembling with such force that the bed shook. I thought he was having seizures. He didn't seem to know we were there. Frank and I stepped out of the room to speak to his doctor said he was having delirium tremors, called DTs for short. Dick was in withdrawal from alcohol. I had never seen anyone in this alarming state. The doctor assured us that in a day or two, it would subside, and he would begin to be more lucid, but we needed to think about putting him in a rehab hospital for awhile. Frank told the doctor that he would need to discuss that with his aunt and grandma because he only had a few days before shipping out for Turkey. The doctor said he understood and assured Frank that Dick would be able to carry on a conversation before then.

Frank visited with his dad several more times the next day. On the second day, the worst of the tremors stopped, and he could hold a short conversation. I didn't go back to the hospital with Frank.

There were only two days left for me to visit with my aunt and family. I deliberately asked Frank when his grandma was present thinking she'd be my ally. Frank's response was, "No, I can't take the time to drive you over there and come back for you. We have to leave from here Sunday to go to New York."

Grandma Honley spoke in my defense, "Frank, she can drive herself there and back. There are cars here to get around in. You can't deprive her family from seeing the girls." She turned to me, "Just be back here no later than early Sunday morning." Frank corrected her and told me to be back Saturday evening.

It was such a joy to see my aunt. She always had a hug and big smile for everyone. She cooed over the girls saying they were precious. I asked about Betty, and found that she was married, and had a child. If time permitted, I'd go see her, but first I wanted to see my mother and sister.

My mother looked haggard and really old. Life had broken her. I had harbored such anger with her for years, but my experiences since I had married Frank had given me a different perspective. I understood the helplessness of women who had children to feed, and how we were economically dependent on men. She insisted that I have a cup of coffee, and put a chipped cup of steaming liquid in front of me. I remembered that boiling coffee she promised me years before and how Al had thrown it in my face leaving my eyes burning and bleeding. I pushed the memory away and focused on the can of evaporated milk she pushed across the table. It appeared to have a week's worth of dried brown milk surrounding the opening, and some fuzz or dust had settled in the fuzz. I opened my mouth to decline the coffee, but the look on her face stopped me. She was making a gift—the only thing she had to give. As I sipped the coffee, I listened to her speak in a halting voice, and noticed her eyes were strangely dead. The anger I had felt for years was replaced by a rush of compassion, and for the first time thought maybe—just maybe, she had let me go because she thought I would be better off, especially if there was someone who would feed and clothe me, and not beat me.

After a reasonable amount of conversation, I left her and Aunt Mary to visit, and Barbara and I went out to the porch to talk in private. "Aunt Mary told me you and Eddie ran old Al off, what's the story?"

Barbara answered, "After you left, he wouldn't leave me alone, chasing me around and saying what he wanted to do to me, then one night after Eddie left for Viet Nam, he threw the mattress off the bed, threw me down and tied me spread eagled on the springs. He started biting on my breasts—it hurt so bad I was screaming. He put things inside me that burned. He did this to me almost every day. I was trying to decide whether I would kill him or just run away."

"Where was mama?"

"She was in the other room. I begged her to help me. She did nothing but sat out there crying and wringing her hands."

I put my arms around my sister and felt such rage that I was nauseated.

"When Eddie came home on leave after Viet Nam, and found out what Al had done, he started beating on him. Then I jumped in and helped. We beat him to a pulp."

"Oh, goodie, I wish I'd been here to help."

"No, Sarah, you don't. When Eddie and I had him on the floor crawling to get away from us, he was bleeding from several places with a broken arm, and his ribs were sticking out of his skin. I'll never forget how he looked. Mama was screaming for us to stop that we were killing him, and that is what I wanted to do, but when I saw what a broken bloody mess he was, I puked my guts out. I was ashamed that I was capable of that kind of fury and of killing someone with my bare hands, even an evil bastard like Al. I had felt such rage that I was shaking. I'm not sure I was human then."

"What happened to him? Do you know where he went?"

"Believe it or not, he managed to crawl to his old beat-up car. As he drove away, we threatened what would happen if he ever came back. Several people told me that he moved in with some old rich woman over near Asheville. I'm sure he told her some big lie that she was willing to believe because she was alone and lonely."

I held her tightly saying over and over, "I am so sorry you were hurt, I'm so sorry." I had begun to feel sorry for mama, I knew what it meant to be dependent on a man, and I knew fear, but I could never allow one of my kids to be abused like that. I would kill him. I didn't know if I could even look Mama in the face ever again.

"Barbara, where is Eddie?"

"He's stationed at Fort Dix up in New Jersey. When he came back from Viet Nam, he was still stationed there. I hope that's not a bad sign that he can be sent back soon. You know that he lied about his age to join the army. I don't know how he got away with it—someone must have falsified papers for him. He was only sixteen years old when he went to Viet Nam. Imagine thinking it better to carry a gun and go to war than to live with Al. He said he wasn't staying in the army when his tour is over. I guess he'll come back here."

"Can you give me his address, I want to write to him."

"I'll give it to you before you leave, if I forget, remind me. To change the subject, Aunt Mary told me what happened to you, and why you felt you had to marry that old boy. I sure hope he doesn't mistreat you."

"He doesn't mistreat me. I mean he doesn't hit me or anything like that, but he doesn't pay much attention to me either. To him, I'm just his housekeeper, and I'm fine with that. Barbara, I only married him because I was pregnant, and had nowhere else to turn, why, I didn't even know him. I still don't know him. What I've learned about him is that he has a dark side, and is not a likeable or trustworthy person. I promised Grandma that I'd get some sort of education before I left him, but there was nothing in the Philippines, and it was even worse at Fort Lewis. I had no money, job or baby sitter so it was impossible for me to go to school. Heck, I don't remember if there were any schools nearby."

"Why don't you just divorce him? You should be able to get alimony and child support."

"I went to see a lawyer this past year—an Army lawyer. He told me that most men do not pay alimony or child support regardless of what may be awarded in court. He said to think really hard about leaving because it would be up to me to support the girls. Let me be a lesson for you, please get an education and a job before you get married or have kids. I hear Marion's got a good community college and a trade school, go there and pick something that you can finish in a few weeks like secretary work or maybe the medical assistant--something so that you can get better than store clerk or factory pay."

"Sarah, at least I don't have to worry about being homeless. This house belongs to mama, all paid up. When Uncle Kay died, he left mama enough money to buy a little house. He stipulated that it should be in mama's name only, and then me and Eddie second. It's not much, a shack really, but it belongs to us."

"Barbara, I know about the community college and trade school because I've been investigating how I could stay here, and manage to get by. I could do it if I didn't have to pay rent. Do you think I could stay here with you and mama for awhile—just until I could get some training and a job? It would just be for a few weeks."

"I don't know if living with mama would be any better than living with Frank, but you should ask her."

When mama and Aunt Mary came out to the porch, I asked, "Mama, could the girls and I move in with you and Barbara—just long enough for me to get a job and a place that I could afford?"

Mama's answer was immediate, "This place is too small, and there are only two bedrooms. Eddie said he was coming back here. Besides that, my nerves couldn't stand two little kids running around."

"Well, so much for that, I thought it was worth a try. Looks like the only option is to go to Turkey and make the best with what I find there."

Mama answered in a dull voice, "I think that's for the best."

Barbara and I said our goodbyes and vowed to write to each other. I promised to come see her whenever we returned from Turkey.

It was late Saturday when I made it back to Winston Salem, and had only a short night's sleep before Frank was shaking me awake. His aunt and grandma busied themselves in the kitchen making us breakfast and a picnic to take with us. They accepted my help and directed me to smearing mayonnaise on slices of bread.

Granny talked non-stop about what a good father Frank was. She said, "I was worried that he would never settle down, but he seems to be doing fine. I think he adores those kids of his."

I thought about this on the long ride to the airport in New York. Since Frank returned from Viet Nam, he did seem to be taking his role of father serious. Before he left, he rarely had anything to do with them, and when they were fussy or cried, he became irritated. I thought some of his scuffling and teasing a bit disturbing, but what did I know?

My first impression of Turkey was that it smelled and sounded wonderfully exotic. Our sponsors, Rose and Bill Andrews picked us up from the airport and took us to the small hotel where they had made reservations for us. After we checked in and freshened up, they took us on a short tour of Ankara. Everywhere we went, I heard sounds that reminded me of a Gregorian chant, but more musical. Rose noticed that I stopped and looked around for the origin each time the chanting started.

"That's the Islamic call to prayer. You'll hear it, I think, five times a day. It's coming from the mosques all around us. Tomorrow, we'll go to the bazaar and we'll pass a beautiful mosque. I'll point out the minaret near the top. That's where the crier or muezzin stands to call everyone to prayer. It's really a beautiful thing. You'll get so used to it later on that you won't even notice it."

The following day, Bill took Frank to check in to his unit while Rose and I went to the bazaar. With Amy clutching one hand and Ada holding the other hand, it was difficult to examine anything up close. As far as one could see, there were stalls loaded with merchandise. The air throughout the bazaar smelled of exotic spices. There were stalls stacked high with brass, people selling jewelry, clothing, and even fruits and vegetables. One old man was selling live chickens. I stopped in front of a pile of Turkish rugs, and told the girls to stand where I could see them while I examined a couple of the small area rugs. Rose said, "A word of caution, Americans buy these rugs to put in front of their entrance door. That pisses off the Turks because those are prayer rugs and only used to kneel on for prayer, not to ever be walked on. It's obvious you like this place."

"Oh, my goodness I love it. As soon as I find an apartment and move out of that hotel, I want to come back here. Bill told Frank there weren't any available quarters on base so we'd have to find a short-term rental in Ankara. Rose, I know it's a lot to ask, but tomorrow would you help me find a place? Bill said you knew some Turkish and knew how to read rental signs."

We moved into a sixth-floor apartment with no elevator which made it difficult to walk the marble stairs with two toddlers and even more challenging with bags of groceries. The land lady lived on the third floor. Sometimes, when I was climbing the stairs, she stuck her head out her door to invite me in for Turkish coffee while the girls played with her kids. Though I spoke very little Turkish, it was pleasant being in the company of another friendly woman while the children played together jabbering away in some language of their own. The Turkish coffee was wonderful. It was like drinking sweet foam.

We lived in the Turkish apartment only three months before quarters became available on the small army base outside Ankara. It was an isolated Army Security outpost which sat on a mountain top overlooking the Black Sea. Someone said If you looked across the sea, on a clear day, you could make out the Russian coastline, but I never saw anything but water. There were two layers of barbed wire surrounding the base, and in the section where the soldiers worked there was a field of listening devices that looked like giant saucers. It was such a small base that I could see vehicles come and go through the heavily guarded entrance gate from my front window, and from other windows, I could see all areas of the base. We had a tiny commissary, PX, and dispensary. The doctor at the dispensary could handle most minor illnesses or accidents, anything more serious, had to be air lifted out. The commissary stocked only canned milk, and the meats were a strange shade of grayish-brown that looked as if they had been frozen for years. The eggs were so old that the yolks were a strange orange color that broke into a runny pool when cracked open. I complained to one of my new neighbors. Anne said, "I know we're told the food isn't safe from Turkish farms, and the cows have tuberculosis, but I go to a farm about a mile from here to buy eggs and milk. They're real fresh. I'll take you down there tomorrow."

The farmer didn't speak much English, but we were able to communicate. I hadn't learned the value of Turkish Lira so I held out my hand for him to take what he needed. He took a couple of coins, but left me with most of it. We had a pile of fresh eggs for dinner, and a glass of fresh milk. The milk had not been pasteurized, but if Ann and her kids had been drinking it for months, I didn't think it was a problem. It was delicious.

True to our promise, Barbara and I wrote to each other about once a month. I had written several letters to Eddie, but had never received an answer. Knowing that Barbara and Eddie had remained close, I asked her if she knew if Eddie had received any of my letters, and if I had the correct address.

Dear Sarah,

Yes, Eddie received your letters, but has no intention of answering. Al did a number on him. He has lots of issues, and doesn't trust anyone. He can't seem to get close to anyone so don't feel offended, it isn't personal. You weren't raised with him,

so he sees you as a stranger. I'd just save the postage if I were
you. Many times, he hurts my feelings and says cruel things to
me.

Love,

Barbara

I did feel offended, and also loss.

It was only a short time after that letter when Frank handed
me another letter from Barbara. My hands shook as I opened it
fearing the worst.

Dear Sarah,

Mama died. I think she had colon cancer, but never did get
a diagnosis from the doctor. Mama was on welfare and I don't
think they did much to help her. She complained of pain and there
was a growth on the side of her stomach. It kept getting bigger
and bigger, and still the doctors ignored it. Finally, when I pitched
a fit, they did a colonoscopy and found cancer. It had gone all
through her. Why did they wait for over a year since her first
complaints? There was no money to bury her, so in desperation,
I hunted down Al. He had moved in with another old rich woman
who lived in Old Fort. He refused to help bury Mama although he
was still legally married to her.

Aunt Mary called Uncle Kay down in Florida, and he sent
the money to the funeral home, and some to Aunt Mary to help
with things. He did come up for the funeral. Eddie came also. I

knew you would not be able to come or maybe you would not want to come even if you could. Aunt Mary talked me into going. I don't know if I'm glad I went or not. I had such mixed feelings about Mama. Sometimes I felt sorry for her, and other times I hated her.

I know you were angry because she left you at Grandma's, but honestly Sarah, you were better off than any of us. I just recently found out that she had a nervous breakdown after Daddy died, and she had no choice but to put us in that orphanage. Aunt Mary told me that Mama didn't go to visit uncle Don or Uncle Kay, she said Mama went into a mental institution. I don't know if you knew about Uncle Ronald. He wasn't such a nice person after all. He kept coming around pestering Mama even right after Daddy died. When she wouldn't play footsie with him, he offered her just around $400.00 for her house. When she refused to sell to him, he told Miss Greer and Grandma that Mama was abusing us, and that she had threatened you with a knife. The welfare had no choice after his report but to take us away and send her to the mental place. I think he pushed her close to the edge, and Al pushed her over. Aunt Mary said that when she got out of the mental institution, she didn't seem much better. I don't think she knew what she was doing when she married old Al. She was so desperately lonely. Aunt Mary told me there were times when she went to visit Mama after she got out of *the institution, she would find her face swollen up from crying. She told Aunt Mary she was so lonely and missed Daddy so much that she didn't want to live anymore. I think when Al came along, he took advantage of her. I think she was half broken by then, and Al finished the job. I don't remember her talking much or ever showing much emotion, just wringing her hands and worrying about everything.*

Well, I hope the next letter has better news. I have been dating a guy for awhile who has mentioned marriage several times. He hasn't asked me to marry him, but I think that's what he's leading up to. I'm not sure how I feel about him, but if he asks me, I am leaning toward accepting. I hope you're not disappointed in me, but I just haven't gotten around to checking out the school. I work full time clerking at the grocery store. It's so close that I can walk to work and don't need a car. I've been too tired when I'm not working to even think about school.

Your sister

I had so many thoughts about her letter. I doubted if she would ever go to school. My feelings about Mama were mixed. I felt sadness because she was my mother, but even with Barbara's explanation about her mental state did not excuse her for allowing Al to abuse Barbara. Why would a mother allow such treatment of her child? Still, I felt sadness over her loss.

There was no time to dwell on the death of my mother because Frank was demanding that I attend an awards dinner with him. I did not want to go. When we were in the Philippines, Frank had insisted I was obligated to accompany him to all events. He paraded me around as if I were a prize, and I always felt humiliated. I told Frank, "I would rather not go--sounds boring to me, and besides, I don't have a baby sitter."

He was quick to respond, "It's your duty to go with me. All the top brass will be there, and I'm looking to get a promotion. You need to get all dolled up and put on your snooty manners to impress the brass so I'll stand out."

"Frank, my manners are not snooty--just manners. My granny always said that good manners were only consideration for the other person."

"Whatever. Your manners are just the thing to impress the brass. Your looks don't hurt either. Kenneth and Jan Goldstein live at the end of the street--they have two teenage daughters. Surely one of them will babysit. Go knock on their door and ask."

Robin did agree to babysit, and several weeks later, she watched the girls for about three hours while Frank and I went to an event at the NCO club. After that time, she was always too busy, and Francis said her mother thought she was too young. Strangely, after that, Frank didn't mention going out to any functions.

One day near Easter, I convinced Anne to go with me downtown Ankara. Frank was on the swing shift and could watch the girls, and I could be home before he had to go to work. Ever since the brief visit with Rose, I'd wanted to go back. When Anne and I got off the bus, there was a terrible smell coming from the field across from the bus stop. When we approached to get a better look, we saw that men were slaughtering sheep right there in the square. There was blood everywhere. The grass was soaked in blood, and the bleating of the sheep, the blood, and the sight and smell of the entrails was almost over powering. One of the men explained that this was an Easter ritual. They gave the meat to the poor and to feed the orphans. I thought it seemed much more Christian than giving baskets of candy. After that, the bazaar seemed dull compared to the Easter ritual.

Frank's behavior was becoming even more inscrutable. When others were around, he still put on an act of good husband, and he was very talkative. He bragged a lot and tried to impress with his superior knowledge, but the minute we were alone, he retreated to his distant world. He did continue to shower the girls with attention. He always seemed to be on guard--from what or whom, I wasn't sure, and he had become an even more insufferable know-it-all expressing his opinion on every subject, and belligerently insisting he knew more than the professionals on every subject. If a new friend invited me and Frank to her home,

Frank made himself so obnoxious pontificating with the husband that we were never invited back. I lost so many potential friends that I just stopped excepting invitations and spent most of my time alone.

Frank started leaving the house around 11 pm saying he couldn't sleep and was going to work. If I questioned him as to why he would go to work in the middle of the night when he wasn't scheduled to work that shift, he said I was being childish and clingy. Someone was always working around the clock at his workplace, and everyone including Frank rotated the hours of work, but I felt bewildered that he would go there in the middle of the night when he wasn't scheduled. One night, I watched him leave the house, my eyes followed his tail lights down our street and watched him turn out toward the gate and disappear away from the base. I had a sick feeling in my stomach knowing he was up to no good. There was more going on than fooling around with women. I asked him where he had gone. He glared at me and denied he had left the base telling me I was delusional. I knew he was an accomplished liar, but I began to question my own sanity.

One day without warning, we were confined to the base. Word was that there was a mole on base. Either it was a soldier, a dependant or one of the civilian workers, therefore no one could leave or enter the base. I tried to deny my suspicions-–telling myself that I was being an alarmist, but if Frank was the spy, that

157

would explain the disappearances, the furtive phone calls, and the times I felt as if someone was watching us. This behavior had been going on since early Philippines. Then there was the evasiveness and lies. I had no proof, and knew that I had to keep my mouth shut--at least until I actually saw or knew something.

After a few days, things were back to normal. Word was not that they had found the culprit, but that things were under control--whatever that meant. Frank stuck close to the base and his work schedule after that, at least for a couple of months.

We had been living in Turkey less than a year when we were informed that the base was being shut down and everything was to be turned over to the Turkish government including all the listening devises and all spy doodads. I was very glad to go. What I had experienced of Turkey was wonderful, but I had been so isolated in the little army base with its surrounding layers of barbed wire, and we never had the money to explore the country. People came back from trips to various sites with tales of exotic and ancient ruins. I didn't even get to see the Hagia Sophia except for a quick view on the way to the airport in Istanbul. Someday when I had plenty of money and no responsibilities, I vowed to return for a lengthy trip. Frank received orders to report to another small Army Security base at Vent Hill Farms, Virginia.

I wanted to go to North Carolina to see Barbara before going to Virginia. Maybe this time, I could arrange to stay there. I asked Frank if we could go see family first but he insisted he was given no leave time and had to report to his new assignment right away. "There's no time. I have to check in first, but maybe we'll visit after we're settled. It's been a long time since I've seen my grandma and aunt."

Barbara's last letter was disturbing. She had married her fellow, but after just a couple of months, left him.

Dear Sarah,

I have left Arthur, and moved back into mom's house. Eddie is living here too. He got out of the army and moved back here. He's working in construction odd jobs.

I didn't know until after I married Arthur that he was a member of a church that was really a cult. He tried to force me to join, but I refused. He told me that everything we owned belonged to the church, that it was a sin for us to own property. He tried to force me to sell mom's house, and give the money to his church. I refused, and he slapped me around. When I cried out and cursed him, he beat me up and broke several ribs. After years of abuse from old Al, no man is ever going to hit me again. I told Arthur that if he came near me again, I would kill him. I should have taken your advice and gone to school, but it's not too late. I've been going to school to be a medical assistant. I seem to have a knack for it. The instructors told me that when I finish, there will be lots of jobs available.

When you get back to the states, please come see me. I'm sorry that I can't offer for you to stay. Eddie is living here, and would never allow it. I'm sorry.

Love,

Your sister, Barbara

I wrote back that we were moving to Virginia and for her to visit me, or I would come down after we were settled in.

We were lucky to arrive just when they opened new family housing, and we moved into a new three-bedroom apartment on base. It was a self-contained base having a PX, Commissary, and small medical unit. Vint Hill Farms Station was fairly rural, and at least a five-mile trip to get to any place off base. It did have a community center where there were regular organized activities, and the small NCO club tried to have some entertainment at least once a month.

When Frank checked into his unit, he discovered that the Goldstein family had arrived a month before, and Kenneth Goldstein was Frank's new first sergeant. He was happy with the arrangement saying Goldstein had a reputation of being fair.

The first occasion to need a baby sitter came within a week. Frank felt he was under obligation to attend a unit party, and told me to find a baby sitter because I was also expected to be there. I thought of Robin and Francis. I had no idea why Robin wouldn't baby sit in Turkey, but maybe something had changed. I walked over to the next street in the housing area and rang the Goldstein's doorbell. Jan came to the door, and after a bit of small talk, I asked if Robin could baby sit on the night of the event. Jan was cordial, but said something that struck me as very odd, "Well, I guess it's ok. She can always walk home or Francis could walk home with her. It's not fair to punish you for something you didn't do."

I asked her what she meant by her comment, but she brushed it aside, and hurriedly said she would speak to Robin, and she would call me. I thanked her and made some more small talk to cover up my dismay at her comment. It would be useless trying to get her to elaborate on what she'd said.

Robin agreed to baby sit. When we returned from the unit party, she insisted on walking home alone. She said, "I need the exercise and my home is just one street over."

The next time I needed a baby sitter, Frank wanted to enter a pinochle tournament and insisted he wanted me as his partner. I yearned for social activities, but I did not want to play cards with Frank. Every card I played, and every bid I made, he belittled me loudly. It would do no good to voice my reasons for not wanting to be his partner so I said, "We can't afford a sitter."

Frank said, "It's not that much money. It's only once a month. Get the sitter."

We drove home afterward in a frightening storm. It was raining in sheets, lightening streaked from the sky to the ground, and thunder felt as if it was shaking the car.

I convinced Robin to let Frank take her home, "I know it is just a short distance, but you can't walk in this storm."

She hesitated, but did agree.

I was brushing my teeth readying for bed when Frank came home. It seemed he had been gone longer than necessary, and he had an ugly scratch across his face. He claimed to have run into a bush or something in the dark when he got out of the car.

The next day, Frank was on the day shift but came home at lunch time which he had never done before. He appeared flustered announcing he just received orders for Alaska.

I was flabbergasted, "We just got here, and I haven't even finished unpacking, and now I have to pack up and move again?"

"You can't go with me. This is a yearlong isolated assignment in the Aleutian Islands off Alaska's coast. I have to leave tomorrow morning so I had to make arrangements for you and the kids. There's an empty apartment at Selfridge Air Force Base in Mount Clemons, Michigan. It's about 4 miles from where my mom lives. You saw her when we visited--she's gotten much sicker, and needs someone to help her. Howard isn't any help--he needs extra help as well. Someone will be here this afternoon to pack up. They have cut my orders so that I can drive you up there, and I have a ticket to fly out of Detroit."

I started to protest, but he cut me short. He had given the order and I was to obey, but I questioned the short notice and the rush to get out of there so I persisted. "Frank, I know this is not normal. The Army doesn't cut stateside assignments with such sudden notice. What's going on?"

"You don't know what you're talking about. I asked to go. The only isolated assignment was the Aleutian Islands, and the slot is closing now. I took it so I won't have to go back to Viet Nam. If I stay here, I'll be shipped back to Viet Nam."

I didn't even attempt to find the logic in what he was telling me. I just knew in my gut something wasn't right, but stopped questioning and figured that Frank was correct, I didn't know what I was talking about.

The next few hours were a whirlwind of packing and cleaning. Fortunately, not all the boxes from Turkey had been unpacked. Both girls were hyper and whinny because they could feel the tension. I repeatedly told them that we were going to live near Grandma. It calmed them for a short time before they started whining again. It was late before I fell into bed exhausted, but ready for the movers early the next morning.

We headed for the air force base first. Frank left us waiting in the car while he went into the headquarters and housing department. He came out holding a set of keys saying we could go to the empty apartment and move in when we wanted to, but our belongings wouldn't be delivered for two days. Since we had no beds, we were compelled to go to his mother's home.

Maude was surprised to see us and tried to hide that she was not prepared for our arrival. She was obviously very ill, and half the kitchen table was an array of pills. Several times during the two days we stayed with her, she was in the bathroom throwing up blood. I was alarmed, but she said, "It's not so much blood—I'll know if I need to go back to the hospital." I tried to convince her to let us take her to the hospital, but she refused saying the bleeding had stopped.

Before Frank left, he instructed me to take care of her as well as Howard who seemed completely helpless for a forty-something-year-old man. He left for work each morning at six or seven and returned around five. Soon after eating supper, he went to sleep in the basement where he had moved a bed. I resented that Frank didn't seem to care that I would be in a strange place caring for two children without help. He did not need to order me to care for his mother, I would have done so out of compassion.

I checked on Maude every day, and tried to cook dinner for all of us as often as I could. Sometimes I cooked it at home and other times, she sent Howard to the store to buy food for dinner and I cooked in her kitchen.

I was in the middle of cooking a meal one afternoon when I heard sounds of Maude throwing up in the bathroom. She sounded feeble when she called out to me. One look in the bathroom and I knew we needed to get her to the hospital immediately. She was slumped on the floor and soaked in blood. I got Howard to help me get her in the car, and gathered up the girls in the back seat because Howard said he could not watch them or go to the hospital as he had to go to bed. I thought he was a cad but didn't say so aloud. The girls and I sat in the waiting room most of the night waiting for someone to help Maude.

I went looking and found her in a curtained triage area. She had continued to bleed and appeared to be only half conscious. This made me very angry that no one had helped her after all this wait, so I guess I created a scene. It did get attention. After the doctor examined her and started a blood transfusion the nurses cleaned her up, and called for someone to take her upstairs. Before she was wheeled away, she clutched my hand and begged me to wash her kitchen curtains and get them back up. Of all things to worry about, but I promised her I would take care of them, and headed back to Maude's to get some sleep. Assuming Howard was asleep downstairs, I dumped Ada and Amy on

Maude's bed with their clothes on, and didn't bother taking off my clothes. I was just too tired.

I slept until eight and woke up hearing the girls talking to Howard. He had decided not to go to work, and asked if I would take him to the hospital. When we arrived, the staff wouldn't let the girls go into Maude's room so I had to stay in the waiting room while Howard went to see Maude. We waited for over two hours for him to come back down stairs. He said the reason for all the blood loss was that several blood vessels in the liver had ruptured and that a vascular surgeon would try to repair them. The surgeon said to call Frank to come home--they would wait to perform the surgery until he arrived. The operation would be tricky.

The Red Cross contacted Frank's commanding officer in Alaska, and Frank was on a plane within a couple of hours. He had almost two hours to visit with Maude before she was wheeled away for the surgery.

Maude died during the surgery. She was only forty-four.

Howard said we should take her back to Marion to be buried in her family grave, and made arrangements for her to be flown back to North Carolina. It was cramped in the sedan for the drive to North Carolina with Howard in the back seat between the girls. When we came to the first rest stop, Frank ordered me to ride in the back with the girls and let Howard up front so he could stretch his legs a bit.

Before Maude's funeral, I had a chance for a hurried visit with Aunt Mary, and Barbara. Again, Barbara made it clear that she and Eddie shared the house and there was no room for anyone else. She said, "I would love for you to live close by, but you would need to find somewhere to rent."

As soon as the funeral was over, Frank hustled us back on the road saying he had to get back to his unit. He had another seven months to complete his year in Alaska. I prayed that our next assignment would be somewhere that had opportunities for me to get a job, and there would be a college--even a community college or a trade school. The girls would be in school part of the day, and with Frank's swing shift, maybe I could solve the child care problem. Mostly, I just wanted to stay put for awhile. I was tired of moving.

Before Frank left for Alaska, he gave me orders to look out for Howard. "He can't get along without help. He has cataract surgery scheduled in two days, take him to that and help him afterward."

He expressed no concern for me or his kids.

Howard suggested that I stay with him for the two days so I would be there to take him early for the surgery. "I need help adjusting to being alone."

I prepared all meals for Howard, for the next two days and did his laundry at his request. The first night, I awoke with a start thinking someone was in the bedroom. I had closed the door before going to sleep, and thought I heard the door click shut when I stirred. I told myself that I was only dreaming. The night before Howard's surgery, we all went to bed early because of the early rising. I awoke when I felt someone kissing me and fondling my breasts. I rolled over away from those hands, and cried out. The bathroom light across the hall was on, so I could see the silhouette of Howard quickly leaving the room before he shut the door.

We all dressed to take Howard to the hospital and I said nothing about the night, neither did he. When the nurse wheeled Howard away for his surgery, I asked the person at the desk, if I had time to run an errand. She answered that if I could be back in an hour and a half to maybe two hours, then yes, there was plenty of time. I went back to Howard's and packed up the clothing we had brought, and put it in the trunk of the car. Then, I went next door to talk with Mr. and Mrs. Dorsey. We'd met before, and they had said they were willing to help Howard any way they could. I asked if they could watch over Ada and Amy until I brought Howard home. "They've spent too much time sitting in the hospital waiting room. They need a snack and a rest."

I took Howard home, made sure he was doing okay, and left him with his neighbors for company and care. I never went back to spend the night and only seldom for a brief check on his welfare.

Frank sent me a copy of the new orders so that I could begin packing, and planning. We were going to Berlin. I wrote to our sponsor family, Tom and Patti Reynolds requesting information about Berlin. Patti's answer sounded too good to be true. "Even divided, West Berlin is still one of the largest cities in the world. There are multiple universities and schools, and the American complex houses a PX, commissary, multiple small shops and they hire mostly military dependants. I work part-time at the PX. My paycheck isn't very large, but it gives me pocket money which I spend at the Ku'damm. Oh, just wait till you see all the fabulous department stores."

The more I thought about her letter, the more excited I became, and said prayers that it was all true.

Tom and Patti met us at the airport. I liked Patti immediately. She had bleached blond hair, wore a mini skirt, and was a chatterbox describing everything we passed. She cautioned that we could not wear miniskirts in any of the military facilities. "Someone stands at the entrance with a ruler and measures to see if the skirt is above the knees. If it is no more than three inches, then it follows protocol. Oh, well, you know we have to be obedient that's why the army calls us dependant wives."

They took us to our new home so we could drop our luggage and freshen up before setting out on a whirlwind tour of Berlin. While Frank and Tom completed paper work to establish the apartment as our new home, I wandered around examining everything. It was a large apartment, and had everything a family could possibly need to live in comfort. There were stacks of bed linens and blankets, towels and washcloths, a large set of china, an eight-place setting of silverware, a fully equipped kitchen that included more pots and pans than I thought I'd ever need or use. Every room was furnished with all needed furniture. There were gold damask draperies on the windows, and oriental rugs on the glossy wood floor. It was overwhelming and felt as if I had stepped into a fairy tale world. Tom said this was how middle-class Germans lived. I saw luxury, not middle class.

We began our tour on the Kurfurstendamm, the major street in the heart of Berlin, commonly called the Ku'damm. Glittering Multilevel stores lined the street on both sides dotted with numerous outdoor cafes. Flower pots and planters were everywhere and overflowing with carefully tended plants. Looking east down the Ku'damm loomed the Kaiser Wilhelm Memorial Church. It had been damaged from bomb raids and sported a large hole through the tower. Berliners left the church unrenovated as a statement against war.

We walked around the church and intersected with Strasse Des 17. Juni. Patti explained, "It was named from the uprising of the East Berlin workers on the 17th of June 1953. They protested salary cuts and increased workloads. They didn't have a chance against the Soviet tanks, East German soldiers, and police."

Patti said, "If you'll look down the street, you'll see the Victory Column and farther beyond that is the Brandenburg Gate flanked by the infamous Wall."

I only glanced at the Victory Column because my eyes were riveted on the Brandenburg Gate and the Wall. East German guards goose stepped across the top with weapons at the ready to mow down anyone who dared come too close. Nothing in my life had prepared me for this sight. Goose bumps raised the hair on my scalp and ran down to my feet. Shocked at what I saw, it was more than I could absorb in a brief minute. Later, standing in Check Point Charlie and watching the Guards examine the underbody of a car with a long-handled mirror to check every inch of the car for contraband or smuggled bodies, for the first time, I felt real fear of communism. I had never felt any fear during the duck and cover drills in school.

Tom had been mostly silent while Patti rattled on being the perfect tour guide, but he got her attention, "It's getting close to the time for their orientation, and we haven't shown Frank where he'll work. We'll skip McNair barracks for now since that's just where the grunts are stationed."

I had to ask, "What are grunts?"

Tom laughed, "Oh, that's what we call the infantry. Frank, all the intelligence groups work in this place where we're going now. The Germans call it Teufelsberg which I understand translates to devil's hill. Apparently, after World War II, the Berliners needed some way to dispose of all the rubble from the bombing so they piled it on top of an abandoned Nazi Military academy. But the Americans call it Spook Hill because of all the security surrounding the place and all the saucer receivers."

Spook hill was impressive. I thought it looked like something out of a spy movie. We parked just outside the guard shack, and Tom told Frank they would go inside so Frank could get a look, and meet some of his coworkers. He indicated that only he and Frank were going inside. "We won't be long, and then we'll go have lunch before the orientation."

Tom talked to the guard for a minute and then he and Frank disappeared inside. I was desperate to pee so thought I'd ask the guard if I could just go to a bathroom.

Patti said, "It's no use asking, we're not allowed inside."

I asked the guard if I could just go inside for the bathroom. His answer was an adamant no. To emphasize his refusal, he placed his weapon across his chest where it was very visible.

I asked the guard, "What would happen if I just walked through the gate?"

He responded, "I'd say halt!"

"What if I didn't halt?"

"Well, Ma'am, I'd just have to shoot you."

I knew he would too. I headed back to the car and found Patti collapsed with laughter. She was wiping tears from her face. "Oh, you're going to be so much fun."

The mandatory security briefing for newly arrived dependants was both informative and humiliating. Two officers, a lieutenant and colonel, took turns briefing the women. The lieutenant began by looking down from the stage, addressing us as dependant wives. If that wasn't bad enough, he continued by asking, "Do spies have big ears? Do spies have big noses? No, no, they look like everyone else. They could be your neighbor; they could be your friend. Berlin is the spy capital of the world, so we are going to give you some information to ease your adaptation to this assignment."

I asked myself the question, *could the spy be in your own household*? I had been suspicious of Frank's activities long before Turkey. I never did find out if the suspect was caught. But by the time of that incident, I had already suspected him of nefarious activities as far back as the Philippines. I couldn't forget the hushed conversations outside the gate, the nights he did not come home or he left in the middle of the night claiming to go to work, the secretive phone calls, or the times our house was under surveillance.

The lieutenant continued his spiel in a voice as if he were talking to a toddler.

"The only way we can enter or leave West Berlin is through Templehof airport or by American Duty Train. If you need to leave, then you are required to request permission a couple of days prior to travel. Then, you will be issued flag orders, so called because the American flag is stamped at top of documents. The French and the British each have their country's flag at top of documents, and they too operate an official train. The American train leaves West Berlin at 8:30 pm and snakes its way through East Berlin and East Germany arriving in Frankfurt at 6:30am the next morning. There are many rumors why it only travels at night, but it's most likely just to remain out of sight. You are forbidden to talk to or make contact with either the East Germans or Soviets—you must remain in your sleeping compartment at all times with the shades drawn. If you are hassled or detained, you are to demand an audience with a Soviet officer."

The colonial stood up and motioned for two soldiers to come on stage. One was dressed in a Soviet uniform, and the other dressed as an East German soldier. The colonial pointed out the possible insignia each soldier could have on his uniform.

Then he told us to be alert for the presence of KGB in the city. "They always drive black limousines with dark tinted windows. If you see one of these cars, call the military headquarters."

The colonial's final warning was about our children, "Most of you live within sight of the wall, and your children will be playing in its shadows. The entire Wall is not a concrete barrier. There are long stretches of barbed wire fencing that is easy for a child to slip through. If you suspect or know that your child has crossed the barrier, call the military. Under no circumstances are you to go across looking for them."

I thought, *no amount of barbed wire or military guns would hold me back.*

Patti and I made faces at each other when we left the briefing, and Tom said, "There's one more thing to show you, and it's in your building."

When we arrived at our building, Tom headed down to the basement, and we all followed. Private rooms lined the basement along both sides separated by a wide hallway. For each two rooms, there was a bathroom.

Tom stopped in front of one of the rooms, pulled a key from his pocket, and opened the door. He motioned for us to step inside for a look. It was a small but self-contained room with a single bed, nightstand, bureau, and a small table with two chairs.

The bed was neatly made with a spare set of bed linens and towels stacked near the foot.

After we had a look, Tom locked the room and laid two keys in my palm, saying "This room is assigned to you. You can arrange for a single girl to live here in exchange for babysitting or light housework. The girls come from all over Europe to attend the Frei University. There's a list of girls who want a room at the headquarters building."

I clutched the keys tightly and was so overjoyed that I didn't hear any more of the conversations. I blindly followed up the stairs to our third-floor apartment. Before leaving us, Patti said, "I live the next street over in the same building as the first sergeant Allen Cooper and his wife, Barbara. She said she would give you a day or two to rest up and then come over to meet you. You'll like her. We go shopping together--now you'll have to come with us. The department stores on the kudam are fabulous. We don't always buy anything--just oogle. After you get settled, I hope you'll visit me."

"'I'd like that, and the shopping sounds fabulous. I thank you both so much for today, but now I am ready to collapse."

Frank saw them out, and we were in bed within five minutes. He and the girls fell asleep immediately, but I lay awake unable to sleep. I had no idea how many hours since I'd slept. I tried counting the hours since we had left the guest house to the time we landed in Berlin. I knew that I needed to add or subtract around six hours to account for the time change, but my fuzzy brain couldn't do the math, and add to that time, we had just finished a long day. And what a day it was. If this was a dream, please don't let me wake up. My new apartment may be how middle-class Germans live, but for me, a kid from poverty, it was luxury.

The UBAHN was just a block away, and there was a bus stop outside the apartment. What freedom! Everything was a short walk, the PX, Commissary, Grammar school, high school, even the theater. I was overcome with Joy over the room downstairs. The girls would be in school, at least for part of the day, but I would have child care when needed. I couldn't fall asleep until well after midnight Berlin time because my mind was whirling.

Each morning when I awoke, I was filled with joyful anticipation of new discoveries, new adventures, and I loved Berlin more than the day before. The girls and I discovered the museums, and we visited every one while reading all we could about the artists. We took rides on the UBAHN just for the novelty. We had never ridden a subway. We sampled German food and became enamored with the canteens where we had curry wurst and potato salad.

Barbara visited three days after our arrival. I liked her immediately. Before another week had gone by, she and Patti had visited me twice, and we had strolled the Kudamm, sat at a sidewalk café for coffee, and shared German pastries.

West Berlin was an easy city to love. I soon felt as if I belonged, and adopted the same tired stories and jokes that Berliners used to cope. For example, frequently Soviet fighter jets buzzed the city. They'd swoop down close to towers and quickly climb to disappear from sight. People looked up, shrugged and someone would say, "You think they are going to attack us?" Someone else would answer, "No, they're just reminding us they're still there, besides, all they'd have to do is post a sign on other side of the wall that says, 'concentration camp.'"

I hired a baby sitter from the list at headquarters. Gabby was from Bavaria, and since her first classes at the Frei University had started, she had been sleeping on a friend's couch. I interviewed her and helped her move in the same day. She understood that when I got a job and started school, we would need to work out a schedule. But I didn't feel as if I could manage a job, go to school, and run the household with the increasing severity of my back pain.

I still had the print outs of the exercises that had helped me in the Philippines when the pain first began after Amy was born. The doctor in the Philippines sent me to a physical therapist and it did help for a year or so. I spread out the instructions and did the exercises faithfully for a month, but there was no improvement in my pain. It just increased, and continued to get worse each day. I had a difficult time concentrating on anything because the pain was so severe. I hurt from my mid back and fanny all the way down to my toes. I couldn't sit, I couldn't stand, I couldn't lie down and get a restful night's sleep. The pain was unrelenting and constant. Nothing seemed to relieve it. Finally, in desperation, I had to admit I needed help so I made an appointment with Dr. Berry, an orthopedic doctor at the military hospital. After taking X-rays, he showed me that three vertebrae had slipped pinching the spinal cord and nerves. He called the pain sciatica and said that I needed a fusion, but Dr. Munston, the chief orthopedic surgeon in Europe, was the only doctor capable of performing this operation. He was located in Frankfort.

Dr. Berry asked, "Can you get to Frankfort in three days? I don't think you should delay this surgery, your vertebra are sitting in a precarious position. I explained the need for speed to Dr. Munston's assistant and scheduler. They can move you up to the top of the schedule, but I have to call them back to confirm. You'd have to take the duty train the night before the appointment arriving early in the morning. I'll arrange for someone to pick you up at the station, and I'll send your records and X-rays to Dr. Munstson today."

Dr. Berry said "You'll probably be in Frankfort for a month--maybe two."

That gave me only two days to arrange to be away. Since I hadn't started working or registered for school, the only thing I needed to arrange was care for the girls. They had started school. Amy was in kindergarten and Ada in first grade, but Frank's work schedule would not provide proper supervision for the girls the entire week. When he worked the swing shift, the girls would be alone from around 3pm to eleven, and when he worked the midnight shift, they would be alone from eleven thirty pm until seven am, and when he was on days, they would be alone after school for most of the afternoon. I planned to work the schedule out with Gabby so that she could be there when Frank was at work, but Patti said, "I think they would be better off with me. Even if Gabby and Frank could work out the hours, the girls need to have proper meals, and besides, my kids would love the company."

Frank argued, "They'll be fine. I've already talked to Gabby and she only has one class that conflicts, so they'll be alone for just two or three hours."

But I did not think it okay to leave a four-year-old and a five-year-old alone for any time. I ignored Frank and accepted Patti's offer that they stay with her until I came back to Berlin. She seemed eager to have them. He grumbled about this, but I held firm.

Frank got the required flag orders for me to take the duty train to Frankfort, and Dr. Berry assured me someone would pick me up at the train station. This was my first trip on the duty train. Too excited to sleep, I sat with my nose pressed against the window staring out into a black East German sky, and sipping coffee from my thermos. The train pulled into the first checkpoint, and all was lit up in the station. I could hear the heavy-booted steps of the soldiers and guards as they boarded the train to check whatever it was they checked. There were three young Soviet soldiers marching on the platform outside my window. We smiled warily at each other then one of them made a gesture toward his mouth. I believed he was asking for coffee and held up the thermos. He shook his head and gestured again. This time I understood he wanted a cigarette. Forgetting the rules, I opened the window and handed him one. With a combination of pantomime and heavily accented English, he made me understand that he wanted to trade his belt buckle for a carton of cigarettes. We made our trade just before the train pulled out. He waved and smiled me out of sight.

The surgery was more painful and extreme than I had anticipated. I bled profusely and had several blood transfusions. Each attempt to get out of bed and stand caused a feeling of faintness. This prompted the doctor to use a tilt table to gradually raise me to a standing position. Once I could stand and walk a few steps, I was fitted for a brace which prohibited me from bending at the waist. Dr. Munston said, "I took a piece of bone from the iliac crest, shaved it up, and packed it around the vertebrae. You'll have to wear the brace until the bone had grown solid. When you can walk to the end of the hall and back, you can return to Berlin."

When the day finally came that Dr. Munston felt I was healed enough to return home, he called the hospital in Berlin to inform them when I would arrive, and requested they contact my husband to be there to pick me up. Patients were discouraged from using the telephone on the ward, but the nurses relented when I told them I needed to call my husband to make arrangements to pick up my kids. Frank answered right away and said he had already been informed to pick me up. I asked him to call Patti and tell her he would pick up the girls on his way to the hospital. He grunted a reply that I took for a yes. I missed Ada and Amy terribly. Frank seemed distracted and cut the conversation short, but promised to pick me up with the girls.

The girls were not with Frank, and I asked if he had left them alone. He said, "No, they are not alone. I'll explain when I get you checked out."

After a medic wheeled me to the car, Frank settled behind the wheel, but instead of starting the car, he turned to me, and said, "I have to tell you what's been going on. I brought the girls home after you'd been gone for three days because that's where they belonged. Between Gabby and me, we managed to have someone to watch them except for the mid shift, and that was not a problem because they were sound asleep before I left for work and I had to wake them up when I got home in the morning."

I gasped, but before I could say anything, he continued, "I imagine the neighbors will be telling you about loud noises coming from the apartment until late at night. Gabby and I were arguing religion and some of the conversation got really heated and loud. I decided it was not a good idea to have her baby sitting until you were home, so I took what was in our savings account and bought a ticket for my pop to come over and help out."

I was stunned. "Can you get a refund on the ticket? I don't want or need him here."

Frank's facial expression was the poor-me-victim, and in his whinny voice, he said, "He is here. He has been here for three weeks or so."

"Frank, I don't know how to react to any of this. Why did you get the girls from Patti? It's not okay that you left them alone for any time, and I can't even process that you would be arguing religion with the babysitter. That seems like such a strange thing to do. You know how I feel about your dad. I don't want my kids near him--I don't want to be near him."

Frank insisted that his dad wasn't drinking anymore and that when he tried to kiss and fondle me, he was drunk and didn't know what he was doing. "He's here and that is the end of it." I knew better than to say more because Frank's facial expression and body language began to stiffen into what I interpreted as repressed rage.

The girls were overjoyed to see me. Amy blurted out, "granddad can go home now." I did not react but instead tried to be civil to him.

The very next day, it was obvious that Dick was going to be a problem. He disappeared around 9am. When he returned, he was drunk and explained he sat at the beer garden next door with a nice German man, and they talked about the war. He staggered to his bed and slept until I called him for dinner. He left the house every morning around nine to sit and drink with his new German friend at the beer garden. When he came home, I prayed he would go to sleep because I was tired of his advances and vulgar language. Each time, I'd push him away and angrily tell him to leave me alone, and he accused me of being a prude. On the afternoons when he stayed awake and the girls were home, his gutter language and mouthy attacks on the girls were hard to deal with. I told Frank to buy him a ticket and send him home. Frank said he didn't have the money for a ticket and it would take a few months to save enough. I felt pure despair. It was hard enough to take his drinking and gutter talk, but he was an added a burden. I had another person to cook and do laundry for. He also caused the household to lose sleep. He wandered the house at night coughing so hard that he would throw up. In addition to his drinking, he chained smoked. Frank reminded me that he had only one lung, and shouldn't be smoking as if I could do something about it.

I got a big dose of courage when he began talking racism around the girls. One afternoon, Amy got into a fight with her best friend, a sweet little African American girl. When Amy came into the house crying that Irma had hit her and she had hit her back, and now she was mad at her. Dick handed Amy a pocket knife and said, "Go cut that little nigger's throat." I was appalled, grabbed the knife from Amy and told her she would do no such thing, and I never wanted to hear her call anyone those names.

I turned all my fury on Dick--told him I never wanted to hear those words in my household, and that I was teaching my kids to settle differences like two smart human beings.

That evening after dinner, I said, "I want your dad on a plane and gone by the weekend. No more excuses. My kids are not growing up with that negative influence. They are not going to be angry racists, and they are not going to be subjected to that drunkard's putdowns anymore. Find the money somewhere. If you don't, I will go to your commanding officer and beg for help."

I had never talked to Frank like this nor given him an ultimatum, but I was so angry that I was shaking, and it gave me courage.

The next day, Frank came home with a ticket for his dad to return to the states in two days. He said he'd borrowed the money. I felt like falling on my knees and giving thanks to God. Not caring to have any type of goodbye, I didn't go with Frank and his dad to Tempelhof. The girls and I just sat in the apartment savoring the quiet. It felt as if the atmosphere had changed and that the stress had gone out the door with Dick. I knew that to be short-lived that when Frank returned, the air would again be charged with a stress and uneasiness that I found impossible to identify. When Frank was around, tension hung in the air.

I began having nightmares. Almost every night, I had the same dream. I was in a large old home, and trying to climb to the top floor of the winding staircase. There was some evil on the top floor that I struggled to see, but in my dream, I was frozen with a terror that always kept me from reaching the top. Every time, I woke up with my heart racing, and drenched in perspiration. I told the doctor about the nightmares when I had my post surgical checkup. He said, "You've been through a lot with blood loss, transfusions, anesthetic, and pain meds. Most people have some lingering sleep issues after undergoing a big surgery."

Other than the nightmares and resultant sleep disturbance, I seemed to be healing nicely. At last, it was time to turn my attention to getting a job and starting school.

There were two university extensions in Berlin--University of Maryland and Boston University. After thumbing through both catalogues, it seemed that the University of Maryland had a better liberal arts offering with more courses of interest. Boston University only offered a business degree in Berlin. There was only a month before classes began for the new semester, I would have to hurry to get a job and arrange the hours with Gabby to stay with the girls when Frank was on the swing shift.

I had not seen Gabby since I left for Frankfort. Strange. I would have thought she'd be up to ask about things. Maybe she felt embarrassed about the loud arguments with Frank. I was healed enough to climb the stairs, but it was a slow go. I knocked on Gabby's door repeatedly. Getting no answer, I was preparing to write a note to leave on her door when the girl occupying the next room came out to tell me that Gabby had gone to Israel and planned to stay for months. Climbing back up the stairs to fetch the room key, I repeated over and over to myself, "Why hadn't she told us? I couldn't understand someone just taking off." When I let myself in, it was obvious she had no intention of returning.

The room was empty of all her belongings, and it was very dirty. The bedding was heavily soiled, there was a granular substance covering the floor, and drug paraphernalia scattered on the night stand. If I could get the room cleaned with fresh linens the next day, maybe I could get the civil engineering group to change the lock before the weekend. If I could arrange that, it was possible that I could hire another college student before the weekend was up.

After much cajoling, Frank carried the vacuum cleaner downstairs and some cleaning supplies. He insisted he had no idea that Gabby was gone, nor did he have any knowledge of why she left. Both girls agreed to help if I promised to give the room to a British lady. They had been watching comedy on the British television, and had become enamored of all things British.

Fortunately, the second person who inquired about the room was Valerie, from Northampton, England. She was attending the Free University in Berlin, and desperately needed the room. I explained that I would need her to stay with the girls from 2:00pm until I returned from work around 5:00pm, and on the evenings I had classes, until 9:00pm. This would only be two out of three weeks. She assured me that this would not be a problem.

I made the rounds in one day filling out applications for any jobs that I thought I could handle. I applied at the American PX, the commissary, hospital, dental clinic, and the Special Services.

All the places had a reputation for hiring military wives. Two days later, I received a call from the PX offering me a job as store detective. The manager said, "If you come in today, fill out paperwork, and sit through an orientation, you can start tomorrow.

On the way home, I stopped at the University of Maryland's business office and asked the lady at the front office if I could talk to a counselor about registering for my first class. She said, "I'm Ruth Hobbs the counselor, receptionist, and sometimes registrar. We run a lean ship here. What can I do for you?"

I introduced myself, and told her, "I've never been to college, and I want to know what I need to do to register for my first class."

Ruth asked, "Where did you graduate from High school? Where did you take your SAT?"

"I didn't take those tests, are they a requirement? When they were given in my school, I didn't have the money to pay for them, and I didn't have anyone I could ask for it." I chided myself for giving too much information. I tended to do that when I was nervous.

Ruth answered, "We try to remove obstacles for servicemen and dependants. Are you willing to take an entrance exam—I can give it to you right now—it won't take very long to complete. It just measures if you have the basic knowledge required to do well in a college class?"

Ruth handed me a couple of sharpened pencils and the test. She said, "You'll be measured in math, English, some science, and some history, and I'll score it before you leave. Depending on your score, we'll discuss the next step."

The test seemed easy, but I watched nervously as she scored it. Ruth was smiling when she reported that I'd answered every question in all categories correct. "It appears you are well prepared to do college work. There are some other exams you can take that will give you college credit if you have a passing score. You can get credit for all your core subjects, so I would suggest you plan to take those tests and register for something outside of the core subjects. Look over the schedule and see if there is something there that interests you."

My heart did a dance when I saw Latin 101 on the schedule. "I had two years of Latin in High school and loved it. Could I take this one?"

Ruth said, "I've not seen anyone get so excited over a Latin course, but yes, you can take that. I think you'll really like the professor. She's one of the favorites."

As a kid, I'd never felt such joy. I wanted to dance and skip home, but then the mental policemen started to crowd in. Doubt. Could I manage to walk around all day? I was still supposed to wear the back brace, but had not worn it for the interview. It was not something that I could hide since it was metal and leather, and buckled onto a large stomach pad. It reached from my neck to mid hips, and was worn over my clothing. I decided not to wear it for the first couple of days to see if I could do without it. I also had to tell Frank. I knew he would be livid, and would try to stop me.

Just as I had anticipated, Frank's first reaction was explosive anger, "You did what? I never gave you permission to be gallivanting off to some low-level job, and don't you think you're a little old to be going to school? Your place is here taking care of me and the kids."

His explosive anger and all the angry gestures startled me because he usually kept his anger controlled.

"I have been taking care of all household duties including washing your fatigues, starching them, and ironing with regulation creases for a long time. I have been cooking your meals which you are constantly criticizing and giving me orders. I have never done anything for myself. I am going to take this job, and I am going to school."

I couldn't believe I had been so forceful. My cheeks flamed with anger and frustration that I had broken my grandma's advice to pick my battles, but I thought she would approve this time. I didn't want to make matters worse, but this battle was worth fighting.

Frank attempted to reestablish control over me, he said, "Are you forgetting our agreement in the beginning? Okay, go to school and get a job, but only if you can keep up the housework and your other duties at home. It's not the job that I object to so much, but the school. What makes you think you're better than I am? A woman's place is at home. Maybe I'd like to go to college, but I can't. Not with my schedule. What about the kids? Did you ever give a thought that if there was extra money for anyone to go to school that it should be saved for them?"

There it was. The anticipated victim, the implied, "Look at how you're mistreating me when I don't deserve such treatment." In the past, I felt guilt when he used this type of manipulation, but I wasn't falling for it this time. I would do this job, and go to school.

My class started two weeks later, and by the end of the first week, I was exhausted, but determined to keep up.

On the two nights of classes, I picked up chicken and potato salad from the German deli on my way home from work. That helped some with meal prep. On weekends, the girls followed me around the house while I recited the latest mythology, or ancient Greek, or Roman history as I did household chores. They loved the stories, and saying them aloud helped me remember, and do better on tests.

The nightmares had become more vivid and frightening. Also, I began having what I called the shakes. Suddenly, I would become weak and shaking. Heat spread throughout my body and I felt as if I would pass out if I didn't get something sweet to eat. Many times, these episodes came on suddenly and interfered with work and class. I needed to get help.

The doctor ordered a glucose tolerance test. The results were in the normal range. The doctor said I did not have a medical problem, but I had anxiety. He wanted me to schedule a visit with a mental health person. Reluctantly, I agreed to join a group monitored by the head of the psychiatry department.

On my first group session, I wasn't sure what to discuss regarding anxiety so I listened to the others talk about what was bothering them. Two women and one man took most of the hour.

Christine was dealing with a son who started fires. He was an eight-year-old arsonist. He had started multiple small fires, but the latest was serious. He lit the contents of a closet to watch them burn. The fire gutted the apartment and caused damage to the nearby apartments. Her husband's commanding officer was pushing to have the boy removed from the home and placed in an institution. She had taken her son to one of the department therapists who specialized in treating children. She had come to this group hoping to learn how to help her child. I had the impression that she had talked through meeting after meeting without any change in her situation. Dr. Hanson, who chaired the group, commented that she might have to face that she and her husband were not equipped to deal with the boy, and that he needed extensive help in a residential facility.

I wanted to put my arms around Christine and tell her not to listen to Dr. Hanson, but to look further for help. Surely someone could help her little boy.

Janice was haunted about her adoption. She had tried to find the identity of her biological parents, but all records were sealed. She had tried multiple avenues to find the truth, but to no avail. She said the parents who raised her, were good parents, and she knew her search saddened her mother, but she could not be at peace until she found her biological mother and asked why she had given her away. One person in group asked her if she had made any more inquiries and gotten any results since last meeting, and Janice answered, "No."

Skip was one of the two men in the group. He complained that he couldn't stand to look at his wife because she had gained about twenty pounds since they were married. He said he was turned off by her fat. He also complained about her housekeeping saying she sometimes left clothes lying on the dryer instead of putting away, and suppers weren't always ready when he got home from work. He also complained that she didn't pick up from their two kids every day, and that the house was cluttered, and they didn't always get their bath before six o'clock.

I asked him if he ever gave her any help to which he said, "No, I have a job. That is her job."

I said, "Well, she's probably very tired. Running a household and raising kids is a big job. It sounds like she could use a little help." He glared at me.

Dr. Hanson asked him, "Do you want a wife or do you want a housekeeper? You can always hire a housekeeper."

I felt like hugging him.

There were only ten minutes left, when Dr. Hanson asked me to tell the group something about myself and why I was there. I really didn't feel like talking about myself, but I said, "I saw a doctor for what I thought was hypoglycemia, but he said my glucose test was normal and that I suffered from anxiety. I don't believe it, but just in case anxiety is causing me to get so weak and shaky, I'll come here for a time or two. I figure it can't hurt."

Dr. Hanson asked me if there was anything in my life that made me feel tense or upset. I confessed that I had these dreams that left me shaking with terror, but once I was awake, I was fine.

He asked, "Would you tell us about the dreams?"

"I'm always in a three-story house. It's an old Victorian--it also has an attic, I think. Maybe it's the fourth floor, but I can never reach it. I'm always frozen in fear and with a sense of foreboding when I reach the top of the third-floor stairs. I wake up shaking with terror, sweating, and with my heart pounding. Sometimes, when I go back to sleep, I repeat the dream."

"Maybe there's some knowledge so dreadful that you've buried it in your subconscious?" This question was from Dr. Hanson, but the other group members settled on this and asked other questions along these lines.

I really tried to concentrate and come up with an answer, but confessed, "My life from early childhood wasn't happy, and many awful things happened to me, but I don't bury them. I just deal with them."

What I didn't share with anyone was my relationship with Frank, and the fear he was involved in something awful like spying. The idea that he might be a traitor sickened me. How could someone in his position betray our country? If I had actual proof instead of just suspicions, I would report him in a heartbeat. But that was the dilemma. If I breathed any of my suspicions to anyone, and there was no proof, both of us would suffer. I just had to be on guard. This was probably the reason for my anxiety, and it was especially stressful since I couldn't discuss it with anyone. There was another reason that I feared the truth. What would happen to me and the girls if he was convicted of spying? How would the world treat us?

Shortly after this, I began having another reoccurring nightmare. I took the elevator down three floors sub basement to be fitted for my back brace. I made a wrong turn down one of the many hall ways. It was a labyrinth down there, and there was not a soul around. My steps echoed as I frantically turned down one hall and then another. I could not find my way out. Then I would wake up. I didn't share this new dream with the group.

The one or two group sessions, I had committed to attending, became a weekly thing. Each week, I'd tell myself it was the last time, but I'd show up the next week. The nightmares continued. So did the shakes until I learned to eat high protein foods and stay away from sugar.

Each semester, I managed to take one class. I had taken the maximum allowed CLEP tests, and received credit for most of the required core classes. After four years, the routine didn't get any easier although the girls were older and could help more, and they could also read the harder textbooks to me as they followed me around. Frank continually expressed his displeasure that I was going to school. He grumbled constantly that I thought I was uppity and smarter and better than everyone around me. I also had criticism from the women in the building. Many had been very vocal in their criticism, and expressed the opinion that women belonged at home not off doing some job and certainly not going to school. I had no friends among them. I was just too busy to care, but was dismayed that criticism was coming from other women. Only Patti and Barbara remained friends. Both said, "The women who are judging you harshly are just jealous, and don't have the smarts or the guts to do what you're doing."

Barbara and I had remained friends and had become even closer, but I had never shared details of my marriage. One evening Frank was working the swing shift, and I had no classes. Barbara called, "Are you home tonight? I haven't seen you in over a week--we need a good visit. Can you spare the time?"

Her husband was Frank's first sergeant and worked the same hours. I really had looked forward to a quiet house after the girls were in bed to catch up on some work, but felt the need for company.

We settled in with our coffee and made small talk until she asked me, "Why do you do it? Why do you work so hard? Why is getting a college degree so important to you? You know not one of the wives around here has a degree, and none seem interested in getting an education. You seem to be more driven than you are ambitious.

I never wanted to discuss my private thoughts nor my goals, but she was a kindly person and I needed a friend. The words escaped my lips, "Barbara, I'm both driven and ambitious. When I was a little girl, and told my uncles that I wanted to be a doctor when I grew up, they patted me on the head, laughed at me, and told me that girls couldn't be doctors—that they had to be wives and mothers. I've been told all my life if I insisted on a career, it had to be secretarial, nursing, or teaching. Even the women around here criticize me because they say my place is at home, that I shouldn't be working or going to school. I would think women would want to be equal in this life, but they seem content with their lot. Society says that I do not have any worth as a human being except for the proscribed role as homemaker. Even the army calls us dependant wives. So yes, I am ambitious. I want to be more than just a servant, but right now, I'm driven because I want to leave Frank, and I can't do that until I can support the girls and myself."

Barbara looked stunned, and I shocked myself that I had said so much aloud. She asked, "Does he hit you or does he fool around?"

"No, he doesn't hit me, but I do suspect he fools around." I had time to slap a monitor on my tongue so I would not utter my real concerns. "He lies to me, and there are times he just disappears and claims he's at work, or he'll get a phone call and talk low so I can't hear. I've seen him ogling other women and mouthing things to them. Some of them ogle back. A few times when I questioned him, he tells me I'm imagining things--that I'm paranoid."

"If you had proof he was fooling around, would you confront him? What would you do?"

"I've suspected it for years and it doesn't bother me anymore. I just want my degree so I can get a decent job, and then just leave him. I don't want any drama or trouble, so no, I'd not say anything to him, but it would make me feel better to know that I'm not crazy."

Barbara said, "I'm supposed to keep my mouth shut. Allen said if I breathed a word of what he told me I could cause a lot of people trouble. He says there are times when Frank is at work, and poof, he disappears for an hour or two." Barbara snapped her fingers and said, "Poof, He shows up and insists he has been there all the time. Another time, everyone left for lunch, and Allen had to go over to McNair barracks for something. He saw Frank sitting at the little sidewalk deli beside the entrance to the barracks. He was sitting with some older man in civvies. Allen didn't think anything of it and started toward him to say hello and maybe join him for a bite, but as he approached, he saw Frank and the man were engrossed in conversation, so not wanting to intrude, he turned around and left. When they returned after lunch break, Allen said to Frank, "I saw you at that little deli at lunch. Is the food decent?" Allen said Frank just gave him a blank stare and told him that he was nowhere near that deli. Allen says Frank gaslights people all the time."

I had to ask, "What is gas lighting?"

"Just what Frank does, insists you saw nothing, you heard nothing, you are seeing things or just what he said to you, that you're paranoid."

"What does Allen think Frank is up to?" I held my breath for her answer.

"He wonders if he's homosexual, not just because of seeing him with the man, but he is too familiar with one of the young soldiers. This young soldier, I think his name is James Talbot, and Frank spend a lot of time together, and even go off together. His wife has called to speak to him, and Allen has to tell her that James can't come to the phone just now, but he'll have him call her back. Allen has counseled Frank, telling him that he's causing trouble in the kid's marriage. Frank just shrugged and told Allen they're just good friends, that he babysits for them. They have two young kids, a boy, and a girl. There have been other times as well, when Frank is nowhere in the compound, but insists he was there the whole time, although no one had seen him."

"Listen Sarah, I can't know all that you go through, but Frank appears to be a good father. He pays those girls a lot of attention. I know he takes them and their little friends to the movies frequently. It would be sad to take them away from their father. Maybe you could just hang in there until the girls are grown. Maybe that would be better?"

"The girls are almost nine and ten. I think they're old enough to handle it. Besides, I'm not ready to leave yet, not until I get my degree."

Barbara said, "I don't think they are ever old enough. I was sixteen when my parents divorced. They had both been good parents and I loved them equally, but when my mother took me and my brother to live a few miles away, I was devastated. I saw my dad regularly, but it was not the same as having him living in the same household. I swore that I would never do that to my kids. I'm not telling you what to do. Every situation is different, just think about it and see if you could stick it out at least until they are in college and ready to leave home."

Since Barbara was in a talkative mood, I had questions that she might be able to answer. Everywhere we were assigned, there was always a time someone was watching our house. Here in Berlin, there were times when I'd leave the building with Frank, and I had a real sense we were being followed. Yesterday, someone took my picture several times as I walked to the bus stop. In past years, I had asked Frank about this, and he told me he was getting a security checkup. He said that all members of the Security group were monitored by the FBI on a regular basis.

I asked Barbara, "How often does the FBI run a security clearance, and do they ever watch someone's house?"

"I think it is every year, or maybe every two years, I'm not sure, but I don't think they would ever have your home under surveillance, that is, not unless you are suspected of doing something illegal. You're not involved in something shady, are you?"

"Barbara, Thanks for listening to me. Anyhow, it looks as if I'll be forced to change my plans. We've been here for almost four years, and Frank says that he can't get another extension. We'll probably have to leave soon. I still have several credits before I get my degree, and the best I can hope for is a college close to where we're stationed. If I can get a job, then I can continue school, and I just hope that I don't lose too many credits in the transfer."

Barbara stared at me open mouthed. "Frank didn't tell you? Apparently, Frank's enlistment was coming up soon. He put in a request that if he reenlisted, he could stay here another three years. He received orders approving this last week. You'll be here long after I leave. Allen's assignment is up, and we already have orders for Virginia. The new first sergeant arrives sometime this month."

This information left me dumfounded. I didn't know what to say to Barbara so I just mumbled something about this news being a nice surprise, and expressed my dismay that she was leaving. I put a governor on my words and tamped down my emotions until Barbara left. Again, Frank had lied and manipulated me. He had said I should not register for the next semester because we would be leaving. He knew this was the last week to register. I had just two days left. It was obvious he intended I miss the registration before he told me about his reenlistment. It was an easy decision not to let him know that I knew, and to quietly register for a class the next day.

I had learned a new word, gas lighting, and took some comfort that I was probably not nuts, but I didn't think Frank was homosexual. The knowledge of his absences at work, and the tale of Frank's meeting with the older man just strengthened my suspicions he was involved in something nefarious. I had also witnessed his meeting with an older man when he was supposed to be at work, and the significance of that meeting baffled me, but also strengthened my suspicions.

I had developed the habit of taking my lunch to a little park near work. The park was divided by shrubs and small trees into what could be called rooms. A person could sit on a bench in one room, but be obscured from vision of anyone in the next section. I was enjoying the flowers, and the quiet, when I heard a familiar voice. I peeped through the shrubs, and saw Frank and an elderly man in conversation. I held my breath not daring to move while watching them move to sit at the park bench just a few feet from where I sat. I could hear their voices, but could not understand what was being said. Frank pulled an envelope from his inside jacket pocket, and handed it to the man. I didn't take my eyes off them, and did not see the man hand Frank anything. If Frank was handing over secret information, what was he getting in return? What shocked and puzzled me the most was that Frank was not speaking English or German. I did not recognize the language. In my earlier conversation with Barbara, I dared not tell her anything about what I saw because I had no proof of anything--I didn't know what I had witnessed.

That Barbara verified what I knew all along about being watched just furthered my suspicions.

The day after Barbara and I had the conversation, I was clearing the table from dinner when the doorbell rang. Frank was home and had retreated to the back of the apartment, so I quickly dried my hands and answered the door. The man was wearing fatigues with the name tag Talbot. He didn't wait to be invited but pushed his way in. His demeanor was insolent when he demanded to see Frank. They went into the back bedroom and closed the door. I heard raised voices but could not make out what was said. Later when the door opened, I caught the tail end of the conversation. Frank was saying, "You just keep your mouth shut and you'll be ok." Both men were loud and obviously upset about something. It seemed that I was called upon to say something, but stupidly asked, "What were you two talking about?"

Talbot gave me a withering look and said, "None of your damn business," as he slammed the door behind him.

Very early morning the following day, Barbara called me. She said, "Remember me telling you about that soldier, Talbot? Well, he was arrested this morning. He's accused of espionage. Apparently, he has been taking top secret information from the building for the past couple of years. Allen just called me. He said that Talbot is being held under guard in the barracks until he's sent to Fort Leavenworth, Kansas for court marshal. Allen said to warn Frank to steer clear of Talbot--do not go near the barracks."

I knew in my gut Frank was also involved, but I couldn't decide what to do. I had been trying to quit smoking, but found a half pack of cigarettes and chained smoked the rest of the pack while pacing back and forth my mind in a quandary.

Finally, I decided I needed to report Frank before Talbot was shipped out because in some way, they were connected. I worked through my lunch time so I could leave early. Gathering my courage, I let my convictions lead the way to Headquarters where I encountered a confusing row of desks in the front hall. Each was manned by a soldier in dress uniform. Approaching one with my voice shaking, I said, "I want to report a spy."

I was immediately ushered into an office and introduced to a colonial who motioned me to sit down. Without any preliminaries, he asked, "Who is this person, and what information do you have?"

I was not going to give him a name until I found out how he reacted to what I had to say. "The person I am concerned about handles top secret information, and I've seen him talking to a person in a language I think was Russian. He gave the man a package. He's been seen at other times with this same man but denied being there."

"Is this man your husband?"

I feigned surprise, "Of course not."

"Do you have anything more to tell me? If this is all you have, then it's far from enough to start an investigation."

I told him about Frank's suspicious behavior, and I told them about Talbot, but I left out names.

The colonial snorted and glared at me, "Missy, are you trying to stir up trouble."

I fled from the building with my cheeks burning with shame, glad that I hadn't given them my name.

Talbot was shipped to Leavenworth within the week, and Frank never mentioned Talbot or what had happened.

Frank had read a lot when I first met him, but his reading had become an obsession. He read only science fiction, and about conspiracy theories. He shared these books with the girls, and then quizzed them on content. I wanted them to be avid readers, but I also wanted them to read about other things. Frank pushed his books at me, and when I had time, I tried to read one or two, but they were just not my cup of tea, and when I told Frank I did not enjoy science fiction, he treated me as if I were an idiot.

I was cleaning Ada's bedroom when I noticed *Stranger in a Strange Land* on her nightstand. I sat on her bed to thumb through the book. Someone had highlighted multiple passages with a yellow marker. I read a couple of these highlighted passages, and felt sick. They were about incest and very graphic group sexual activities. Certainly not something an eleven- and twelve-year-old should be reading. I practically threw the book at Frank, "Why would you give your little girls something so disgusting to read? They are way too young to be reading this stuff. I'm too young to be reading such stuff."

He gave me a derisive look, "You are such a prude."

"I just might be a prude, but do not give that book back to either of them." I shoved the book into his hands and considered the subject closed.

Frank's commanding officer told him he had to attend the NCO Academy in Bavaria if he expected another promotion. Promotion was the only way to get a decent pay raise.

Before Frank left, Valeria told me girls were being attacked in the basement of all three American housing buildings. This had occurred several times in the past month. The German guards and the military police had put extra patrols on the buildings, but the man was slippery. He seemed to disappear quickly. They thought he must live in one of the buildings because someone had gotten a glimpse of him, and reported that even though it was such a cold winter, the man wore only a light shirt.

I felt fearful over being alone for so long, and wanted Frank to install a chain lock on the door. He snorted, "No one is going to bother you."

I considered installing it myself but didn't know where to buy it in Berlin. What do the German's call a hardware store? Valarie stayed with the girls while I had my class. I didn't relish walking alone after dark even though it was only a half mile to the high school, but I had a final exam.

It wasn't quite dark when I walked to the high school, but when class was over, it was nine o'clock and completely dark. It wasn't scary because it was well lit and the German guards were patrolling, but as I neared my building, I could feel the tension. I feared opening the door to the dark stairwell. I had to walk a few paces forward into the hallway, and then to the left wall to press the button for the light. When the stairwell lit up and I could see there was no one there, I blew out my held breath and hurried up the stairs. Valerie told me that all was quite in the basement, and no one had been accosted this week, but she didn't know if they had caught the man.

Frank had been away for three days attending NCO Academy when I found the book again on Ada's night stand. Ada said her dad had given the book back to her and told her to read carefully the highlighted sections and they would have a good discussion when he returned. He was due to return in about eleven days. I took the book from her and told her she was not to read any more nor discuss it with her dad. I asked if she had questions that I could answer, and if she wanted to discuss the book with me, but she insisted she didn't like what she had read and did not wish to discuss it with anyone.

I tore the pages from the book and buried them in the bottom of the kitchen garbage. My stomach tightened over debasing a book. I had a lifelong love of books and treated them with respect--all books but not this one. It wasn't really the book, but it was that Frank wanted his twelve-year-old daughter to read and discuss the incestuous family with him. Maybe I am a prude, I thought, but I felt sick to my stomach, and needed to discuss it with someone. Barbara and Patti had left Berlin leaving me feeling empty. There was no one else I could talk to. I decided to bring it up in my next group therapy meeting. The members of the group had changed several times over the last six years since I had been in the group. The only person who had been there longer than me was Dr. Hanson. His wife was from Berlin so I guess he was allowed to have an almost permanent assignment. I only attended twice a month, some months, not even at all due to my job and school. It met in the evening to accommodate those who couldn't leave work, but I was usually away two evenings a week, and felt that the other evenings should be spent with the girls.

The sick feeling I had over the book had not left me, so when the group assembled, I blurted out my concerns, and asked the group if they thought me a prude. Maya looked at me with a look of horror, "No, you are not a prude, but maybe a coward. If that were me, I'd stuff that book up his ass. That is just sick."

Everyone else expressed similar thoughts. Dr Hanson was studying my reaction to the comments, but he didn't offer any of his own. I had other things bothering me, and needed to talk, and get other's views, but decided to think about them for a while longer. Maybe next time.

My suspicions that Frank was a spy were just too dark and dangerous to discuss with anyone. I was still rattled about the meeting I had witnessed in the garden, particularly that Frank gave someone a packet and was speaking a foreign language. I had tried to adopt a casual tone later when I asked him if he spoke other languages than English. His answer was a smirk and, "Why would you ask that? Of course not." His denial disturbed

me more than anything. I took it as a sign he was hiding
something.

Frank had always baffled me, but lately what disturbed me
most was his parenting skills, and how he was treating me. I had
not found the courage to bring this up in the group. He belittled
me to the girls, and it seemed that he was trying to turn them
away from me. He would say things like, "Your mother thinks
she's better than anyone else," or "your mother is more interested
in getting a degree and working than spending time with you."
The girls had started repeating the many accusations. Many
times, when I had looked forward to spending time with them and
promised to take them somewhere special like one of the many
museums or parks in Berlin, Frank whisked them away to a movie
or some other activity. I chastised myself for thinking this a
problem, after all, his grandma, and many of the people we knew,
had commented that he was a good dad. He even invited the
neighborhood kids to go along with them to the movies or to the
park. Was I being unreasonable or a prude? Based on my
background, what did I know about parenting? Still, I could not
shake the feeling that he was a bad influence on the girls. I
especially didn't like it when he wrestled with them. He would get
both on the floor, tickling and rolling around until I demanded they
stop. I lectured that they were young ladies and much too old to
be on the floor wrestling, even with their father. He always snorted

and called me a prude, but would stop until the next time. I felt that this was wrong for so many reasons but could not find the words for my discomfort.

When Frank came back from NCO school, He seemed to have forgotten about the book. Instead, he was concentrating on getting a promotion and doing paperwork to extend his tour in Berlin. We had been living in Berlin for almost eight years, and Frank was doubtful that the army would allow him to remain any longer if he received a promotion.

Frank did not get a promotion or an extension. His first sergeant gave him a negative review saying that he did not show commitment to his job or to the army, and didn't deserve to be promoted, and since he only contributed what he felt necessary to his job, he was not needed in Berlin.

I was only six credits short of getting my BA when Frank received orders to leave Berlin for a post at Fort Devins, Massachusetts. I was devastated. My plans had been to have my degree and prospects for a decent job when we returned stateside. I also had begun to feel as if Berlin was my home. We only received three weeks' notice. Three short weeks to sort and pack, and say our goodbyes. I wanted to send for school catalogues, but there wasn't enough time to receive them at an APO address. It would have to wait until I got to Massachusetts.

Amy begged, "Please, can't we stay here and let Dad go back to the states?" The sobbing of both girls broke my heart, and I felt like crying along with them. "I'll ask around and see if that is something we can manage."

But after numerous inquiries, I had to concede that we had no choice but to go to Fort Devens as a family. If the girls and I remained in Germany, we still had a military ID so we could shop in the commissary, and PX and we'd have access to the military hospital, but I would have to move from the apartment, and get a better job to afford rent. Also, we would not be German citizens.

Ada, Amy, and I took a walk the length of the Ku'damm to say our goodbyes to Berlin. We walked past the bombed-out church, and sat at a café near the Brandenburg gate. The three of us were tearfully saying goodbye to a city that had become part of us. They had spent most of their formative years here, and I had grown up and become a different person

Frank used a low-cost military service to ship our car to the NY port. The car would be driven to a kiosk section of the Kennedy airport where we would pick it up when we arrived.

We left Berlin at 9am Monday, February 6th, and allowing for the time difference and travel time, we arrived at Kennedy Airport around 9am Monday, February 6th. It was very cold and snowing, and lacking boots, gloves, and hats, we were not dressed for the weather. Our winter coats were too light-weight to be adequate for the cold, but I thought we could turn the heater on once we got on the road, and be warm enough until we reached Fort Devens. Surely, we could get some heavier clothes from the PX. The year was 1978. We had lived in Berlin almost eight years. The girls were more German than American in their acquired culture, and I had done lots of growing.

The airport shuttle dropped us off at a kiosk at the far end of the airport parking lot. The man who checked us out, cautioned Frank, "Drive carefully, it's snowing heavier north of here. Weather reports say that in Connecticut, Rhode Island and Massachusetts it's accumulating fast. I wouldn't stop if I were you--just drive straight through."

By the time we reached the Massachusetts border, the car was slipping, and it took all of Frank's attention to keep it on the road. We saw multiple cars off the road. Some were just on the shoulder, but many obviously needed to be pulled out. Frank said, "I can hardly see the snow is coming down so thick, and I'm almost out of gas. If I see a gas station open, I'm going to stop. Everyone go to the bathroom, and find something to eat in the station. None of these roadside places are open." Shortly after we turned onto route 2, Frank saw a neon sign off the exit flashing they were open, and we pulled into there.

The man at the station waved his arms wildly into the air and yelled something at us as he stomped toward our car. Frank rolled down his window and yelled back, "I need gas and food, and they need a bathroom."

The man threw his arms in the air, "What are you doing out here? The governor shut down the state. Route 128 is at a standstill. Dozens and dozens of cars stranded for hours. *Nobody* should be out here."

Instead of Frank's usual argumentative tone, he actually restrained himself, "I have orders for Fort Devens. We just got back to the states--picked up my car in NY. We haven't eaten for hours. I just need some gas and to get to Fort Devens."

Frank was wound so tight that anything could set him off. When the man motioned us to go inside, I quickly herded the girls into the station. When we returned, the man was telling Frank to stay off the back roads--to take the exit off route 2N--that it would point to Fort Devens. We passed numerous cars either on the shoulder or well off the road in ditches. They appeared to be abandoned. I wondered where the people were and if they had waded through the thigh-deep snow. We were traveling at a crawl, and sitting rigid with tension. No one wanted the cheese crackers or anything else I had purchased from the gas station. All eyes were riveted on the road and silently praying the car would stay on the road. When we finally pulled into the gate at Fort Devens, it felt as if we had reached paradise.

The two military police on duty were shocked to hear that we had just driven from New York through the storm. The ranking MP did all the talking, "The electricity is out on the whole base-- probably the whole state, and the best I can do for you at this hour is put you up in the guest house. I don't think there's anybody else there. Follow me. I doubt you'll be able to park anywhere until this snow is shoveled, but you can leave your car on the road side in front of the guest house. Just be sure to move it early tomorrow after the lot is plowed."

I took just the overnight case, and the bag of milk and cheese crackers. Frank grabbed the suitcase containing his uniform, and we trudged through the snow. It was still coming down, and drifting with the wind. Snow covered the door handle and lock. I didn't know if it was piling up that high or if the wind had caused it to drift, but the MP and Frank kicked at the snow and used their feet and hands as shovels until they could get the door open.

When I woke up, it was daylight, but I couldn't tell the time. All was eerily silent for a military base. Frank was in his dress uniform ready to report for duty. He said, "I'm going to walk to the headquarters building to report in. I'll find out about our permanent quarters, and where we can get a bite to eat."

He returned about an hour later and began searching for his fatigues, "Everyone on base is ordered to report in work clothes. We're joining the National Guard, and going to the shore. There are 15 and 20 ft waves hitting the houses along the shore and they're all flooded. Apparently, there are still people in the houses waiting to be rescued. Some of us are going to route 128 to help the stranded motorists. They're hooking up a generator for the commissary--should be open in an hour. They're only going to be open for a couple of hours. I'll show you where it is. You can get something for breakfast and enough to last a couple of days." He tossed a few bills on the bed, "Here's all the money I have to spare. You'll have to walk. None of the roads on base are cleared, and they won't be until we get back from the shore or wherever they send me."

I asked, "Any chance we can move into our quarters?"

Frank snapped at me, "Whadda you think? It's going to take several days to get the mess from the storm cleared away."

We subsisted for over a week before the plows cleared Fort Deven's streets, and restored electricity. I thought enduring a blizzard was the end of troubles, but evidence of a negative environment just kept revealing itself. When the base and the little town outside the base were back in business, I took the girls to register for their new school. We encountered a policeman and a German Sheppard standing guard just inside the entrance. On our walk through the halls to the principal's office, we saw two or three more officers with their dogs. The atmosphere was tense and the woman who registered the girls was grim-faced and unsmiling when she glanced at their papers and registered them.

I sat in the car for a long time fighting with myself. I wanted to run into the school and grab the girls. I could not shake my reaction to the dark and tense atmosphere that pervaded the school.

The rest of the day was spent visiting the two colleges within reasonable commuting distance. I wondered at my ignorance. I had thought if I only needed six credits to get my BA through University of Maryland, that I could take them at any other school and get the degree. I found that I would have to fulfill the new school's requirements which would put me back fifteen or more credits. I felt like a real idiot, and even more so after scanning three newspapers for possible employment. The liberal arts degree, that I had coveted and worked so hard for, appeared to be worthless. I didn't appear to be qualified for any jobs that I couldn't get without the degree--all low paying, go nowhere jobs.

One of the newspapers had a large ad advertising a free certificate program in computer programming. IBM was sponsoring the program, and had worked it out with a local community college to give courses in coding, and other data processing subjects along with a few liberal arts courses. The college would give credit just short of an associate degree. IBM was sponsoring this course to address the shortage in computer programmers. The catch? Applicants would be required to take a test in logic and mathematics, and only the top thirty scores would be chosen. The ad said those interested in scheduling the test should contact the office of the college I had just visited earlier in the afternoon. I excitedly called the number and scheduled to take the test. As I waited for my test appointment, I began to doubt my ability to pass a test in logic and math. Math had never been my strong suit. Actually, I barely passed all my high school math courses, and had avoided math in college.

When I sat down in the classroom to take the test, my heart was pounding, and I clasped my hands together tightly in an effort to stop the trembling. Looking around at my competition, I saw that I was the only female in the room which further lowered my confidence. When the start buzzer sounded, I opened the test and read through the first page. It appeared to be some type of puzzle. There were a series of wheels and pulleys. The first question asked if the wheel in the middle turned a certain way and the pulley attached to it was also attached to the wheel at the bottom, which way would the wheel turn. I turned the page sideways and then upside down to see if I could figure out the answers, and forgetting that I was taking a test, became lost in puzzle solving. There was some math, and I answered the best I could. When the proctor called, "Time," I sat back with a huge exhale, glad it was over, and sure I had flunked. When a week went by without any news, I told myself to forget about it because my chances of scoring in the top thirty were nonexistent.

My thoughts returned to getting a job. Most of the jobs listed in the newspapers required a degree in a certain specialty, and only a handful required no degree or certificate. I applied at a local blanket factory because it was closer to home, but hoped that I wouldn't get the job. When I received a call from the personnel office at the factory offering me the job, I agreed to the minimum wage, and agreed to be there at 8 a.m. Monday. Immediately after hanging up the phone, I felt remorse and was tempted to call back to decline. Was this what I worked so hard for the past several years? Two hours later, I received a call from the college informing me that I had one of the top thirty scores, and that classes would start in three weeks. They would run from 6:30 p.m. until 9 p.m. because many in the class worked during the day. The call made me feel differently about the factory job. It was a bridge to a better future. The minimum salary would allow me to save for first and last month's rent, in a different town with a better school system, and away from Frank. It would also pay for gas money or bus fare to my classes. Every other expense for the certificate program was free, even books.

Amy and Ada came home almost every day terrified because bullies stalked them with threats of violence. Ada's hair was loose and she had red scratches across her face. I asked the names of the kids attacking them. "I'm going to the principal to demand they be punished and never come near you again."

"Please, Mama, don't," Amy begged, "That would make things worse, and they would really hurt us then. We'll take care of it. Please don't."

I began taking them to school and picking them up, but with my new schedule for school and work, it would be impossible. Maybe Frank would. He worked close to the school and had flexible hours.

He said, "That's ridiculous. They can ride the bus. You can fix their breakfast and make sure they're ready before you leave for work. It doesn't matter which shift I'm working, I'll be around to see they get on the bus. I need to get some rest."

I had an hour in the evening to fix dinner, get the girls settled doing homework and then get to class. Fortunately, I only had classes Tuesday and Thursday. Twice a month, there was an all-day Saturday class.

I managed to siphon off part of my salary, before Frank got hold of it, to save in a carefully hidden pocket in my underwear drawer, and it was growing slowly. I hoped to have enough to get us into an apartment in a better school system, when I received my certificate for computer programming in six months. That should allow me to get an entry level job in the field, and I could take other computer languages or advanced courses later. Things were looking up for me and the girls, so why did I feel as if there was something terribly wrong in my household. I still had the nightmares, and if I believed the therapist back in Berlin, there was still something in my life that I could not consciously acknowledge, but lately, I had little time to think about it.

The day finally came when I received the precious certificate in computer programming. Immediately, I began putting together a resume, but didn't have any relative experience to list. I'd need to convince the hiring person that I was smart, and a quick learner. I rewrote the resume several times until I was satisfied with it, then Went to the community college to take advantage of the counselor's service to edit and make copies for me. The counselor handed me a list of potential employers along with addresses and phone numbers. I sent a resume to everyone on the list along with a cover letter requesting an interview for an entry level job. Only two on that long list responded. I returned home despondent after both interviews because things didn't seem to have gone well, so I set about compiling another list of potential employers.

Almost a week later, I had a call from one of the places I'd interviewed asking if I could come in for a second interview. The interview only lasted fifteen minutes before the interviewer, who would be my new boss, offered me the job. It was entry level pay, not much more than I had earned at the factory, but I would get a pay review in six months, and a yearly review after that. The best thing about this job was the chance for advancement. Promotions would come with pay increases. I had every intention of getting those promotions and increases. A bonus was that I could be home with the girls in the evenings. My new boss, Mel, said if I could be there at seven thirty and take only half an hour for lunch, I could leave at four. Since I had an hour commute, this would put me getting home at five in time to cook dinner and help with homework.

I gave my notice at the blanket factory, and when I walked out of that building for the last time, it felt as if a huge weight fell away.

Frank's interruption of our meals had to stop. If I spent my time to cook a meal, then everyone would sit down and eat it. There was another thing I intended to put a stop to. Frank had resumed his wrestling with the girls. He would get them on the floor, roll around and tickle them until they were begging for him to stop. Each time I told him to stop because it was not appropriate activity for two teenage girls and a grown man even if he was their father. He scathingly called me a prude and other unflattering terms, and he continued with the wrestling matches. But now, that I had found my voice, I told Frank, "It will stop. I don't care if I am being a prude and unreasonable, it makes me uncomfortable, it will stop, and not only that, the girls will not go out to eat unless I say we are going out. I spend my time cooking a nourishing meal and you take the girls out for a hamburger instead of eating the meal. That will stop."

Frank was visibly startled by the fierceness in my voice and the blood in my eyes, and he wilted, muttering, "Okay, okay."

I wondered why I hadn't been this fierce before, but I knew it was because for the first time in my life, I had a sense of independence and hope for the future.

That night he left for work hours before he was due using his old excuse that he had work to finish. I knew he wasn't going to work, but I no longer cared. I had noticed the two men watching our house when I came home. They left when Frank left. Once, I had wondered if Frank was having me watched, but now after years, I knew someone was watching Frank. When he wasn't home, there was no surveillance. If I knew they were there, other people could see them. Whoever they were, did they think they were invisible?

Ada's sixteenth birthday was on a Thursday, but I could not beg off work. My programming job had started off smoothly with me able to leave at four, but once I was put on a project, I had to stay late and work long hours in order to make the deadline for completion of the project. I asked Ada, "Will you be upset if we have your party Saturday? You can send out the invites for Saturday around 2 p.m. I'll order a cake to pick up Friday on my way home from work, and Saturday morning, we'll go to the store for ice cream, punch, nibbles, and whatever we need. We should be able to decorate and be ready by 2 p.m. What do you think?"

Ada responded, "Yea, fine. I only have five or six people to invite--just the friends I've made on Fort Devens."

"What kind of cake do you want?"

"Can I have chocolate with chocolate frosting?"

I stopped at the bakery after work Thursday to order the cake. The owner said that was really short notice, but I convinced her to have it ready the next day by four.

I was late getting home and knew I would have to rush to cook dinner, but was so tired that all I wanted was to fix myself a cup of coffee and watch the news. When I walked into the apartment, I was astonished at the mess. There were paper plates everywhere--some with half eaten cake, and some with the remnants of melted ice cream. Paper cups were everywhere, and someone had spilled something red on the table. It was dripping toward the floor.

I was shaking with anger when I asked, "What's going on?" But it was obvious that Frank had Ada's birthday early without my presence or knowledge.

"You know how much I wanted to share my daughter's sixteenth birthday, it was really important to me."

Frank simpered, "Her birthday was today. She deserved to celebrate today, not two days after. Seems a mother would understand that."

"I have to cook dinner, but not in this messy kitchen, it had better be cleaned up by the time I finish my coffee."

Frank offered, "We'll just go out for dinner,"

"Like hell you will. Get the kitchen cleaned and then I'm cooking." Wow, I heard myself, but could hardly believe that was me talking.

I slammed the kitchen door, and moved to the television feeling as if I had been punched in the gut.

Things with Frank had been really bad for the past couple of months. It seemed that he was deliberately taking over all parenting and pushing me out of the picture. I would spend time in the kitchen cooking a nourishing meal, and when I called the family to eat, Frank announced that he was taking them out for a hamburger. I was left with an uneaten meal and eating alone. I was simmering over that and determined to find a way to put an end to it. That disturbed me, but this latest felt like physical blows. I wanted my kids to have a nourishing attentive father, but my gut didn't think anything he did or said was nourishing. After these thoughts, I'd feel guilty and conflicted, remembering his grandma and even some of my past friends had commented on what a good father he was. Maybe I'm being childish and unreasonable like Frank had suggested many times, but then I'd remember my grandma's words, "If your gut tells you something is wrong, it probably is."

After dinner, Ada went immediately to her bedroom and shut the door. I had promised I would help her with English homework, so I pecked on the door. She was crying, and made an effort for me not to see. I sat on her bed and pulled her to me, "What's going on?"

"Mama, I didn't mean to hurt you with the birthday party. Dad said that you didn't care, and that you told him to have it. I didn't know."

I smoothed back her hair, "It's not your fault, honey. Did you have a good time?"

I helped her for about half an hour with her English homework, but it was obvious she was way behind and struggling. I hoped that I could find someone to tutor her and that it would be affordable.

The following day, I received a phone call from her principal. She said she was calling me at work to set up a conference with her and a couple of teachers because she wanted me to come alone. I think you should not tell your husband that you are coming. He seems to get upset and has a short fuse when we have had conferences in the past. Ada has gotten behind and needs some extra help. We need to talk about it before we get into the spring of the school year.”

“I have to talk to my boss and see if I can leave early. If I can see you at 4 p.m., then I won’t have to miss much work.”

The words she said didn’t sound too bad, but there was something in her tone that had me on edge, and why didn’t she want Frank to know?

There were three teachers in the conference room and the principal. I had met them before at a conference but couldn’t remember their names. Frank had gone to the conferences since I started working, and I assumed he shared everything discussed with me.

Immediately after we sat down, the principal said, “Ada has missed one hundred days of school, and will fail the junior year unless we put things back on track and she goes to summer school.”

 I gasped. “I’m not aware she has missed any school. There has to be some mistake. I fix her breakfast, and make sure she’s dressed and ready to get on the bus. I have to leave for work, but her dad is always there to see her onto the bus regardless of which work shift he’s on.”

Ada’s English teacher and her math teacher looked at each other knowingly, and then the principal said, “There have been several times that she has shown up quite late in a taxi. We haven't counted those days as absent, but it is reflected on her grade because she didn't know the subject."

I felt stunned. "A taxi?" We simply could not afford them--especially for transportation to school when there was bus service. I needed to get home and confront Ada and Frank. There must be some misunderstanding. I needed to think. I assured the teachers that I would get to the bottom of things and then see what we could do for Ada, and stumbled out of the school.

Frank was working the swing shift and had already left for work. I asked Ada to come sit with me. "We need to talk."

Ada leaned her head on my shoulder. Her body shook with the force of her tears. I let her cry it out, before quizzing her further. She said, "The kids bully me and call me stupid and dummy. I feel dumb because I don't understand what the teacher is saying or reading. I feel like I'm locked up inside of myself and can't get out."

"Do you want to talk to me about it?"

"No, I can't. I don't know how to explain it."

"Do you want me to make an appointment with someone for you to talk to? Sounds like you just need to get some help with reading and a little help with other subjects. Moving from Berlin to this strange school has probably not been the best move."

Ada sat up, and looking at me pleadingly said, "Yes, please. I don't want to repeat the grade."

As promised, I called the psychology clinic at the base hospital the next day. I explained, "Ada was diagnosed with dyslexia in Berlin, but with extra attention, she learned to read and seemed to be doing well, I didn't realize she still has a problem, but she isn't adjusting in this new school."

The psychologist, Cecil Paul, assured me that he would talk to me after her appointment about a treatment plan, or give me some contacts to reach out to for help.

I dropped Ada off, and had just enough time to make a quick run to the commissary before picking her up. She was waiting for me in the hallway, but made no effort to stand up to leave. I tried to interpret her facial expression to see if something was wrong, but she motioned toward a closed door and said, "He wants to talk to you."

Dr. Paul opened the door before I could knock, and motioned both of us into his office. He had gathered a stack of papers and flyers which he handed to me, "I think the dyslexia is the problem, and there's plenty of help for that. There is an excellent school in Beverly called Landmark--it's about an hour from here. They deal only with dyslexia so admission requirements are a one-on-one IQ test administered by a qualified Psychologist and an MRI which shows something about the brain.

I'm not sure what the purpose is. I'm not qualified to administer the test or give specialized help, but I can refer you to someone, and make the first appointment for you. Dr. Diane specter is an education specialist. Her office is about an hour from here."

I asked, "Will the army pay for the tests and MRI, and is there a chance I could get her into Landmark for summer school?"

Dr. Paul answered, "Yes, tests and Dr. Specter would be covered, but you'd need to come up with tuition. I think the summer session is around $5,000.00, and if I can get the needed tests scheduled for her, and you get her application in by the end of this month, yes, I think she could get in for summer school."

I gulped at the amount, and knew we didn't have the money, but determined to sell my soul to get her the help needed.

"Yes, make the appointment for her with this doctor, and tell me what I need to do to get her accepted."

Dr. Specter confirmed that Ada had dyslexia, and sent Landmark the paperwork. I received confirmation that she was accepted for the summer semester, and met with her principal to compare the Landmark curriculum with what her high school required. Her principal said it would get her a pass for her junior year and she could proceed to the senior class in September. Surely this would be acceptable to another school because I intended to find a way to move before the next school year. I had just received a small pay increase with my six-month review, but that still wasn't enough so I reluctantly took the rest of funds from my hidden stash, and cashed in my small life insurance policy.

Amy and I took Ada to Landmark at the end of May, and attended the parent's orientation. Frank insisted he needed to sleep. Ada wandered off, and when I spotted her, she was in rapt conversation with a girl about her age. It was wonderful that she was making friends already. She didn't seem at all perturbed that I was leaving, but seemed upbeat about the prospect of summer away from home.

Ada was allowed ten minutes phone time on Saturdays which she split between me and her sister. She insisted she didn't need to talk to her dad.

Amy moped around missing her sister. Frank said he would take her emerald mining in North Carolina before Ada came home. I thought it would be good to get away from my job for awhile. I really needed a vacation, and I hadn't seen any family for a couple of years.

A little over two weeks before Ada completed the summer at Landmark, Frank announced he was taking Amy to North Carolina, and leaving that weekend.

"Can't we wait until Ada finishes the summer school? There's another three weeks before school starts, and besides, I don't finish our big project for another week and a half. I need to ask for vacation time at least a week ahead."

Frank was adamant that I was not to come. "This is a special trip for just me and my daughter. I've promised her this trip for a long time. It'll be fun to see if we can find some gems. People have found diamonds, emeralds, garnet, and other gems in the North Carolina mines. I'm planning on visiting Granny, and my aunt--staying with them for a couple of days, and then we'll go mining for two or three days."

No matter how much I pressed him, Frank would not relent. Only he and Amy were going on this trip. I pointed out to him that he would have the only car. "How am I to get to work?"

His answer was, "The bus stop is only two blocks away. Take the bus."

Amy didn't appear too excited for this trip. She asked me, "Can I borrow a night gown--one with long sleeves and full length?"

I said, "Frank, she is growing up--a young lady now, and feeling modest. If you insist on going alone, you have to get her a separate room."

Even though Frank agreed to the separate rooms, I wasn't convinced that he would follow through so I said to Amy, "Honey, I don't have any granny night gowns--just have these flimsy short things. If I have time and the money, I'll see if I can find you a granny night gown, but I told your dad to get you a separate room. And if he doesn't, the rooms will have two beds so you can get undressed in the bathroom, turn off lights and run to get under covers.

They left Saturday morning before Ada called. She seemed extremely upset that I had not gone with them, and seemed to be overreacting and stressed over the trip. I tried to explain that I was not wanted on this trip--that her dad said he promised Amy a special trip to go emerald mining.

Amy had asked about decorating her bedroom with a space theme. I thought it would be a nice surprise for her, and also keep me occupied instead of wandering around in an empty house feeling lost without them. She called me Wednesday evening as we had agreed. I asked her, "Did you find an emerald today?"

She sounded really depressed when she answered, "I didn't go mining today."

"What's bothering you Amy, are you sick?"

There was a too long pause before she answered, "I just don't feel good. I want to come home now."

I asked to speak to her father. "Frank, do you know what's wrong with her? Does she have a fever? Are you still at your granny's house?"

Frank said, "No, we were there, but came up here to the mines yesterday."

"Frank, she wants to come home, and since she's feeling sick, I think you should head back home tomorrow."

He said he agreed, and would leave early the next morning.

I said, "If you leave early in the morning, and spend the night somewhere in Pennsylvania, then you should be home sometime Friday afternoon. If Amy's feeling bad and running a fever, then there'll still be time to take her to the dispensary."

I was getting ready for bed Thursday night when I heard the front door open. Terrified, I grabbed a glass bottle from the window sill, and started down the stairs. I came face to face with Frank. Amy followed looking gloomy. She gave me a quick hug, and headed to her room saying, "I'm not sick--just very tired. I'm just going to bed for some sleep."

Frank explained that he drove straight home, that he left North Carolina early morning and only stopped for bathroom, snacks, and gas. "Amy rode in the back seat. Most of the time, she appeared to be asleep. She said she wasn't feeling good."

Amy stayed in her room most of the day Friday, and ate very little. I took her temperature several times, and it was normal. I asked, "Can I take you to sick call?"

She insisted, "I'm feeling much better—just needed some extra sleep."

Saturday morning, she sat by the phone waiting for her sister to call, and insisted on talking to her first. I left her to go into the kitchen, and when she called me there was only about two minutes left for the phone call. I assured Ada that we would be there early the next Saturday to bring her home.

There would be a little more than three weeks before a new year of school started. The principal had said Ada could continue to her senior year, but I didn't want Ada or Amy to go back to that horrible school. My plan was to have moved to a new home and a new school by now, but circumstances had changed, and the upfront money for rent was spent for Landmark tuition.

Most rentals required first and last month's money up front. Thoughts kept going around and around in my head, how could I get the money—then I remembered the Krugerrand in my jewelry box. I had purchased this in Berlin as an investment at the urging of coworkers. Our pay checks were sent to an account at the Berliner Bank. On pay day, we'd all go to the bank, withdraw our money in dollars except for enough marks for lunch, and then we'd go as a group to eat. On several occasions, someone would buy a Krugerrand for investment saying that it was a solid gold piece and would always increase in value. I could only spare the money to buy one coin before it became frowned upon. We learned about the apartheid in South Africa, and joined a growing number of people in boycotting these coins. I had forgotten about the coin until searching for something in my jewelry box, I came across it. Excitedly, I called the bank to see what gold was selling for, and learned that it was over $800.00 an ounce. After cashing in the coin, the girls and I would go together to check out apartments. I wasn't sure how to tell them that we would move without their father or how they would react.

The following week seemed to pass so slowly. Usually, when Frank was on the day schedule, he left for work some time after I left. His work place was just the next street over. But this week, he left half an hour before me explaining they had some problems at work he needed to straighten out. When I got home, Frank still wasn't home, and it appeared that Amy had just slept all day. She and Frank had been avoiding each other since they returned from North Carolina. When I questioned Frank, he said, "Well, she didn't want to stay at Grandma's because my pop was staying there. He went on a weeklong drunk, and was fired from work. So, we went to a hotel just outside of the mine entrance, but she claimed she was sick and didn't want to go mining. She's pouting because I told her that she had ruined my vacation."

"Frank, that is really selfish--she can't help getting sick, and none of us wants to be around your dad. He's a real creep." I should have gotten used to Frank's poor me reactions, but it still galled me that nothing was ever his fault. Why did there always have to be a fault?

I knew Frank was shallow, but this was so terribly self centered and uncaring that I was reminded of why I wanted to get away from him.

Amy and I were up early Saturday anticipating our reunion with Ada. Frank said we'd have to go alone because he started a midnight shift tonight and needed to get some sleep. I didn't say so but I was relieved, and Amy seemed to liven up a bit. The girls sat together in the back seat interrupting each other in their eagerness to catch up. When we got home, they went to Amy's room, sat on her bed, and continued to talk.

They didn't look up or acknowledge me when I told them, "I'm going to cook an early supper since we haven't had lunch. Also, your dad needs to be getting up."

I was in the kitchen when Ada came in to announce she was going to see Dr. Specter, and that Amy was going with her. I tried to argue with her, "Honey, this is Saturday afternoon--I'm sure she doesn't have office hours now. I thought you were finished with her--that she was just getting you into Landmark."

"She called me at Landmark and wanted me to make an appointment to see her after I left there. She said I should continue seeing her."

I said, "My understanding was that she was a specialist in education. She should have called me instead. If you still want to talk to someone, I think the Fort Deven's therapist can help or recommend someone."

I was angry that Dr. Specter had been so inappropriate and pushy.

Before Ada could respond, Amy and Frank came up behind her, and I could tell both girls had been crying. Frank announced, "I'm taking them," and he quickly hustled them out to the car calling back over his shoulder that they would be back in a couple of hours. They were gone before I could say anything else or react.

I left the half-cooked meal, and sat down listening to the empty house. Something in this household was terribly wrong, and I had no idea what it was. Had something bad happened to Ada or Amy? I had suspected for years that Frank was having multiple affairs everywhere we moved. Here at Fort Devens was no exception. Had one of the girls found him out and confronted him? I suspected that was the problem, and that it bothered them much more than it bothered me. Months ago, a man called the house and asked for Frank. Frank talked to him briefly and when he hung up, said he had to go to meet this man's wife. He said she was a young recruit in his squadron--barely eighteen going through a mental crisis of some sort. Frank said she was asking to talk to him. My response had been, "If she needs professional help, then refer her to a therapist who is qualified to help her. Why can't she talk to her husband?"

"I can't do that because she'd lose her clearance. That's why her husband calls me--she will not talk to him, but asks for me. I guess I'm a father figure to her."

I listened to this explanation, but didn't believe a word. It sounded fishy. Over the months, her husband called Frank multiple times, and each time, Frank left the house for an hour or two. Was this more than what Frank claimed, and had the girls found him out? They were fifteen and sixteen and had friends scattered over the base, it was logical they would hear gossip or even see something. But why go to see Dr. Specter? I felt totally strung out and my heart raced with the stress. All I could do was wait.

I didn't have the will to get up and busy myself, but instead just sat and stared with my mind racing for what seemed hours until I heard them returning. Ada and Amy came into the living room and sat on the sofa with me, but Frank went upstairs. He came down dressed in his uniform and announced he was going to work.

"You don't have to be at work until 11:30, and it's only six."

He said, "We have a problem we're working on--I need to be there early." He stormed from the house as if someone had hurt his poor feelings.

"Ada took my hand and said, "Mom, we have to tell you something." I was prepared to hear about their dad's infidelities, but my world turned upside down and crashed by what she had to say.

Ada continued, "Mom, dad has been forcing me to have sex with him since I was about four or five years old. Remember when you went to Frankfort to have back surgery? He came and got us from Mrs. Patti's house, and that night he raped me. I didn't know what was happening to me—seemed like I'd dropped into hell, and a monster was tearing me apart. He hurt me so bad, Mama, I still remember the pain—it felt like burning and ripping, and I screamed and screamed. I'm sure the neighbors heard me. He threatened me that if I told anyone, horrible things would happen to you and Amy. He said you would go to jail and so would Amy. Then when I got older, he started telling me that no one would believe me, and if I didn't keep quiet and let him, he would get Amy. He raped me every chance he got--all these years up to when I went to Landmark. That's why I was so glad to leave."

I managed to ask, "Amy, do you remember hearing anything?"

Ada interrupted, "Mama, I think he drugged her, because she slept for two days. I couldn't get her to wake up."

"Oh, dear God, my poor babies. I wish I'd known. Oh God, what irony—people kept telling me what a good father he was. I'm so sorry. I wish I'd known before he hurt you. I wish you could have told me. I'm so sorry."

Ada said, "The main reason I didn't tell anyone was because he threatened to go after Amy if I told. But he just did anyhow when he took her to North Carolina. I was so worried about that trip--I thought about telling you then. I feel so guilty that I didn't tell. Mama, He tried to rape her, and when she fought back, he pulled her hair and forced her onto the bed. Amy bit him a bunch of times, and he left her alone, but made her sleep on the floor. That's why I'm telling you now. That's why I wanted to see Dr. Specter, I didn't know what to do or who to tell. Amy went into her office with me and told her what happened on the trip."

Amy spoke up, "That's why we left North Carolina early and drove straight home. I wasn't sick--just sick of him. He pulled my hair so hard that he had handfuls of my hair. I have a couple of bald and bleeding spots on my scalp, and he slapped my ear so hard it bled and hurt for days."

She began rocking back and forth and wailing. I felt as if a giant clawed hand had reached inside me and yanked me open. My heart actually hurt as if it were being crushed, and I felt that I couldn't breathe.

Ada was sobbing and could hardly talk, "Mama, about those hundred days of school I missed--when you left for work, he would force Amy to get on the bus, but make me stay home. He'd rape me several times, and then make me get cleaned up before you or Amy came home. Sometimes he sent me to school late in a taxi. He was getting worse, and doing horrible things to me that hurt terribly. Sometimes, I hid in the closet hoping he couldn't find me. It was hell."

Oh, my poor babies, the agony they've been through. I should have saved them from this monster. I thought he was lacking as a human being and had secrets, but I could never have imagined that he could do this. What evil. How could a father do this to his child? How could any human being do this to a child?

We stayed up all night talking and sobbing. I promised them they didn't have to be around him ever again--we would move away and find a town with better schools.

"Today is Sunday and the newspaper has a larger classified. We'll mark anything that maybe we can afford and that works for us. I'll go into work tomorrow and ask for a couple of days off then I'll come back for you. We'll look at apartments, and by the end of the day, we should have a place to move. Let's concentrate on getting out of here first, and then we need to go to the police and file charges--he needs to be locked away."

Ada spoke up, "Mama, please don't. Dr. Specter told me not to. She said I would be put on the stand and torn to shreds. She said women never win, and it would do me no good to be treated that way. I don't think I could stand going through that."

"I don't have a good feeling about Dr, Specter. She was supposed to only administer a test and a letter to Landmark. She was not supposed to see you again. On the other hand, I'm glad there was someone you felt safe to talk to. Let's get out of here and talk more about it later."

Around seven, we heard Frank coming in. We were still on the sofa just like he had left us. He took a look at our swollen faces and proclaimed, "Well, I guess they told you." The tone of his voice was the same as if he was asking for a glass of water.

I jumped up and confronted him, "You are to go upstairs, pack your clothes, and go to the barracks to live until we can find somewhere to move."

He seemed startled by the degree of my anger, and backed away. Then he turned and went upstairs. I could hear him moving around presumably packing. Then it got very quiet for too long. Had he fallen asleep up there?

I tip toed up the stairs to have a look, and saw that Frank had emptied the contents of my jewelry box onto the bed, and was sorting through it. He had the Krugerrand in his hand.

"Give me the Krugerrand."

He spat out the words, "No, I'm keeping it, "as he stuffed it in his pocket.

I was desperate and tried to grab it from his pocket, "I worked for it, and I bought it with money I earned. I need it for rent."

Frank bent back my reaching arm until I yelled with pain, slung his duffle bag over his shoulder, and left the house. I could hear that he took the car. I dropped to my knees in despair. I had no idea where to turn or where I could get help. "Please God, show me the way, what can I do?"

Ada and Amy joined me upstairs. Their faces were twisted with grief and also despair--emotions that a 15- and 16-year-old should not have to confront. I knew then looking at those faces that I had to reach down and find some courage or at least be able to fake it for their sake. I rose off the floor, sat on the bed and said, "I am so tired that I can't even think straight. Let's see if we can manage to get a little sleep even if it is just an hour or two. I'll think of something. Later, we'll go through the Sunday paper and mark anything that we might afford. I want to look in Andover, Sterling, and Tewksbury because they're supposed to have really good school systems, and all three towns are actually closer to my work."

Ada looked at me dubiously, "Mom, he took the car, how are we to get around?"

"I have a set of keys, if I have to, I'll walk around base until I see the car, and just drive it away. It must be either in front of the headquarters building, or the NCO barracks. We'll just go after it later today after we get some sleep--no, actually, it's best if we wait until Monday morning when we'll go off base--that way he can't come get it during the night."

We managed to sleep for about four hours. Ada was up first and had started a pot of coffee, and I could smell bacon frying. Suddenly, I realized that I was really hungry not having eaten since lunch yesterday. I doubted that they had eaten either. I lay there reliving the events of yesterday, and remembering my despair over the loss of the Krugerrand, I tried to plan the day tomorrow. I would go to work, beg for a couple of days off, and go to the finance department to beg for an advancement of my pay. I had overheard a couple of my co-workers saying they had done this more than once. That should be enough for first and last month's rent. We'd empty the refrigerator and the cabinets. Thankfully, I'd just been to the commissary and there was enough food for a week or so. I'd worry how to pay the bills next month, and feed us on a shorter paycheck.

After we had bacon and eggs, and a pot of coffee, Ada went to the little quick store to get a newspaper. We spent the rest of the day, poring over the classifieds, marking anything that might work and that we could afford. We started looking for a two-bedroom place before becoming very disillusioned. We simply could not afford two bedrooms. It appeared that we could not afford a one bedroom in Andover or Sterling, at least according to what was listed in the paper. "Okay, I said, "we'll just have to stick to a one bedroom in Tewksbury, and look at the layout to see if the living room could double as a bedroom for me, then you two could have the bedroom. We need to go back to the store to get some maps of Tewksbury.

Monday morning Ada volunteered to go with me to look for the car. We didn't have to look far. It was parked in front of the NCO barracks just as I suspected. I dropped her off in front of the apartment, and promised to be back around mid morning. "Be ready to go at ten,"

As soon as I left the main gate and pulled onto the highway, the tears started again. I could barely see to drive and could not will them to go away. I realized that I was wailing loudly and sobbing. I had done nothing but cry with the girls since Saturday afternoon, and it felt like my eyes were almost swollen shut. As I pulled into the parking lot at work, I knew that I could not go into the building like this. The towel used to wipe foggy windows would have to do to dry my face. Pulling out a compact from my purse, I put several layers of powder on my face. I still looked bad, but it was better than nothing. I took a deep breath knowing what I had to do and entered the building. My boss looked up at me startled. The look on his face told me he could tell I had been crying and the powder wasn't going to fool anyone.

"I have a family emergency and have to ask for a couple of days off to settle some stuff."

"Well, you have vacation time coming--take the time you need."

I was grateful, not only that he would not make me schedule the time, but for his kind tone.

I then made my way to the finance office talking to myself, "Dear God, I don't want to do this." I felt like a beggar, like I was requesting something dishonest, but then I told myself I would work for the money. It wasn't as if I was asking for a handout.

Mrs. Tate, head of payroll, looked at my tear-stained face and just answered, "Sure sweetheart, how much do you want advanced?"

"I think maybe $800.00 will do, could I get $800.00?"

I did a quick calculation and realized that was more than two weeks pay, and couldn't live for that long without some money. "Could I pay it back over a couple of months so I could get some of my pay check?"

Bless Mrs. Tate. She filled out a form showing how It would be paid back, and typed in $800.00 on a blank check. I thanked her profusely and headed for the parking lot hoping not to run into anyone. I was trembling violently and crying again when I reached the car. I laid my head on the steering wheel and sobbed so loud that it was good that I was in the car where hopefully no one would hear me. "What will we do? This money would be gone by the end of the day if we have success finding a place, and my paycheck will be short for several weeks. Then I remembered. How could I have forgotten that we have a joint checking account and there should be around a thousand dollars in there. I had been putting the majority of my paycheck into that account. I didn't think he took the checkbook. I needed to rush home to get it and go to the bank. If only I had advised the girls to put the chain on the door and not let him in. I reached for the dirty towel to dry my face and headed home. When I tried to get into the apartment, I couldn't because one of the girls had slid the chain in place. After several minutes calling through the crack in the doorway, Ada came to the door. She said the perp had been there demanding to come in to get more clothes and other things he needed, but they told him to go away. He said he'd be back and that the car was his.

Ada and Amy had started calling him 'the perp' Saturday evening and had referred to him as that since.

I rushed to the drawer where we kept the check book and was elated to find it there. I looked at the register and saw that there was almost $1300.00 dollars in the account. Apparently, Frank had yet to pay the bills. Stuffing the checkbook into my purse, I urged the girls to hurry so we could get stuff done and not leave the car unattended. I drove to the bank first and withdrew all the money. It would be safe in my purse for a short time, but after today, I would use a trick my granny had taught me years ago. I would roll it in a handkerchief and pin it in my panties. Both girls howled with laughter when I told them this, but I explained that the perp would search every nook and cranny to find the money. I said he has a bed in the barracks and food in the mess hall. We need the money more.

We drove to Tewksbury and checked out apartments in the order we had arranged yesterday. Each time coming away disillusioned. The one-bedroom apartments were more like efficiencies with one tiny bedroom not large enough for the two of them, and the tiny living rooms weren't large enough to hold the sofa which I intended to use as my bed. There were only two more places on our list, and the next one didn't sound promising. I was tempted to skip it. It was described as being converted from an old warehouse with high ceilings and a certain charm. "Oh well," I said to the girls, "let's see what a charming warehouse offers us." The building super let us into the advertised apartment which was full of surprises. Not only was there a large bedroom, but there was a large loft which the girls thought would make a great bedroom. The kitchen appeared to be an afterthought squeezed into a closet-size space with a small stove, a small refrigerator, and about a foot square of counter space. There were two upper cabinets and one lower cabinet not counting the one under the tiny sink. I had already decided to take this apartment if she would rent it to us. The loft sold me. That and the $425.00 rent. I asked how much money did I need up front, and when could we move in. She answered," If you give me first and last month's rent, and sign the lease, you can move in today if you wish."

On the way to the car, I said, "We can go back to Fort Devens, pack all the food, pack our clothes and get some linens. If Special Service is still open, we can see if we could borrow cots just until we can get our beds and some furnishings. I fear the perp will steal the car if he sees it unattended in front of the apartment."

Amy spoke up then, "Mama, why don't you just tell him you're keeping the car. You should tell him how he is going to act or you can have his ass hauled off to jail. You don't have to actually do it, just threaten him."

She did have a point. "Okay, let's get some boxes and go pack what we can get in the car. We don't have room for cots-- just pack enough blankets and pillows so we can sleep on the floor. I'll make sure we have a bed to sleep in tomorrow night. Grab the coffee pot and basic kitchen needs. If he comes over while we're packing, I think he'll come in to look for the checkbook and anything else he can carry out. I'll confront him then about the car."

He did come by while we were packing, and wanted in to get some things. I decided to let him in knowing he'd go for the checkbook. I thought we might as well set things straight now, but he just tossed the checkbook in his suitcase along with some more of his clothes and some books. He said he was taking the car.

"Give me my jewelry and the Krugerrand. Just so you know where you stand, you don't dictate anything to me. Tomorrow early morning, you are to arrange some furniture delivered to us. We will need our beds, dressers, the sofa, somewhere to sit and eat, and more of the kitchen things. The car is mine. I need it to get to work. You only have to walk a couple of blocks."

I hid my shaking hands by burying them in some towels. I was shaking all over. He took a step toward me, but thought better of it. Instead, he played the victim by whining that I was taking advantage of poor him.

"The girls are already calling you the perp. Don't give me any trouble or I'll see that your ass is in jail."

I had planned to spend the night in our new apartment, but since I had managed to sound so fierce, decided to stay here for the night and sleep in a bed.

As Frank was leaving, I repeated, "That car had better not leave the parking spot, it is mine, and I expect a truck with loaders to arrive here before noon tomorrow morning."

Frank whined, "How am I supposed to get any one without more notice?"

"I don't care how you do it, just have somebody here before noon."

We worked well into the night sorting and packing, and slept late in the morning. Frank didn't show up with the truck until 1:30. I didn't say anything, but knew it would be late this evening before we unloaded and unpacked the essentials.

For the next several weeks, we slogged from one day to the next just hoping that day would not present any challenges. I talked to an attorney, and filed for divorce. I asked if I could get something in child support and alimony. He said he would ask for it, but men rarely paid alimony, and even if child support was granted, the father rarely paid that. In most cases, the mother was fully responsible. I think I'd already figured that out.

Amy had called her friends at Fort Devens soon after we moved, but had not received a return call from any of them. Her friend Molly called three weeks after we had moved and asked if she could come for a visit. I told Amy to invite her to stay for dinner so they could have a good long visit. I knew Molly's household was always in turmoil, and that she had some emotional issues, but I didn't know any details. They could benefit from each other's company.

When they went into the bedroom and called for Ada to join them, I just thought it typical teen behavior. After about forty minutes, I called them for dinner.

They came in, sat down at the table, and pushed the plates and utensils back. Three solemn faces registering despair.

Amy talked first, "Mom, the perp got another car and moved off base into an apartment. He took Molly to North Carolina and he and his friend Johnnie Burk took her out on a boat and raped her repeatedly. She was bleeding so badly and could hardly walk when the perp brought her back to Massachusetts. She came back three days ago and is still bleeding and in pain."

I felt as if I had been socked in the gut again, "Molly, can I take you to a doctor?"

Molly's shoulders slumped and she looked like a little girl defeated, "No Ma'am, I'll be okay."

"Molly, I think you should see a doctor, and then the four of us go to the police. How old are you."

She lifted her eyes which registered not only defeat, but also panic. "I'll be fifteen next month. Please don't report this or tell my parents. I lied to them and told them I was going with Amy. At the time, I thought it was just a little white lie. Mr. Honley said

Amy and Ada were already down in North Carolina with their grandma, and they wanted me to come down for the last week. He said I didn't need to make any phone calls because Ada and Amy were expecting me, He took me to my house and waited outside in the car while I packed a bag and told my mom that Amy had invited me to go to North Carolina with her. I told her that I'd be back in a week, and left without giving her a chance to ask any questions or stop me. I don't know why I lied. I don't know why I believed Mr. Honley. My parents won't believe anything I say, and they'll blame me just like Ada's dad said. He said I would be labeled a bad person and maybe go to jail. My parents will throw me out--Ada's dad said so. I have to keep this secret. Please, please don't tell anyone."

Amy spoke, "Don't call him my dad--he's a perp."

Ada snorted, "That's exactly what he said to me time and time again--that I would be blamed and go to jail because I was committing a crime. He also told me that mom would throw me out. Imagine, a four-year-old committing that crime. I spent all those years terrified. I wish I had told years ago so that Amy and Molly would not have been hurt."

I persisted, "Will you girls testify against him if I report him. If we don't throw his ass in jail, I just might kill him."

Neither of them was willing to report him. Amy said, "Dr. Specter said men get away with everything--I would be put through a wringer and it would be horrific what the court would do to me. Mom, I can't take anymore. They would treat me so bad and say it was my fault."

Is there no end to the depravity of this man? Again, I was shaking from the revelation of more evil than I could comprehend.

"Molly, I persisted, at least let me take you to Planned Parenthood for some help with the bleeding and pain. They will not force you to report to anyone--they'll just help you heal."

She seemed eager for help if it wouldn't require police or confession. After she called home to tell them she was spending the night, we all went with her, and waited while she was examined and treated. I felt that the staff were angels of mercy by how gentle they were with Molly. I thought of the pain that my poor Ada and Amy had suffered and with no one to help them, and shed more tears.

I could hear the girls talking, and crying most of the night. I was so very glad that at least they had each other for an iota of comfort and understanding. Especially since I intended to stop Ada's weekly visits with Dr, Specter. I was miffed that she visited Ada at Landmark, and insisted Ada continue therapy with her without consulting me, but I decided to swallow my anger and continue taking Ada for weekly visits until I could find someone closer to home who specialized in trauma. But Ada came home from these visits angry and agitated because Dr Specter said there was no way I had not known she was being abused all those years, and that I had knowingly allowed it to continue. It seemed to me Dr. Specter was doing a great harm to my daughter. I decided to take the coward's way out to avoid a confrontation—simply refuse a return appointment.

Instead of asking to reschedule Ada for the following week, Dr. Specter handed me a business card and told me to call that doctor for an appointment. I said I could not afford the time or the co-pay, but she sternly told me that if I did not see this doctor, she would start proceedings to remove my daughters from my care. I started to slide the card into my pocket, but she said, "I gave you the card to call now and ask for an appointment next week. You can drop off Ada and then go for your appointment. He is only a couple of miles from here."

I said, "It's after seven--no one will be in his office at this time. I'll call him tomorrow."

Dr. Specter said, "He works from home, and I've already talked to him. He's expecting your call."

The woman, who answered the telephone, did not identify herself so I assumed it was his wife. Without hesitation, she gave me an appointment for the following Wednesday. Dr. Specter wrote the time and address on an appointment card and shoved it at me. I was so stunned that I took the card without comment, accepted the return appointment for Ada, and left in a fog.

The following week, I dropped Ada off at six twenty--a little early but she could sit in the waiting room for ten minutes.

The handwritten directions were almost useless since there were no street lights, and in many instances, no road signs. It was a rural area with a maze of roads, and it was a complete moonless night. After driving in circles and convinced I would never find Dr. Hammond's home, it was suddenly right in front of me. It appeared that all the lights in the house were on, including outside spots. What a welcoming beacon with all the surrounding darkness. Dr. Hammond answered the door before I could ring the bell. He introduced himself and guided me into his office.

"The doorbell upsets my son. I hope you don't mind if I leave the door open so I can keep an eye on him--my wife has a school board meeting. He doesn't talk or make a sound."

A little boy, who looked to be around nine years old, sat cross-legged on the floor. He was arranging and rearranging dozens of tiny figurines. He didn't look up but appeared engrossed in his activity.

Dr. Hammond said, "Sit anywhere you like. Dr. Specter gave me a summary. I know that your husband raped your daughter when she was four and continued until recently. I know that he attempted to rape your youngest daughter. I also know that he is in Army security holding a top-secret clearance. Before we continue, I do need to ask you, are you here because you feel the need to talk or are you here because you feel forced?"

"I'm here because I was forced to come or lose my daughters. Last week was to be Ada's last visit--I had intended to find her another therapist, but Dr. Specter threatened to take my kids. I don't want to lose my kids--that's why I'm here. Dr. Specter told Ada that I knew about her dad all those years and just ignored it. I'm here because everyone will believe her since she's a doctor. I'm not sure why she wants me to see you."

Dr. Hammond said, "She wants me to write a letter confirming that you knew, and did nothing. She thinks a letter from me would give her legitimacy with social services to remove your daughters from your home. You can rest easy. I will not do that. After our visit, you can decide if you might gain some benefit from seeing me. You can be assured that what we discuss will remain between us, and is of no concern to Dr. Specter."

Dr. Hammond's son began rocking back and forth and crying. He excused himself, went across the hall, and knelt down beside his son. He stroked his back and talked to him in a soothing voice, then pulled out another set of miniature figurines from an old chest. He spread them out onto the floor in front of his son. The boy stopped rocking and looked up at his father with a smile. Dr. Hammond returned to his desk and said, "I'm really sorry for the interruption, but he'll be quite happy for the rest of the hour."

I dropped my guard when I saw how gentle he was with his son, and talked nonstop for most of the hour covering my life with Frank. I told Dr, Hammond things that I had not dared say aloud to anyone. There was no time left to get feedback or ask questions, but there was always next week. I did not like or trust Dr. Specter, and I also knew she had an ulterior motive sending me to Dr. Hammond, but he seemed to be a kind and trustworthy person, and I hadn't realized how badly I needed to talk to someone.

Dr. Specter was livid that I was ten minutes late. She raged, "This is never going to work. When seven thirty comes, I want to turn off lights and lock up."

I pointed out that she had insisted I see Dr. Hammond, and it had to be during Ada's appointment. That didn't calm her down. As we were leaving, she said, "You'd better work something out, I'm not going through this again."

Ada's visits to Dr. Specter were being billed to CHAMPUS which was a civilian medical health program of the military. I received a statement from them the day before Ada's next appointment. It showed Dr. Specter had billed for daily appointments instead of once weekly. According to the billing, Ada had seen her fifteen times in the past month, and would soon reach the yearly limit. The letter stated Dr. Specter would need to submit a request for a greater number, and give reasons why they were needed. Not only was she a harmful therapist, but was also dishonest.

I took Ada to her appointment the following week, and continued on for my appointment with Dr. Hammond. I wanted to talk to him before firing Dr. Specter. If he said she could not take my kids, then I would never bring Ada back to see her. I also wanted to ask him what to do about the fraudulent insurance claims.

Dr. Hammond said, "Absolutely don't take Ada there again. No, she can't remove your daughters from your home. If she pushes the issue, call me. There are several very professional trauma specialists, close to your home. I'll give you names and contact information before you leave."

"Dr. Hammond, how could I have been so stupid? Since he didn't touch me after I became pregnant with Amy, I thought he fooled around with grown women—not babies. I also thought he was a spy. I told you last time about all the suspicious actions and people. I knew in my gut that the only answer was that he was a spy. Now that I look back over the years, there were glaring clues he was a pedophile. How could I have been so stupid? Over the years that I plodded along I'm sure he hurt other children, and stole the life and soul from his own kids. If I had not been so blind and stupid, I could have saved all those kids from the bastard."

Dr. Hammond said, "He was in the perfect profession. Keeping secrets. He fooled even the professionals. Every year or so, he was re-evaluated for a top-secret clearance. No one caught this because he was so adept in hiding. He manipulated everyone, even the psychiatrists who passed him along as no threat for black mail. I haven't personally examined him, but based on what you have told me, he appears to be either a sociopath or a psychopath."

I asked, "Is he evil or sick?"

Dr. Hammond said, "Depends on who you ask. Law enforcement says he is evil, and the current thinking in psychology is that he is sick, and can be helped. I do not go along with that thinking. I did attempt to treat pedophiles early in my career, but later refused because I became convinced they were both evil and sick, and could never change. Also, the thinking has been for the victim to confront her abuser in a protected and supervised environment. The last time I allowed a pedophile in my office, I became physically ill when I saw the degree of evil and manipulation of that man. I had a client, an eight-year-old girl who had been sexually abused by her uncle. He had been in court ordered therapy for a couple of years and was reportedly making progress. I brought together my client and this man so that she could confront him with how much he had hurt her. His therapist accompanied him to the meeting. He strutted into the room and sat with his legs spread, and when my client told of her hurt, his response was, "What do you expect. You paraded around in your little skimpy outfit just begging for it."

"I could have lost my license over my reaction. I shook my fist at him and chased him out of my office. I said to his therapist, "You call that progress? He blames his victim—a child?" I never again agreed to treat pedophiles or rapists."

The following week, that conversation played over and over in my mind. It was chilling that I had spent years with a psychopath and subjected two innocent, defenseless babies to his evil. It did not matter that I didn't know. All that really mattered was that I had not protected them.

Ada, Amy, and Molly refused to testify against him, and I could not hurt them further by insisting, but maybe if I could find two or three people who would agree to testify, then maybe Molly would feel safe in speaking out.

Some memories were dim and names eluded me, but I was determined to compile a list of people to contact. The first person that came to mind was Robin because I was never able to get a satisfactory answer to comments her mother had made, and why was Robin so eager to babysit in Turkey, and then after only two times, she was too busy. Why was Frank shipped to an isolated assignment with only a one-day notice, and that was right after he had taken Robin home? The next people I wanted to find were the young soldier at Fort Devens and her husband. Frank's story never seemed to make any sense, and most of what he said was nonsense. There were three or four more people I wanted to contact because of strange comments or suddenly not letting their kids play with Ada and Amy if Frank was the only parent home. I had to render this monster impotent so he could no longer hurt anyone.

Dr. Hammond offered the use of his office phone saying it was a business expense, and he offered help tracking down the people on my list. He said, "Think of the last place where you knew them to be, and any parents or relatives' names." He found Robin through her father's obituary in an old *Stars and Stripes* newspaper. Robin's married name and her spouses name appeared in the obituary. She lived in Florida. Dr. Hammond made inquiries and phone calls and found an old phone number.

My heart pounded when I dialed the number not sure if it still belonged to her, but she answered on the first ring. I introduced myself and explained why I was calling. I told her what Frank had done to my girls and to Amy's friend and I wondered if there were more victims—more to the point, was she a victim? What could she tell me if anything. Robin began talking immediately as if she had been waiting for my call.

"He had made inappropriate comments and suggestions in Turkey. I told Mama, and she said I couldn't baby sit for you, but when we were in Virginia, Mama said it was an easy walk home or else she could send Francis to walk with me. That particular night, it was a real bad electric storm, so I took his offer of a ride home. I didn't think he would bother me since I lived only a couple blocks away, and my dad was his first sergeant. He went a couple of miles past my house and parked in a dark parking lot. He ran his hand up my skirt and grabbed my crotch before I could react, and he said, "How would you like to make an extra twenty?" I screamed for him to take me home immediately, and tried to open the car door, but I couldn't get it open. He put his hands back on the steering wheel and said, "Okay, stop screaming, I'm taking you home, but if you tell anyone, something really bad will happen to you." I was shaking all over and terrified. I was only thirteen then. I told my dad and brother as soon as I got in the house. If you remember, my dad was his first sergeant, so the very next day my dad arranged to send him to an isolated assignment in Alaska. The orders were cut that very day. They decided not to tell you because my mom and dad thought it would hurt you and the kids. My dad's only concern at the time was to just get him far away from me. I wish they were still alive so you could talk to them. When you wanted a sitter in Virginia, Mama said you seemed like a nice person--she didn't think you knew what a cad he was, and I could walk home alone or have Francis meet me. I wish I had called Francis or even my brother that night, but I was rattled by the storm and not thinking clearly."

As she talked, I could feel her anxiety, and realized that just talking and remembering was still traumatic. I didn't want to cause her more hurt, but needed her help to stop him, so I asked if she would testify against him. She said, "I can't do that. I have a family now, and don't want to stir things up. I only want to forget, but good luck to you."

It was a relief to actually hear the truth, but I felt a stir of anger toward her parents for not telling me. Because of their silence, the hurt continued.

The young man, who called the perp for his wife, was Justine Andrews, but I couldn't remember her name. Dr. Hammond had many contacts at Fort Devens, and found that Justin was still assigned to the base, but lived in an apartment not far from the main gate. As he handed me Justine's phone number, he said, "I didn't get his wife's name, but if you call this number, you'll probably be able to talk to her."

Justine answered the phone, and when I identified myself, I heard a sharp intake of air and thought he was hanging up. Quickly, I asked to speak to his wife because I thought maybe there was more to Frank's stories regarding their meetings.

Justin said, "My wife is dead. Summer took her own life because of what that bastard did to her. She was only eighteen years old. Sergeant Honley wormed his way into her trust and confidence, and when she confided that she suffered from depression and was thinking about seeing a therapist, he told her if she did see a therapist, and if that information became known by the commanding officer, she would be droned out of the Army Security Agency. He came up with a cock and bull scheme that he would take her to see a therapist he knew who would keep the sessions private. The first time she met him to take her secretly for therapy, he took her to a motel instead and raped her. He told her if she told anybody, he would ruin her career. She was terrified of him. At least once a week, Summer was instructed to have me call the bastard at home to take her to the therapist. Why he concocted such a scheme, I don't know. She left me a note explaining everything and wrote that she didn't want to live anymore knowing how she had betrayed me, but she couldn't see a way out. She begged me not to report him. She didn't want anyone to know how stupid she had been."

I asked Justin, "Did you ever say anything to him? Did you report any of this?"

He answered, "I did threaten him. He just smirked at me. One night, I went to his apartment to confront him—he'd moved off base by then. I had a loaded gun concealed in my pocket. I rang the doorbell multiple times and got no answer so I sat in my car waiting for him to come home. He pulled his car in beside me, but took no notice of me. There were two men who went into his apartment with him. I went home."

"Justin, would you testify if I brought charges against him? He hurt so many people and he hurt my babies badly. He has to pay."

He said, "I can't face that right now—for Summer. Maybe I should just kill him for all of us. I'm sorry for what you've been through, but I can't think."

I told Dr. Hammond, "I don't know where to turn, if no one will testify. He needs to be taken off this earth, I should go and cut off his balls--maybe that will render him harmless."

Dr. Hammond chuckled, "I fear he would just find another way to abuse, and you would be the one suffering."

With each day, both girls became angrier. They were angry at the world, but threw the anger at me. Ada reminded me every day that Dr. Specter believed I knew all about the perp, and had asked, "How could she live in the same household for all those years and not know what was happening?" Both Amy and Ada took up the accusation. They blamed me for everything negative that had ever happened in their lives. There were days that I felt so alone, that I could hardly breathe. I yearned to be held and told that everything would be okay. I had not made friends in

Massachusetts. I never had time. My coworkers were friendly, and we had camaraderie at work, but I didn't have time or resources to socialize after work. I used to think that I had the girls love and respect, but that had disappeared.

Thank God for Dr. Hammond. He kept me from going off the cliff. When I told him about the girl's anger, and that they had turned against me, he assured me they were just trying to work out their upside-down world. "Children often gravitate toward the abuser. In their mind, if they express the anger toward them, they don't know what will happen, but they feel assured of your love and they don't think you will abandon them. They will work it out at some point and come around."

I hoped he was right. I didn't want the anger to influence their future. I wanted them to find contentment and even joy. I wanted them to have a good life. Would this nightmare ever end?

Months went by with us stepping lightly around each other, living in the same household, but not sharing much except for a profound hurt. Hurt hung in the air.

My attention turned to helping Ada get into college, and finding the money. After much research, she settled for Westfield in western Massachusetts. I helped her apply for every scholarship that we thought might apply, and she applied for student aid. She was turned down for several of the scholarships because I made too much money. What a laugh since I barely made above poverty level. Her application for student aid yielded the same results except she did get a work study program that promised to be a big help. I borrowed the rest with a parent's loan.

Gradually, the girl's anger toward me subsided. At least we were talking and sharing.

When we moved Ada into her dorm, I exacted a promise for her to call me collect every Friday. "I want to hear your voice and know you are okay. Amy and I will be there to get you for Thanksgiving with bells on."

This brought a smile which was the first one I'd seen for a long time.

Amy and I were beside ourselves when we headed to Westfield to pick Ada up for Thanksgiving. We both almost ran up the stairs to her dorm room, and stopped suddenly when we saw her. In just three months, it looked as if she had lost fifteen or twenty pounds, and her skin was an ashen color. We hugged her close and grabbed her belongings to take home. Neither of us said a word about her appearance. Amy and I looked at each other wondering who would be the first one to ask about Ada's health. After we had caught up with news and had been on the road for half an hour, I broached the subject of her health. "Ada, are you sick? Did you lose all the weight on purpose?"

She confessed that she didn't feel well at all. "I have constant cramping like I'm having a period, and I have to wear a pad all the time because I bleed all the time."

Those symptoms sounded ominous to me, "I'm taking you to a gynecologist tomorrow, so you can find out what's causing the problems, and then you can begin to get well."

I took her to the hospital on Fort Devens because she didn't need an appointment--just show up and wait. She still had her dependant ID, so the medical was free. She asked if I could stay with her for the exam. I held her hand while the doctor did a pelvic, took a pap test, and drew some blood. He said her cervix was inflamed and showed erosion. But couldn't tell what the problem was until he got the tests back. He said he was putting a rush on the tests and should have them next day, and would call for us to come in. He gave her some pills to calm the cramping.

We waited on pins and needles for the call back, and when the doctor didn't call the next day, we were strung out anticipating bad news. We received a call from the doctor mid morning two days later asking if we could come into his office around one o'clock. On our drive to Fort Devens, we went back and forth, it was good news, no it's bad news. We were called into the doctor's office as soon as we arrived. Doctor Bragg had a bunch of papers spread across his desk along with a blue folder that appeared full. Amy's medical record was open beside these. Our eyes were riveted on his face in anticipation of bad news.

Ada had advanced cervical cancer. Dr. Bragg said, "I suspect it has spread to your uterus and maybe even your ovaries. I don't have the expertise or the facilities to perform surgery, and you need to have surgery right away. I've contacted a doctor I've often worked with at Mass General. She's an expert in gynecological cancers, and she's already arranged for an operating room Friday which is only two days away. You'll need to be here at 7am Friday morning, and I'll have transport to Mass General. Your car will be safe parked in front overnight. All the prep instructions are in the blue folder—you can read through them when you get home today. You'll have your cervix removed, and probably the uterus. After Dr. Liz gets a look at the ovaries, they may have to come out also. I know all this comes as a shock and it's just too much to process right now. I'm really sorry to have to deliver this news, but I assure you that you are in good hands. Dr. Liz is the best in the country."

Amy started rattling off questions, but Dr. Bragg held up his hand and interrupted. His face showed indecision, but then he said, "There's evidence your cancer is caused by the HPV virus. It's a recently acknowledged fact that this virus causes gynecological cancers, and can be in the body for years before causing problems. It's spread through sex, so, Ada it's almost a sure thing that you got this virus from a sexual partner. You should contact him to get a checkup."

Ada was trembling and teary-eyed so I quickly gathered all the papers from Dr. Bragg so I could get her to the car before she had a meltdown.

When we were safely in the car with windows rolled up, she began screaming. Amy and I waited until she quieted before I asked her, "Is the perp the only one?"

She glowered at me, but I needed to ask the question even though I knew the answer, and I had carefully chosen my words.

"Of course he's the only one. Don't you remember that any time a boy asked me out, he would find some excuse to keep him away. He wanted me all to himself. Even now, he's ruined my chances of having a boy friend because I can't stand the thoughts of a male coming near me. No, I don't want to warn him. If he has cancer, then that is just karma as far as I'm concerned."

The three of us were at Fort Devens before 7am eager to get this over and very grateful to Dr. Bragg for arranging the transport. Massachusetts General Hospital was a sprawling place with a confusing maze of hallways. We were met at the entrance and given details about what to expect. Ada was checked in and someone escorted her to the surgery prep unit.

Amy and I were shown where to wait, and told that Dr. Liz would talk to us when the procedure was over, and then someone would escort us to the recovery room.

We waited, and waited, and paced, and tapped our feet, and sighed for what seemed hours. It was such a relief when we saw Dr. Liz coming toward us. I couldn't read her facial expression when she sat down between us. She said, the cancer has been there for a long time, and very advanced, it affected the cervix, the uterus, and her ovaries. "I'm so sorry, because of the extent of the cancer, I had to remove cervix, uterus, and the ovaries. She'll need further treatment. I'll talk to you before releasing her back to Fort Devens.

"I asked, "Dr. Bragg said her cancer was caused by an HPV virus. Is there any chance it was caused by something else? There's a rumor that the water and soil on Fort Devens is contaminated with heavy metals and petroleum products."

She said, "No, those are serious concerns and can cause many health issues, but I'm ninety nine percent sure that this cancer is from the HPV."

Amy and I planned to sit with Ada for the rest of the day, then catch one of the last trains back to Fort Devens, but we learned the last train had already left Boston. I asked if we could stay in Amy's room with her. The personnel at Mass General had already been kind to us, but they went out of their way to bring in two cots for us, and even a small kit with toothbrush and paste. Early the next morning someone even brought us a voucher for the cafeteria so we could get breakfast while the doctors made their rounds. We had not slept very well. Ada had groaned in pain most of the night, and seemed to be only semi conscious.

When we returned to Ada's room, the doctor was still with her. She said, "I'm notifying Dr. Bragg to send the ambulance transport to get her. I'm not discharging her, only transferring to the hospital on Fort Devens. She had a big surgery and needs a few days to recover enough to go home. Because the cancer was so advanced and extensive, she will need post op treatment. Dr. Bragg will arrange for that."

I was grateful for the good care Ada had received, and asked Dr. Liz if I could give her a hug. She grinned and said she would love a hug.

We rode back to Fort Devens in the ambulance with Ada, and stayed with her until she was safely in her new room, and Dr. Bragg acknowledged he knew she was there. Amy and I desperately needed a good night's sleep, a shower, and a hot meal. We went to the lobster claw and stuffed our faces with a pile of fried fish and a gallon of tartar sauce.

The dean at Westfield said they would keep Ada's spot open until the summer semester, and they would also keep her work study program. I didn't think she would be ready to return to school because she didn't seem to be getting better. She never missed a radiation treatment or chemo treatment, but she appeared to go downhill. Her clothes hung off her, and her expression was dull. She showed no interest in anything until one day she exploded with fury, "I hate him. He took everything from me. Now I can't have children--I'm afraid to let a guy come near me so it probably doesn't matter. But I did want kids."

I said, "I'd like to cut his balls off a little at a time and then see the rest rot."

Amy looked at me in astonishment. "Mama, I've never heard you talk like that, but sounds like a good idea."

I let Ada rage close to an hour before she was exhausted and fell asleep. As I watched her sleep, I thought, "Yes, he stole her childhood, and he stole her adulthood as well."

When Ada had her first checkup with Dr. Bragg, he was alarmed at how she looked, and her lack of energy. He ordered a bunch of tests, then after he had a chance to look them over, called us back into his office.

"I need to admit Ada because preliminary test results indicate that more extensive tests need to be done. These tests take longer to accomplish and it would be easier on Ada if she spent a day or two here. I hope to find why she's not getting better. Depending on results, we'll decide further treatment."

Ada was a patient at Fort Devens for a day and a half before Dr. Bragg reviewed all the test results. When I sat down with him, his face showed bad news so I braced for the worst. He said the cancer had spread to other areas of her body, and he wanted to send her back to Mass General so they could give her more extensive tests and scans to identify the extent of the spread, and to recommend treatment.

Amy and I found ourselves back at Mass General sitting on the same seats waiting. It seems we were always waiting--afraid to exhale. The day before should have been a good day, but it was marred by my sense of waiting. I had my review at work, and I had feared a bad review although I had concentrated and worked as hard as I could. I'd had to take so much time off for family emergencies that I feared it would count against me. Instead, I received a very good review and a pay raise. The irony, I then had to ask for a day or two off to take Ada to Mass General. So there Amy and I sat again anticipating bad news. Ada was so weak now that she could hardly walk from her bed to the bathroom. I had made sure she kept every treatment appointment, and I spent extra time planning and cooking nourishing meals. But none of this seemed to make a difference.

Amy and I spent another night in Ada's room. Frequently, a technician came to draw blood, or take her for a scan or special test. Amy and I waited by her bedside for her to return. The three of us spent a restless night. It was around midmorning before Dr Liz came to talk to us about the results. Her grim expression foretold bad news. She pulled up a chair opposite us and began to explain the cancer had invaded multiple organs which tests and scans showed to be the liver, kidneys, and lungs. "I didn't order a brain scan, because I felt she had already been exposed to too much radiation, and I assume it has reached the brain, and should be treated as such. Without treatment, Amy will die. With treatment, she has only a slim chance of living for a few more months, and as far as long-term cure, miracles do happen."

She spoke directly to Ada, "You can stay here and we can start the treatment immediately, or you can go home with your mum and sister. I spoke with key people at Lawrence General Hospital, and they are prepared to begin your treatment tomorrow if you choose to go home, but your mom would need to take you in every day, and someone would need to be with you at home. This is a big decision. I'll see another patient, and come back in to hear what you've decided. Talk about it, and give me an answer when I come back."

I spoke up, "I thought cervical cancer was very treatable. I don't need to think about it, I'll take her to Lawrence for treatment."

Dr. Liz said, "It is if you catch it early, but Ada's cancer was at stage four and beyond before diagnosis."

Amy glared at me, "Don't you think it's Ada's decision?"

I knew what Ada's decision was. She had given up months ago, and I didn't want to hear or accept it.

Dr. Liz looked directly at Ada, "Talk about it with your mom and sister, and you can give me your answer when I come back."

We argued and cried with Ada but she had firmly made up her mind. She had obviously thought a lot about this. "I have nothing to live for. The perp took my life already. You heard Dr. Liz, if I had treatment, it would be horrible, and make me even sicker and weaker. She can't guarantee I won't be in severe pain, and even after going through that, it still may only buy me a month or a few months. I want to go home with you and see if we can't have a few good days. My mind is made up, no more treatment."

We took Ada home. I worried how I could be in two places at same time. I had to work or else we didn't have a roof over our head. I toyed with the idea of calling my sister, Barbara. I didn't even know if she was still in North Carolina. We had written off and on for years, but since I'd been in Massachusetts, the letters from her dwindled, and I hadn't heard from her in over a year. Maybe she had married and had a family.

Amy had the solution. She insisted she was dropping out of school, and would take care of Ada.

I insisted she was going to school, "You only have one more year, and then you can go to college."

"What good is that?"

"It gives you options. Every woman should have options. If you have an education and a career, you can control your own life and future. Amy, please stay in school, I'll work something out. I'm going to make a few phone calls, and see where we can get some help."

Amy would not listen. She insisted she would not go to school for another day. You cannot make me. I'm staying here and taking care of my sister."

It was useless arguing with her so I arranged for her to get instructions in hospice care from Dr. Liz--mainly on how to keep Ada comfortable, and when she should alert me that she needed more pain control. I know I was in denial, but sometimes, I begged Amy to promise she would please go back to school when Ada was better. She would shrug and give me a non committal, "maybe." Well, that was better than no.

Knowing that both girls used to like board games and cards, I bought a couple of their favorites so they could play during the day. This kept them occupied for a few weeks, but then I'd come home from work to find both of them asleep in front of the television.

Ada's nineteenth birthday was coming up and I asked her if she felt like having a party. Would she like to invite friends from Fort Devens? I promised to bake her favorite cake. She liked the idea but didn't know if she could get in touch with them. "They have scattered after graduating high school. Jeannie is going to Mount Holyoke, and Phyllis planned to go to Mount Wachusettes. I'm not sure if Connie is still living at home. I'll see if I can talk to them tomorrow and ask if they would like to come. I'm pretty sure Molly would come."

She talked to all three of them, and they said they would love to celebrate her birthday. Amy called her friend Molly who said she'd love to come. Ada seemed to perk up some. Maybe it was because I wanted it so badly, but she seemed to have more energy. Her birthday was on a weekday, a work day for me, so we agreed to have it Saturday so that we could celebrate all day. I hummed as I planned for her party. On the morning of her birthday, she was still sleeping when I was ready to leave for work. I thought about letting her sleep, but decided to wake her to say, "good morning birthday girl, I left you a little something by the coffee pot." When I pushed open the door to the bedroom, I saw Amy flung across her bed snoring loudly, but Ada was strangely still. I gently bent over to give her a kiss, and felt her cold to my touch and not breathing.

Instead of planning a party, I had to plan a funeral.

I could not cry or express my grief in any way. If I allowed myself to feel, it would consume me so I stuffed it deep inside to be felt another day. I had to remain stoic for Amy's sake and for what needed to be done. Arrangements for Ada's funeral was set for a week away so I had to hurry. Amy said, "The perp read the obit and dared to call me. He insisted he was coming to Ada's funeral."

"Good, I thought, it spares me the trouble to go looking for him."

I went to the only store near me that sold guns. I picked out a rather small pistol, and asked if it could kill anything. He assured me it could. I liked it because I could conceal it in my purse. I asked the sales person to show me how to handle it and how to load it. He took me to the back of the store where there was a target on one wall. After he had me load and then unload the gun following his instruction, he gave me five minutes of target practice. When he saw me weaving about and that I missed the target by a foot, he suggested that I find a place where I could get some lessons and some target practice. I assured him I would do that, but I had neither intention nor the time to waste. I would practice on Frank. I could just aim for the middle of the chest, surely, I could do some harm.

Amy said, "We've received condolences from lots of people. Some people from Fort Devens are coming to Ada's funeral—even Molly and Justin Andrews.

Frank wasn't in the church during the service which I took as a blessing because I didn't want to cause a disturbance during a solemn service. When we reached the cemetery, and all milled around the grave site, I still didn't see him. When the first shovel of dirt hit the closed casket, I looked away, and saw Frank lurking on the edge of the cemetery closest to the parking lot. He turned to retrace his steps, and I slipped away from the small gathering.

Frank had reached the road and was about to step off the curb to cross to the parking lot when I reached into my purse for the gun. I lifted it to point at him and called his name. He looked up and sneered at my shaking arm. He looked across the 20 feet separating us with his usual expressionless face, "Put that thing away if you don't intend to use it."

"Oh, I intend to use it--I'm going to blow you into hell where you belong."

His face showed no emotion--only his eyes and voice glinted with cold dismissiveness, "people, who intend to use a gun, shoot—they don't try to talk you to death."

Evil surrounded him, and at that moment, I understood what had disturbed me so much about his cold piercing eyes. Dr. Hammond was correct, I was looking into the eyes of a psychopath—a mad man who was a threat to anyone with the misfortune to come near him. The world needed to be rid of him.

My hand shook so violently that I had to raise the other hand to steady the gun. All I could see was a red blur of fury when I aimed the gun toward his chest. I meant to shoot him in the heart, but didn't have the sense that I had hit anything. He turned away from me toward his car, and then I heard two or three more shots in rapid succession. Frank slumped to the ground, and I could see he was bleeding from the groin area. His pants had been ripped open from the bullets exposing a mangled bloody mess where his genitals were. The gushing blood soaked the grass turning it into a red carpet. It appeared that the bullets had struck the femoral artery causing blood to spurt like a garden hose left in the sun too long. By the time he hit the pavement, his pants were blood soaked. The blood streamed into the gutter beside where he fell. It appeared that I had blown his balls off which I had threatened to do many times, but it didn't seem to me that I had fired those shots, although I must have fired through a fog of grief and fury. I heard someone say, "Call the police," and I looked up at the crowd staring at me in disbelief. I dropped the gun to the ground, and sat on the sun-heated curb waiting for the police.

Two policemen came, sized up the situation quickly, and reached to put me in handcuffs. I heard my boss Mel and his wife Maureen pleading with the police. "Please don't put those on her; she'll go with you quietly. Amy, if you will ride with your mom, I'll drive your car back to your apartment."

Amy stooped to grab my purse for the car keys. We were briefly at eye level. Her eyes bored into me with such hatred, and she proclaimed loudly, "I'll drive myself back. I don't want anything to do with her." She gave me a look so filled with hate that I felt it like a punch, and then she turned and ran to the car.

I heard a scream. It sounded far away like a trapped hurt animal, and then I realized it was me. Screams ripped from deep within. All the years of repressed anger and loss, all the abuse, and mostly the loss of my two daughters that had been my anchor. The loss of a reason for living fueled those screams.

Mel and Maureen lifted me to a standing position and Maureen wrapped her arms around me and held me tight. "Amy doesn't mean what she's saying. She is so torn into pieces. Her world has collapsed, and she feels alone. She needs you more than ever right now. Mel will go with you, and I'll go check on Amy."

At the police station, I was processed and put into a small cell that had only a cot and a toilet. There was only one thing to do, curl into a fetal position on the cot, and grieve for my babies. It seemed that hours passed, I must have fallen asleep. A guard was unlocking the cell and tossing me my clothes. "Get dressed. Your attorney is here to accompany you to your arraignment. I stumbled behind the guard into a room where a man stood up and introduced himself as my attorney, Jake Halloren. He guided me to the front of the room where someone sat at a tall desk. Jake advised, "Let me do the talking. If you are asked a question, only answer with a "Yes," or "No."

I was only vaguely aware of the back-and-forth conversation. I just knew it was about me. The man who sat at the tall desk was speaking to me, and I tried hard to concentrate on what he was saying, but missed most of it. Jake whispered, "I'll explain everything when we get in the car. The person at the tall desk said, "Your bail has been paid. You are authorized to go home and will be notified when your trial date is set. You may go to work, you may go to church, you may go to the grocery, but you may not leave town."

Jake Halloren guided me out of the building and into his car. I asked, "Did you pay my bail?"

He held out his hand, "Howdy, I'm Jake Halloren. I will be your defense attorney, and I just made your bail compliments of Safe Harbor."

"What or who is Safe Harbor?"

"They're a group that provides help for abused women and children. Your boss's wife, Maureen is one of the founders. She initiated their help and authorized the money for the bail. I volunteer legal services. Maureen asked if I would take you home and have a talk with Amy."

The front door was locked and I remembered that Amy had taken my keys. I had to press on the doorbell for a long time before she came to open it. She was shocked to see me and stammered with too many questions. Before I could answer any of them, Jake introduced himself to Amy and filled her in.

"Amy, your mother's boss is married to one of the founders and current head of a group who help abused women and children. Most of the women they help are being stalked by their husbands or boyfriends with threats on their life. They operate under secrecy hiding the women and children from the abusers. They have a vast volunteer group. I'm a volunteer, but I'm not the only attorney who volunteers to help so you and your mom don't have to worry about payment. I don't know how long before your mom's trial, but she can go back to work. This group also provides therapy for both mothers and children. Maureen wants to offer you support--someone to talk to. She asked me to give you this card with phone numbers if you decide to accept help."

Amy sat frozen trying to absorb what she was hearing. She took the card from Jake and sat quietly playing with it.

I saw Jake to the door, "I'm grateful for this help. Please thank Maureen for me."

He said, "Maureen will be in touch with you tomorrow. I will also call you tomorrow after I check with the court for an update--I want to see if they have scheduled a trial date or picked a prosecutor, then we'll begin working out a defense."

Amy was twirling the business card in her hands, and I saw her face was tear stained. "Sweetheart, I will spend my time arranging for your future. You need to finish your senior year and apply for college. I'll help you apply for scholarships. I know we don't have relatives to turn to for help, but I think Maureen and her group will be a huge help."

I put my arms around her and held her tight. The hug was as much for me as for her. She leaned against me and said through tears, "I'm so sorry, Mom, for what I said and for how I've been acting."

"I understand, honey, you've had a horrible year, and bad just keeps happening. We both need time to get our head straight. Hold on to that card, maybe you should talk to one of Maureen's therapists."

The next day was busy. Early in the morning, Mel called me, and asked if I could return to work. He said, "I see that you have vacation time you haven't taken, why don't you take the time, and return to work a week from today?"

I felt like hugging him. I had feared that I would be fired. I needed to keep this apartment for Amy until she finished school and got a job.

Maureen called next and asked if Amy and I could come in the next day. She had arranged for Amy to have an initial visit with one of the therapists, and advised me, "Call that therapist that you've been seeing, and set up an appointment--the sooner the better. He may come in handy for your trial."

Jake called me after dinner. He said he'd had a hard time getting in touch with people at the courthouse, "But I found out they are reviewing and setting the schedule. Your case will be slated within two months, and due to the nature of the case, they don't think the trial will last long. That two policemen witnessed you standing over the victim holding a gun, and several people saw the same, they think this will be a speedy trial."

"Does that mean I am sure to go to jail in two months?"

"Sarah, I won't lie to you this is going to be one of the hardest trials that I have been involved in. Could you come into my office tomorrow to talk. I want you to tell me everything about your ex--everything leading up to now. I'm beginning to investigate and looking for evidence that he had so terrorized you that it was justifiable homicide."

"I can't tomorrow. Amy and I are going to Maureen's office, and Amy has an appointment with one of the therapists there. Later, I have an appointment to see a therapist that I've been seeing for a long time."

I heard a sharp intake of breath on the other end of the phone. "He just might be your savior. Would you mind if I talk to him? Would you give me his name and contact information?

When you visit him tomorrow, would you give him permission to talk to me?"

I met several wonderful people at Safe Harbor. Vera seemed to be in charge. She asked me to wait while she introduced Amy to Elise, her therapist. When she returned, she said Amy would be in there for about an hour, and we could talk in the meantime. I left feeling relieved, and grateful for the support— especially grateful that Amy had a support network. Vera assured me that if I was incarcerated, they would make sure Amy had a home, and whatever she needed to finish school, and they would be there for Amy as long as she needed them. I had just enough time to take Amy home and get to Doctor Hammond's office.

I hadn't seen him for about a month, and he knew nothing about what had happened. I sat down in a chair opposite him and blurted out, "Ada died, and I shot Frank."

Dr. Hammond looked startled, but quickly said, "I'm truly sorry about Ada. Tell me about the shooting, is he dead?"

Apparently, I shot his balls off and he bled to death."

"What do you mean by apparently, what happened?"

"Well, you know he gave Ada cancer--passing along that HPV virus, and when she died, I couldn't take anymore. I knew he had to leave this world. I bought a pistol--I think the store person called it a colt. Amy told me that he was coming to Ada's funeral which didn't give me time to find a place where I could practice. I thought if he came, then I wouldn't have to go looking for him, and if I just aimed and hit anywhere on his torso, I could do some serious damage. At least that was the intention. He stayed a distance away from the grave site, but when he turned to leave, I followed him. I called his name, and when he turned toward me, I shot him. My hand was shaking so hard that I had to steady it with both hands. I pulled the trigger, but I didn't think I had hit him because he didn't show signs he'd been hit, instead he turned to cross the parking lot, and I heard three shots and then he was laying on the ground. His crotch area appeared mangled and he was spurting blood. I don't remember much that day—I was in such a fog. People at the funeral saw me with the gun in my hand and saw Frank on the ground bloody and dead. There was nobody else there, so apparently, I fired those shots."

"Were you still standing in the same spot when the police came? What happened?"

"I dropped the gun and sat on the ground waiting for the police. They saw, and so did everyone at the funeral that I had shot him. They were going to handcuff me, but my boss, Mel, asked them not to. I was only in the jail for a few hours before I was bailed out. Mel's wife Maureen runs a safe house for victims of abuse. Her group put up the money for the bail and sent one of their lawyers to bail me out and take me home."

"Who did they send?"

"Jake Halloren."

"I know him. He's a good man. We've worked together before on abuse cases, and I know Maureen and her group. She does wonderful things."

"He asked me if I gave permission for him to talk to you. I guess it's alright for you to talk to him. He says this is a tough case that he may have to use some type of mental distress defense."

"I think he and I need to discuss that, I don't want to use a defense that would have the judge put you into a mental institution. I wouldn't put my dog in one of those places. Can you tell me what you were thinking and feeling when you sat there?"

"I was thinking I was glad he was dead, but he died too quickly. I wanted him to die slowly and for him to know I was the one killing him. Actually, I felt as if I was in a dream world. Nothing seemed real—not even the people who came to the funeral. I knew I had killed Frank, but couldn't remember doing it."

I didn't hear from Jake or Maureen for the remainder of the week, and braced to return to work. I didn't know how my coworkers would react to me. The first morning, everyone avoided me. I don't think they knew what to say. At lunch, I took my sandwich to the break room and sat alone. Lynn saw me sitting alone and came over to ask if she could sit with me. Before she sat down, she said loudly so everyone in the room could hear,

"I'm sorry about Ada, but I'm glad you shot the bastard's pecker off."

No one in the room moved. No one said anything for a long pause, and then all erupted in laughter, and all agreed with Lynn. The tension was gone.

Jake called that evening. He wanted a list and contact information for the people Dr. Hammond and I'd tracked down. He said, "If I can get several of these people to take the witness stand, I'm thinking that I can make a case for mental distress--that you felt threatened."

I felt a rush of disappointment, "Dr. Hammond said if you went for the insanity plea that I might be sent to a mental institution. He didn't like that idea at all."

"I don't want to see that either. We talked about that, and that's why I want to interview these people. I'm trying to formulate a case of extreme desperation that you were driven to it."

"Do I need to talk to any of them?"

"Not at first--let me make the first call. Your trial has been scheduled. I'm surprised it's so soon--about six weeks away. We'll have to move fast. Can you think of anyone else that might be helpful. If you can remember the name and the last place you knew them, I have some military contacts that may help me track them down."

On the first morning of the trial, I could not stop trembling, and refused Amy's offer to cook breakfast. Jake picked both of us up and walked in front of us into the courtroom. I noticed Mel sitting with Maureen, and even Dr. Hammond was sitting with them.

The prosecutor told the court that there were multiple eye witnesses to my brutal and planned murder, and that his first witness was the policeman who rushed to the scene and made the arrest. He called the policeman to the stand who told the court that I was sitting on the curb with the murder weapon beside me. He put the weapon into an evidence bag, and then arrested me-- that I did not protest or resist.

Jake was asked if he wanted to cross examine the witness, but he replied he reserved the right to question him later, but not at this time. When he made his opening statement, he said he would prove that I had suffered extreme mental duress from the victim, that the victim had a history of sexual crimes against underage girls, including his own daughters. Jake looked at the jury when he said, "I am calling several of Frank's victims to testify."

There were multiple objections from the prosecutor. He repeated several times that the victim was not on trial, but his ex-wife was on trial for murder. Most of his objections were over ruled. It seemed that the first day went fast. On the way home,

Jake said the cards were stacked against me. He said, "I watched the faces of the jury intently today, and I didn't see an ounce of sympathy for you. Amy's friend Molly and Justin Andrews will be in court tomorrow. They have agreed to testify. I'm putting them on the stand, and I think they will be compelling witnesses. I haven't decided who to put first, Amy's friend Molly, or Justin. I also talked to Robin, and have a video of her testimony. They all agreed to testify after hearing what's at stake. I'm saving the video testimony from Robin last."

The next day, the jury saw that Molly was obviously still traumatized. When she said she was fifteen now but was fourteen when Frank took her to North Carolina, the jury was obviously moved. Some appeared to be wiping their eyes. At the end of the day, there appeared to be sympathy for me, but Jake cautioned not to get too optimistic, he still had to do more convincing.

The next day was Saturday so no trial. Amy took a bus to Fort Devens to spend time with Molly. I told her that I'd pick her up and we could get a hamburger on the way home. I was busy vacuuming so I didn't hear the phone ringing until I switched off the vacuum, and heard the answering machine pick up. I couldn't tell if it was a man or woman because they were disguising their voice with a raspy whisper. They said, "You did not kill Frank. The police did shoddy police work. Check the coroner's report. Check the forensic report."

My hands were shaking as I replayed the message several times. The voice was vaguely familiar, but I didn't know why. I called Jake, "I don't remember anyone mentioning a coroner's report or a forensic report. I don't know if there was one."

Jake answered, "Sit tight. I'm making some calls and paying some people a visit. I'll get back to you."

I didn't get much done except for floor pacing and clock watching. At three o'clock, I had to leave to pick up Amy, and I still had not heard back from Jake. I was out of the house only an hour and a half, but when I returned, there was no blinking light on the answering machine. "Amy, do you mind if we have a sandwich for supper? I'm listening for an important call."

Amy seemed to anticipate the call, "Jake?"

It was almost bedtime before Jake called. He said he had spent the day making calls, visiting the coroner's office, and the police forensic lab.

"Well, what I found out is a real bombshell--a good bombshell for you. Before I explain, I want to tell you how sorry I am for not doing my own investigation. It seems that when the two policemen saw you sitting near the victim with the gun on the ground by your side, they made assumptions. They were fooled by what they saw and by what bystanders told them. The coroner took three bullets out of the corpse--none of them came from your little gun. The police chief sent the two cops back out to the site to look for the bullet from your gun. It must be out there somewhere because it was not in Frank. They were also ordered to do a drawing of the lay of the body and verify the direction of the shooter. It's probably too late to get an accurate drawing because it has to be from memory and maybe corroborated by someone there. You've heard the expression that assumption makes an ass out of you and me? Well, the two policemen were asses, and so was I. I am so sorry that you didn't have better representation.

"Do I still go to court tomorrow?"

"Yes, all this will be presented to the jury. I'm calling the coroner, and everyone involved to the stand. You should be able to walk out of there tomorrow."

The next day, I was so uptight that I could hardly walk into the courtroom, and I had to make an effort to control my trembling. Jake called the coroner to the stand, and asked him, "What bullets did you retrieve from the victim's corpse?"

The coroner answered, "I retrieved three 5.56 mm cartridges."

"What type of gun fired those?"

"Those bullets are used in an M16. I think you need to affirm this with the forensic people."

"Did you find any bullets from any other type of weapon?"

"No."

"Is it your determination that these were the bullets that killed him?"

Jake dismissed the coroner and called a person from forensics to the stand. "Do you agree with the coroner? Can you tell me more about the use of this weapon?"

"It's an infantry assault weapon. It's accurate at a distance, so sharp shooters particularly like this weapon."

"Would you say that the person who shot this victim was a sharp shooter?"

"Yes, he or she hit a very small area three times dead on, and from a distance."

"Did you examine the pistol which the accused used?"

"Yes, it was a Smith and Wesson model 39, and had been fired one time."

"Did you retrieve the bullet?"

"Yes, we went back to the scene yesterday to search the area, and found it lodged into the back of a park bench."

My mind leaped to what that testimony meant. I was not guilty. I tried to bring my attention back to the witnesses and follow the proceedings, but my thoughts worried with who else hated him enough to kill him in the manner they did?

Jake interrupted my thoughts and motioned that I rise for judgment. I was free to go. All charges were dropped.

Amy and I headed out of the courtroom, but Jake herded us into the small cafeteria adjacent. He said he needed to discuss the day's events, because he wasn't sure I had heard anything in today's proceedings. "When I looked at you for reactions, I saw a blank stare, so I feel like I should discuss what just happened so that both of us can process. Besides, I owe you a proper plea for forgiveness. This case should not have gone this far if only everyone involved had done proper investigation."

I said, "Jake, you don't owe me any apologies. I owe you for all your patience and kindness. Thank you so very much. Do you think they will charge me with anything like attempted murder?"

"I seriously doubt it. After the jury heard the testimony of his victims, and heard what he did to his own daughters, I could see by their facial expressions that the jury thought getting rid of him was a good thing--even the judge and the prosecutor hated the man they just heard about. I think they all desperately wanted a reason to excuse you."

"Will they find out who killed him?"

"I think they're obligated to investigate, but it will take a long time since they say they are short handed, and then after a while, the case will go cold. No, it seems doubtful they'll ever arrest anyone for the murder."

After dinner, while Amy did homework, and talked on the phone, I sat in the rocking chair. The back-and-forth motion was calming and it helped me think. I was still processing everything. I was in such a state on the day of Ada's funeral. My brain was fogged by hatred for Frank--it was a red fog of fury, and grief over losing my baby. It felt that I was sleepwalking. I also assumed that I shot Frank, and in a state of bewilderment questioned the other three shots. After all I was the only one there with a gun, and Frank lay dead at my feet. I felt cheated. I had wanted him to know that I was killing him--slowly. I wanted him to feel fear. I had planned to take my time killing him. But someone hated him so much that they shredded his genitals. Too bad they were so accurate that he died a sudden death. It must have been one of his victims with hate to match mine—I hoped they were never caught. Something had been niggling around my thoughts, something about Amy. When everyone else came down from the grave site to the parking lot, where was Amy? My boss and Maureen had called for her to go to the police station with me, but she was not around. She showed up when the police came and was coming from another direction. I called her to come into the living room to talk with me for a minute, and asked, "Amy, where did you go after the graveside service?"

"I stayed with Ada until they lowered her casket. I didn't want her to be alone when they covered her up. Then I went looking for a bathroom, and was heading to the car when I saw the crowd hanging around the edge of the parking lot. Why do you ask?"

"Nothing, just wondering. As far as I know, the perp's apartment and stuff are still down there the way he left it, and I think his car is in the police pound. How about us going down there tomorrow to see if there are any things you would want. I'm looking for my jewelry and Krugerrand, and I want a look at his checkbooks and bank statements. If there is anything in them, it belongs to you."

"How can we get in if it's locked?"

"I think we should go to the police department tomorrow, and ask for his belongings. There should be a wallet and a set of keys. Then we can talk to someone about getting his car out of hock."

"They're not going to give that stuff to us."

"Well, we don't know until we ask, do we?"

To our shock, all we had to show to get Franks possessions were our ID cards. We decided not to get the car until we searched Frank's place and went through paperwork. If Frank owed too much on the car, then we wouldn't pay to get it out of hock.

On the drive to Frank's apartment, I opened the conversation, "I've been thinking about all the people we know who could have killed Frank. The person was a sharp shooter and had access to military weapons. The only person who fits that description is Justen Andrews. He hated the perp with a passion, and he had easy access to the base--he was probably a sharpshooter. Your friend Molly hated him enough but I doubt she was a sharpshooter. What do you think?"

"I've thought about it too. I hope it wasn't Molly. There were others--lots of others, they lived so far away, and how would they have known where to find him just at that time? It makes sense that it was Justen. I hope they never find out."

We found military policemen guarding the building, and there were several FBI agents searching the apartment. The MPs blocked our entry. Amy put her hands on her hips and demanded entrance, "I am his daughter and this is my mother, we have a right to go in there and get our belongings."

The MP called into the apartment for the person they called Henry. Henry came into the hall and his jacket identified him as FBI. He asked if we could show dependant ID cards. Amy had her ID handy, but I had to fish in my wallet for mine. I had not given up my card when I left Frank. Thank goodness I hadn't ripped it up. The MP and Henry moved to the side talking so low I couldn't catch what they were saying. They scrutinized the IDs, and then Henry said, "Okay, I can give you half an hour. The guys need a break so we'll leave you alone so you can hurry. I'll be right outside, and will need to see and authorize anything you take out of the apartment."

When Amy and I were alone in the apartment, I said, "Why are they here? What's going on? I need to go out there and demand some answers."

Amy shook her head and continued to move into the bedroom and straight to the dresser. "I think this is where we'll find all the paperwork we need. Don't stop looking, mama. We don't have much time. You can ask them all the questions you want after we get stuff out of here. I don't see any boxes, take this garbage bag--start loading."

"Amy, I want to see if he still has my jewelry and Krugerrand. He had a little wooden box he kept his watch and brass in, where do you think it is?"

Amy motioned to the night stand. I located the box but there was nothing in it. Now my next pursuit was to find checkbooks and bank statements. Those appeared to be in the dresser where Amy was already stuffing all the paperwork from the two upper drawers into the garbage bag. She held up two check books and a stack of bank statements secured with a rubber band.

I grabbed handfuls of papers and helped Amy stuff the garbage bags. I asked her to keep her eyes peeled for a safe deposit box key. Then I went through the place opening every drawer and closet grabbing anything I could carry.

We each dragged three large trash bags out into the hallway. Henry saw us and held up his hand, "Wow, we need to go through those bags." One of the FBI agents stepped up and asked us, "Where did you get this stuff?" He opened every bag and riffled through it.

When we said we'd gotten everything from the dresser drawers, he told Henry that they had already gone through that stuff and taken pictures of any papers that might be relevant. He asked us if we had taken any of the papers from the closet floor.

"No," I answered, "We were going to put these in the car and come back for those."

He addressed Henry and not us when he said, "We searched through those, and there does seem to be papers that might be of interest to us, but we haven't had a chance for a close inspection."

Henry turned to us and said, "Okay, take these bags, but leave everything else. I will contact you when you can come back for the rest."

"We're looking for a title to his car or any payment books. We don't intend to get it out of hock if there's money owed on it. By the way, why are you here?"

He said, "The car is in FBI possession to be searched. Your husband has been under scrutiny for years. We had evidence he was selling or giving away classified information. We were ready to move in on him when he was killed."

I told him about the many times I thought my home was being watched, and I thought maybe Frank was having me watched. Henri said, "No ma'am, we weren't watching you."

I asked Henri, "Did you know he was a pedophile?"

He shook his head, "No, we found out with this trial. I'm glad you were exonerated."

"After I found out he was a pervert, I went to a therapist who said he was in the perfect career--dealing with secrets. I guess he was good at keeping secrets."

All the agents and even the MPs started laughing. One of them said, "Well maybe not so good after all."

"He's dead now. Why are you still looking? If you suspected and had him under surveillance for years and years, why haven't you arrested him?"

"We've never been able to find out who his contacts were. They've been elusive, but we did have someone in our sights and were going to move in on them and Frank when he was killed." Now, our goal is to determine how much damage he has done, and if there's information out there that could put anybody or the country in jeopardy."

Henri helped us put our bags in the car, and said, "Someone will contact you when you can come back to close out the apartment. I know you have many more questions, but I've already said too much."

Amy and I drove home in silence. We were both trying to process today. We dragged the bags into the middle of the living room, and then Amy fell back on the sofa saying, "What a hell of a day."

"Yes, it has been, starting with our trip to the police station. I was shocked that they gave us Frank's wallet and keys without more pushback. The FBI was a total shock. I'm surprised that FBI fellow, Henri, told us anything or let us take anything out of there."

After we ate dinner, Amy said, "Mom, I'm gonna leave you to sort through the bags, I'm going to see if I can get some studying tonight, and I have to spend all day tomorrow studying because I have a big test Monday."

I dumped the contents of the garbage bags in the middle of the room, and sat Indian style on floor checking each piece of paper, each bank statement and the checkbooks, and cancelled checks. Around midnight, I finished, and the cramping in my legs was so intense, I could hardly stand up. What a disappointment. I hoped to find money in some account for Amy's college tuition. She had worked so hard to make up for the time off school, even taking on a part time job and summer school. She had volunteered at Safe Harbor since shortly after Ada's funeral. She didn't have direct contact with the clients but contributed by sorting and pricing clothing for the thrift store. Her association with Maureen, her therapist, and Jake had influenced her in a positive way, and she wanted to major in either psychology or social work. Maureen told her when she finished school and had received her license, she could work for them. I just had to find the money somewhere. I had expected to find some from Frank, but there was nothing there--at least not in this pile of papers. What did he get out of giving up secrets, if not money?

I really needed to talk to someone. Thankfully, I had an appointment with Dr. Hammond later in the week, but I would prefer to talk to my granny. After all these years, I still thought of her as the wisest person I had ever known.

Amy came home from Safe Harbor excited because Jake had given her a list of possible scholarship money. He said if she needed help applying for these, and I didn't have an objection, he would help her fill out the applications. She chattered nonstop about the clinic and about school. She hadn't shown such excitement and happiness in a long time.

"Mama, most of the men around here seem to be good men—even your boss. I see Jake almost every day that I'm at Safe Harbor. Everyone there likes him, and he seems to treat people decently. He asks about you every time I see him. One time when I'd questioned something you'd said, he told me to listen to you because you are smart, strong and a beautiful person. Do you think you could ever be sweet on him?"

"Oh, no honey, I'm not ready for that kind of relationship."

The ringing of the phone interrupted us. As I went to answer, I told Amy that our conversation was to be continued.

Jake was on the phone and he sounded excited, "Turn on your television to the local news. I'll call you back afterward." Then he abruptly hung up.

I turned on the local news, and saw a group of people standing in front of a microphone. There were several men in FBI uniforms in the group. I recognized Henri standing in the background. One of the agents was speaking into a microphone. I heard Amy half groaning, half crying pointing to the banner at the bottom of the screen. I caught the name Frank Honley, and some more that I didn't have time to read before it scrolled by. The man at the microphone was speaking, "We have James Talbot in custody and have charged him with the murder of Frank Honley-- he is also charged with espionage. Talbot was once a member of the US Army assigned to the Army Security Agency where he dealt with top secret information. He and Frank Honley were coworkers. I can't give you any more information at this time. This public briefing is just to inform the public that Frank Honley's killer has been arrested. I'm sorry, but I cannot answer your questions at this time. Later when we close the case, we'll be able to tell you more."

The scowling face of Talbot scrolled across the bottom of the screen. I shuddered because I could not tear my gaze from his eyes. They had the look of insanity and a mean hard hate. I gasped and dropped to the sofa. The memory of that hate-filled face and scathing voice, long forgotten, came rushing back.

Amy was startled and asked, "What is it mama?"

Before I could answer, Jake called, and since Amy was eaves dropping, I answered her by explaining to him.

"Jake, I met that man in Berlin. He was in army security, and worked with Frank. Apparently, they were close. The night before he was arrested for espionage, he came to see Frank. He pushed his way into the house. He and Frank went into the bedroom and had a loud, sometimes angry conversation. The only thing I could understand were parting words when they opened the door, each demanding the other not to talk. The next morning, he was arrested for espionage, and escorted to Fort Leavenworth, Kansas prison. I was told he was court marshaled, but I didn't know the details like how long his sentence was or anything else. It's only been four or five years—seems a short sentence for such a serious offense. What's he doing here? Why did he kill frank after all this time? He must have hunted him down."

"Jake, I need to find out more about who and what Frank was--not just for me, but Amy needs some answers. I tried to find Henri, the FBI agent, after we went down to close out Frank's apartment, but the FBI seemed to have just disappeared. I need to make some sense out of the past years, but I have no clout. You were the first lawyer on Franks murder, so maybe more people will talk to you. Would you please try to gather some information for us?"

Jake was quick to respond, "I've made a few connections in my practice, and I also would like to know more. Let me nose around, and call in a few favors. I'll get back to you, but I think this may take awhile. Sit tight."

I hung up the phone and turned to Amy. She was ashen with silent tears wetting her face, "Mama, I don't know who my dad was. I can't wrap my mind around it. He was a total stranger. For awhile when I was younger, I thought he loved me, and I loved him as well, but after the trip to North Carolina, I know he didn't love anyone. Elise said he was grooming us all those years when he showed us so much attention. He did everything to turn us against you. I see that now. It rocked my world when he tried to rape me, and to find out about him being a pedophile, but now they're saying he was a spy. What else did he do? Who was he? Mama, I am so ashamed—I don't want anyone to know my name."

I put my arms around her letting her sob on my shoulder. If I had the power to pull all the hurt, disillusionment, and grief from her and take it into my own body, I would in a heartbeat. "Amy, listen to me. You are loved. I love you more than you'll ever know, and everyone who meets you ends up loving you. You have nothing to be ashamed of. The shame belongs to him. A man can squirt his sperm into a Petri dish to fertilize an egg then his role is finished. The woman carries the fertilized egg in her belly under her heart and it becomes part of her. You grew inside me under my heart--you are a part of me and I love you dearly. You could have been fertilized in a lab."

Amy was shaking with laughter. "Now you're telling me I'm actually a lab rat?"

Her tears were mingled laughter and grief. I held her tighter glad that she could still laugh.

"I didn't really mean it like it came out, but since it made you laugh, I won't take it back."

Sleep was illusive that night. I had to get through a day at work whether I slept or not. My mind would not let go of all the questions. I tried to make sense of the past years and come up with some plausible explanation of who Frank was. How could I have lived under the same roof with someone for so many years and not be able to say who he was? How could I not have known he was a pedophile? I didn't even know the word pedophilia until he was revealed. Fathers wouldn't do that to their own children. Would they? All the signs were there. How could I have missed them? Dr. Hammond said even trained psychiatrists were fooled, and passed him along approving his security clearance. He fooled everyone. Our frequent moves, Frank's shifting work hours, and his security clearance gave him cover. That he had a wife and two children gave him the final legitimacy.

I knew in my gut he was a psychopath, but I didn't have the words to name it. Grandma told me, "Always listen to your gut," and my gut beat and screamed to me through the nightmares warning me of the monster on the upper floor, but I didn't have the knowledge or words to understand that Frank was that monster.

But I should have known. Mothers are supposed to protect their children, I failed them. I remember all the furtive phone calls, the disappearances, the lies and gas lighting. My suspicions were correct about giving sensitive information away, but I never suspected he was a pedophile. Who did he give this information, and what did he get for it? I had checked thoroughly for hidden bank accounts and found nothing. The FBI had also checked, and they found nothing, or at least nothing they told me about. What did he get in return? What else was he guilty of? I felt as if my brain would explode. I needed someone to talk to--someone to put their arms around me and carry just a little of the burden-–just for awhile. I felt so alone and floating in space ready to fall without anyone to catch me. Tomorrow, I had the appointment with Dr. Hammond. I felt safe talking to him, and a lot had happened since the trial. The thoughts of seeing him quieted my brain, and I fell asleep for about an hour before the alarm went off.

Dr Hammond's first comment was, "I saw the news report last night about the arrest of Frank's killer. Did you know that person?"

"Yes, well, not really. I met him one time in Berlin, the night before he was arrested for espionage."

I repeated the story about Talbot, and said, "I have no idea what he is doing here, and I don't understand why he is out of Leavenworth. I don't think he worked at Fort Devens—at least not in the military."

Dr. Hammond said, "I remember that you thought Justin, the husband of one of Frank's pedophile victims, had killed Frank, and you were hoping that he wouldn't be found out. How do you feel now that you know it was this other person?"

"I'm madder than hell. I wasn't too happy when I thought it was one of his victims, but I could understand the anger. Talbot killed either to keep Frank's mouth shut, or else in revenge. This puts it in a whole new light. It deprived me of my revenge. I had every intention of seeing Frank's blood and life seep away slowly and with great suffering. I had wanted him to know I was responsible for his pain, but instead, he died almost instantly. I

314

have felt anger for a long time, but now—even now, sometimes I feel rage."

"How is Amy taking this?"

"When she saw the news Last night, she started shaking and crying--she was devastated. She had not come to grips with her father, the pedophile, who was responsible for her sister's death, but revelations in the news conference, that Frank was a spy, shocked her. She turned to me and asked, "Who was he? What else did he do?"

"How did you answer?"

"I told her that I didn't know either, but Jake is nosing around for some answers. He has contacts with a couple of military lawyers and some FBI folks that he is trying to get information from. He didn't promise me anything--just that he would try to get enough information so I could fill in the gaps."

"Have you considered that you may never know who he was--that maybe no one knew him?"

It took over two weeks for Jake to get back to me. I was almost ready to give up on him when he called and asked if I would meet him in the little coffee shop near me. He said, "I'll buy you a cup of coffee and share everything I've been able to dig up."

He was waiting for me and had already ordered coffee and pie.

"Sarah, you have to try this banana cream pie. It's the best I've ever eaten. Well, I'll just get right to it. I've contacted every soul that I have ever met or done business with connected to the military or FBI. I also talked to some people I'd never met. I made a real nuisance of myself with some of them because I knew they had information we wanted. A couple of people talked freely, but some, I had to force tid bits out of them. I'm going to tell you who and what Frank was based on piecing together all these conversations. Some things, are what the clues point to, but I cannot prove them.

Probably the reason you could not find a stash of money was because he never got any money--instead, he gave away our secrets because he was being blackmailed. Let me rephrase that—no one ever found a stash of money. I did manage to get in to talk to Talbot after multiple tries. That man is a real cocky jackass, and he talks nonstop. He told me Frank had been blackmailed for years by one or more foreign agents. I believed him because one of the FBI agents, I think he was the one you talked to, Henri, told me there were always foreign agents hanging around all the military security groups. Often enough, they could find someone to slip them classified material.

Henri said that the FBI had evidence of Frank being blackmailed as far back as Fort Bragg. One of the floating spies must have observed him engaging in something illegal or immoral. That was probably pedophilia. Henri said they found a large collection of child porn hidden in his apartment. They had him in their sights but wanted to catch his contacts. He said the information Frank turned over was less important than catching the foreign agents. Each time Frank moved to a new assignment, there was always someone there to receive the information.

Talbot was and is a foreign agent. He had joined the army security services years before Berlin—don't know how he passed the rigorous vetting and background checks. His contacts in Berlin were also Frank's. They worked together to smuggle out loads of information. The military brass wanted to bust Frank, but they wanted more to get all the contacts and they wanted Talbot even more. Talbot claimed that Frank was always a foreign agent. I don't know if that was true—no one in the FBI told me that.

Talbot told me that Frank did not finger him in Berlin. He said when he got out of Leavenworth, his handler ordered him to Massachusetts to take care of Frank because he was on the verge of turning himself in and giving up the names of all his contacts, both present and past. He had to stop him before he could reveal any names."

"Jake, that doesn't make much sense. Why would Frank go to such lengths to hide—even giving away secrets for years, and now decide to turn himself in? That doesn't make a bit of sense."

317

"I don't know how much of this is true. I think it's just too simple to say Frank was a pedophile and a spy, but that is all I can deduce. Sarah, I don't think you will ever learn who he was."

"Dr. Hammond said the same thing. I guess I'll have to settle for this bit of information, and thank you for all your time and effort. By the way, I agree, this is the best banana cream pie I have ever eaten."

Amy was fixing lunch when I arrived home. She grinned and asked, "How was your date?"

"It was not a date. He wanted to tell me what he found out about the perp which didn't amount to much more than we already knew. It seems he was being blackmailed for years. Either he gave away classified information in exchange for silence about his penchant for children, or else he was a foreign agent all along."

"Mama, it wasn't a date to you, but I'm pretty sure Jake was hoping it was, He is obviously smitten with you. Every single time, I am working there, he goes out of his way to ask me about you. Are you still not interested?"

"Amy, Jake is very handsome and he is a fine man, but I have other things on my mind. I never finished my college degree so I thought maybe I could finish it now and maybe go for the masters. I'm not sure what to major in--something along the lines of what you are going to study, but I don't want to work as a social worker or therapist. I find it appalling that there aren't more places like Safe Harbor for women and children. I would like to help get similar places in all states and even in all cities eventually. I want to fight for women's rights, equal opportunity and pay, child care centers, the right to control their own body which means laws need to be passed. I'm fighting for all that. I have an appointment with a counselor to discuss the best degrees for me to pursue. So, you see, I'm gonna be busy working and being a student again. I'm not going to have time for dating."

Amy looked at me as if I had two heads. "Don't you think that's a bit much? How can you do all that? You'll probably be in some of my classes."

"Not at the same time. I'm going to the extension school—night classes."

"Sounds to me as if you need to go to law school if you're gonna get all that done. Mama, I've been dying to ask you a question, would you give me a straight answer? You have called certain men tomcats, and when you shot the perp, you said over and over that the tomcat was dead. What did you mean? Do you hate men or cats?"

"I don't hate men or cats--well, I don't hate all cats or all men. I had a bad experience with tomcats when I was seven or eight years old, and I haven't liked male cats since then. My grandma, your great grandma, always had several cats in the barn. She called them her mousers. There was always a litter of kittens. Each time a cat had babies, I visited them every day starting even before they opened their eyes. I watched them getting bigger and bigger until they were busy catching mice in the barn. There was a litter of five kittens that I especially liked because they were such different colors. I ran over to grandma's house at least twice a day just to see the kittens. One day, the babies weren't there, and grandma explained that the mama cat must have moved them so the old tomcat couldn't find them. She didn't want to tell me, but I kept pestering her. She said that sometimes the tomcat would kill kittens if he thought they would grow up to challenge him."

I told Amy what I had witnessed on my walk home. "The image of that slaughter was burned into my brain. I suffered trauma that stayed with me my whole life. The first time I thought of men as tomcats was when old Al came into our lives. I always thought of him as slinking around ready to strike little kids and women. He hurt us all so bad, and Mama too. I've known many tomcats in my life--Men who had an evil streak in them and hurt women and kids. But the perp was the worst of all. Sometimes, I can't breathe when I think of his evil. But I have also known good men. There are so many good men in this world Amy, and I hope someday you find one to love. I don't think Mama, Barbara, or I knew how to recognize them. We were so vulnerable and innocent."

Amy asked, "Was your dad a tomcat?"

"Oh no, well, only if you count drinking himself to death, and leaving us vulnerable and unable to cope with the world. I didn't know until after Mama died that she didn't visit uncle Don, but was checked into an institution for mental problems. Aunt Mary said she had a nervous breakdown and that's why we went to the orphanage. They didn't do much for her--she was still vulnerable when she met Al. He took advantage of that and instead of helping her recover, he broke her. The last time I saw her, she was just a shell of a human being. I wish I had understood that when she was still alive. I wish I had been more understanding and helpful."

"Mama, there's a woman who helps me sort and tag clothes for Safe Harbor. She talks all the time. She acts like she knows all about us and even what we think. She's always telling me that you and I have to let go of our anger and forgive before we can move ahead."

"Is she a therapist?"

"No."

"Well, I think considering all you've been through, you're doing just fine. You can always talk to me, or Elise."

For days, I thought about this conversation, and about questions of anger, forgiveness, and who was Frank. He had no personality of his own, and adopted the persona needed to control and ensnare his victims. Frank was evil. Frank was nobody. I will never forgive him, and I hope heaven does not forgive. My hatred for Frank will remain with me forever. I will wrap it around me as a coat of armor to propel me forward to accomplish what I need to do. Even after Frank's death, his evil remains. He stole innocence and trust from his victims who are left to grapple for years. Perhaps a life time.